THE ORINOCO URANIUM

THE
ORINOCO
URANIUM

STEPHEN O. SEARS

Editors: Josh Owens, Deborah Froese
Cover and Interior Design: Emma Elzinga

Indigo River Publishing
3 West Garden Street, Ste. 718
Pensacola, FL 32502
www.indigoriverpublishing.com

Ordering Information:
Quantity sales: Special discounts are available on quantity purchases by corporations, associations, and others. For details, contact the publisher at the address above.

Orders by US trade bookstores and wholesalers: Please contact the publisher at the address above.

Library of Congress Control Number: 2022914874
ISBN: 978-1-954676-38-1 (paperback) 978-1-954676-39-8 (ebook)
First Edition

With Indigo River Publishing, you can always expect great books, strong voices, and meaningful messages. Most importantly, you'll always find . . . words worth reading.

CONTENTS

Author's Note VII

Prologue. XI

Chapter One 1

Chapter Two 11

Chapter Three. 23

Chapter Four. 41

Chapter Five 51

Chapter Six 59

Chapter Seven. 69

Chapter Eight 79

Chapter Nine. 87

Chapter Ten. 93

Chapter Eleven. 99

Chapter Twelve. 107

Chapter Thirteen 117

Chapter Fourteen. 119

Chapter Fifteen. 125

Chapter Sixteen 135

Chapter Seventeen. 141

Chapter Eighteen. 151

Chapter Nineteen 159

Chapter Twenety 165

Chapter Twenty-One 175

Chapter Twenty-Two 185

Chapter Twenty-Three 191

Chapter Twenty-Four. 205

Chapter Twenty-Five 211

Chapter Twenty-Six 219

Chapter Twenty-Seven. 227

Chapter Twenty-Eight 233

Chapter Twenty-Nine 241

Chapter Thirty 253

Chapter Thirty-One 259

Chapter Thirty-Two 271

Glossary. 275

About the Author 277

AUTHOR'S NOTE

and Acknowledgements

VENEZUELA, THE LARGEST exporter of oil to the U.S. during World War II, remained a neutral country until February of 1945 when it declared war on the Axis powers of Germany, Italy, and Japan. American and European companies pursued production of crude oil during the war, primarily in the Lake Maracaibo basin with some exploration of the Orinoco River delta to the east. Argentina was also a neutral country until March of 1945, although sympathy for the Axis and its welcome of escaping Nazis are well documented. The German effort to build an atomic bomb, including the construction of a helix of uranium cubes suspended in heavy water, was cancelled when it became apparent it would not be successful in time for the war. While many of these uranium cubes were recovered by the Allies after the war, approximately 650 are still missing. One cube mysteriously turned up in the United States in 2013.

Some historical settings and facts are modified or fabricated for this novel. References to well-known historical and public figures are intended only to provide a sense of authenticity and are used fictitiously, as are the situations, incidents, and dialogues concerning these persons. All other names, characters, places, and events are solely the products of the authors imagination.

I would like to thank Ana Riquer, Emma Richardson, Thomas Jacks, Karl Steinen, Nancy Steinen, and Barbara Sears for reading early versions of the manuscript and providing comments and suggestions. The Shell staff in the Maracaibo office introduced me to the city, the lake, and the surrounding countryside during several visits. I would also like to especially thank Deborah Froese for her meticulous editing, feedback, and encouragement; and Joshua Owens, who has now contributed his editing expertise to the two novels that I have written. The cover design and interior layout benefited greatly from Emma Elzinga's originality and expertise. And I would like to express my deep gratitude to my wife, Barbara, for her support and encouragement during the writing of this novel.

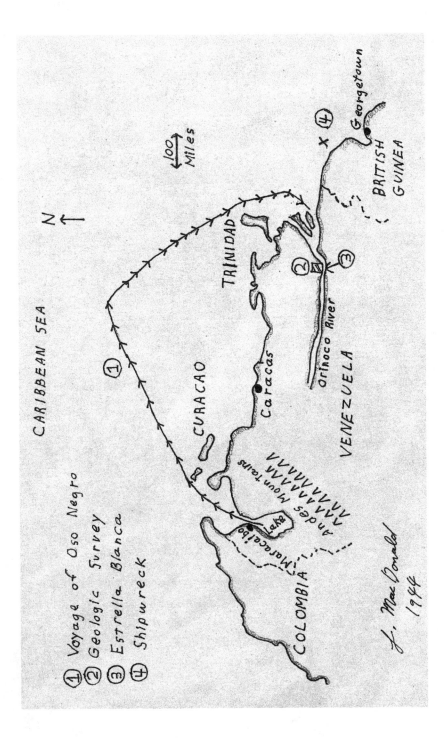

PROLOGUE

Berlin, February 1944

A LARGE CIRCULAR tank occupied the center of the laboratory, hidden from passers-by on the Berlin sidewalk by boarded-up windows. The boards replaced the glass that had been shattered months earlier by a British night raid. Despite electricity rationing, incandescent bulbs brightly lit the room.

A wooden step ladder allowed a technician to climb to the top of the open tank which appeared to be full of ordinary water. A helical network of over three hundred dark gray metal cubes, each uniformly machined to a two-inch width, was immersed in the liquid. Instrumentation wired to the sides and top of the tank, as well as to probes submersed in the water, measured a variety of data. Some information was easily understood—temperature, pressure, and the weight of the structure. Some was intelligible only to a trained physicist with dials calibrated in a unit labeled as *Roentgens*.

Several pallets of wooden boxes were stacked on the wall opposite the door. The boxes were made of a cheap yellow wood—perhaps a species of pine—measuring about a foot high and twice that in width and length. An iron strap wrapped each box, providing reinforcement and a hasp for a padlock. Whatever they contained was heavy. Eight boxes filled a pallet, and those pallets had been moved into the laboratory by the forklift now parked in a corner.

Two men stood next to the tank, reading the dials intently. One recorded data in a notebook. The other, Ernst Dussell, a visitor to the laboratory, stood with his hands in his pockets. He wore a look of intent interest, obviously understanding the measurements. Dussell was a tall man, heavy set with curly brown hair. He wore steel rimmed spectacles with the line of a bifocal lens hinting at approaching middle age. Clean shaven and immaculately groomed, he carried himself like a man with a military background, a common trait among German men in 1944.

"Well, do you see any indication of fission, Dr. Becker?" Dussell addressed the question to the most famous scientist in Germany, a Nobel Prize winning researcher in the field of quantum mechanics.

"I'm not sure." Becker looked up from his notebook. "The data are not unequivocal. I think we need more cubes."

"Do you really believe this will work?" Dussell asked.

Becker ignored the question. "I'm going to have it taken apart tomorrow and redesign it. There are another four hundred cubes in those boxes. Adding those to the ones already in the tank might create sufficient mass to induce spontaneous fission."

"There's no time left," Dussell said. A physicist, Dussell had worked on a parallel effort to develop a German atomic bomb. So far, neither effort had been successful. It was becoming obvious the war would end, to Germany's detriment, without a savior arriving in the form of a nuclear weapon.

"We've been ordered to send all of our uranium to Düsseldorf for the manufacture of anti-tank weapons. I imagine you will get the same directive soon," Dussell said.

"We'll see," Becker replied. Accustomed to obedience within his sphere, he was not prepared to simply hand over material from years of work so that it could be blown up as artillery shells.

"Well, we don't think the Americans are going to be successful either," said Dussell. "I'm going back to Gottow. Good luck with this."

Dussell put on his overcoat, opened the door to the street, and left without another word. He was not a friend of Becker, and the two engaged in an intense professional competition. Becker might not know what to do next, but Dussell had a plan. He made a show of locking the door from the outside. When the lights turned off inside the building, indicating Becker had returned to his office down the hallway from the laboratory, he unlocked the door again.

Three hours later, a German army truck backed up to the unlocked laboratory door. Four burly men climbed down and opened it. Using muscle power instead of the noisy forklift, they raised the heavy boxes packed with five-pound cubes of uranium metal into the back of the canvas-covered truck. With the loading completed, the men climbed into the back and sat on the yellow pine boxes.

The engine cranked, coughed twice, and settled into a noisy clatter. Moving slowly through the bombed-out streets, the driver made sure that a briefcase containing permissions and authorizations for fuel lay securely on the seat beside him. He followed a penciled route on a prewar highway map that led through Germany and occupied France to the coastal port of A Coruña in Spain.

CHAPTER ONE

The Orinoco Delta, April 1944

TWO MONTHS LATER, the steel hull of an ancient freighter pushed onto the muddy riverbank of the Orinoco River in Venezuela, immobilizing the vessel while allowing the propeller at the stern to remain in deep water. The anchor winch was inoperable, never needed when tied up at a wharf in any of the remote locations the ship visited.

As soon as forward motion ceased, a tall, red-haired figure on the bridge yelled down a voice pipe, "Shut it down, Esteban." Gordon was the ship captain and part owner of the decrepit vessel.

An unusual quiet overtook the freighter as the vibration from the oil-fired steam engine ceased. Accustomed to the constant din of the machinery, the crew looked uncertainly at each other. There were twelve of them, not including Gordon, who had navigated them into this strange place after leaving the Spanish port of A Coruña three weeks ago. They were planning a return to their home port on the Rio de la Plata, upstream from Buenos Aires. Argentina was still technically neutral in the summer of 1944, although often accused by the U.S. of favoring the Axis.

Once the ship had departed Spanish waters, they faced no interference from American or German naval vessels, although either side might have stopped and searched them. But a series of heavy storms and huge seas precluded the elderly vessel from voyaging south of the equator. The violent motion of the ship broke one of the steering cables controlling the rudder, and a makeshift repair only allowed steering in calm seas. The need to stop in a secure location to repair the cable, combined with a desire to avoid encounters from the U.S. Navy, led them to enter the Orinoco River and travel upstream.

The lower part of the river flowed through a mangrove swamp. The short trees, adapted to the harsh environment of the intertidal zone, were perched on a network of twisting roots that lifted the dense, dark green leaves above the high tide mark. The mangroves formed a forest of twisting channels with no place to moor the ship or step ashore.

Further inland, the terrain gave way to a grassy savannah with sandbars bisecting the river channel. Sandy riverbanks rose to a small bluff marking the edge of the grassy plains. This was where the ship's captain had ordered the helmsman to steer directly toward the shore, the freighter halting when the bow grounded in the shallow water. The stern was visible to any passing river traffic, bearing the name of the vessel: *Estrella Blanca*. White Star. Home port, Buenos Aires.

The captain relaxed as evening quiet replaced the constant vibration of the moving ship. He acknowledged a grease-stained individual who had appeared in the steel doorway leading downward into the freighter's machinery space.

"Well, Liam. Can we splice that cable?" Gordon asked in English. Spanish was the crew's usual language, but Gordon had grown up speaking both languages. He liked to practice English with those who spoke it. According to his mother, his English-sounding name was after his grandfather, a wealthy Englishman who had come to South America to manage a copper mine in Chile. He had met Gordon's grandmother on holiday in the Lake District, and they married a year later. An old family painting depicted him riding toward hounds in the English countryside with his red hair visible under his helmet.

"Aye, if we had a bit of spare long enough to mend it. But we don't," Liam replied with a cockney accent. Short and stocky with thin hair and pock-marked skin, Liam was born in the East End of London. He had moved to a suburb of Buenos Aires as a teenager but still retained the speech of his youth. Like the rest of the crew, Liam's home was the ship. He had worked his way up to the position of first mate and engineer, making him responsible for maintaining the aging mechanical plant that drove the vessel. The ship's location on the world's ocean never appeared to matter much to Liam, except for their proximity to an interesting port, but Gordon noticed that he seemed unsettled by the swampy delta wilderness.

Another man entered the bridge, looking irritated and impatient. Porcine and red faced, he spoke English with the accent of one who had learned the language in school.

"Kapitan, we have to deliver the cargo to Buenos Aires, not this godforsaken swamp," he said heatedly. "You were chartered to deliver us to Argentina. We need to get out of here before the police show up and want to look around."

Gordon tried to mollify him. "Herr Strock, we will be gone as quickly as we can. But there is no point in trying to head south in the Atlantic during the winter with a steering system that will certainly break again. We're stuck here until we can locate at least thirty feet of steel cable."

He didn't like Karl Strock, who had boarded the vessel in A Coruña and shepherded a shipment of heavy yellow pine boxes onto the ship. Acting nervous but self-important, Strock carefully inspected the cargo hold before telling the captain where the boxes should be stored, asking how high the water might be in the bilge, and what other kinds of cargo would be carried. He accepted Gordon's suggestion to put the crates on the bottom of the hold and covered with bales of wool cloth. No one would find the boxes without unloading the entire ship

Apparently satisfied with the cargo's arrangement, Strock had given Gordon a briefcase of gold coins. "You will receive the remainder when we dock in Buenos Aires."

"That'll be fine," Gordon replied. He wasn't surprised that Strock had wanted the wooden crates concealed. He had paid a fortune in gold to have them transported to South America, chartering the *Estrella Blanca* without quibbling over the price. As the eventual outcome of the war became clearer, influential Germans had increased their efforts to send valuable cargo, including art, gold, jewelry, and records of hidden bank accounts to safe havens in South America, particularly Argentina. Gordon didn't know what the wooden boxes held, but because they were reinforced with iron straps and locked with massive padlocks, he assumed they held cargo looted from Nazi-occupied countries and would be stolen or seized if discovered during a search of the ship.

As the *Estrella Blanca* captain for the last ten years following a promotion from five years in Liam's position, Gordon's only loyalty was to his ship. Accustomed to transporting cargo that usually some sort of contraband at best, and stolen property seized by violent encounters at worst, his decisions upheld the best interest of the *Estrella Blanca*.

The freighter called at out-of-the-way ports where few questions were asked. An outwardly amiable man, Gordon had made friends around the world at these ports, but he gave his allegiance to whoever paid for his ship's service, regardless of his personal likes or dislikes. On occasion, he had dissuaded or physically stopped people, some he counted as friends, from interfering with the *Estrella Blanca's* mission of transporting cargo or passengers.

Gordon would put up with Strock, regardless of the man's disagreeable manner. He could understand Strock's discomfort, but there wasn't much he could do about it until the steering was repaired.

Looking at a chart of the Venezuelan coastline, Gordon retraced the *Estrella Blanca's* route. They had passed through the delta's mouth two days ago and travelled the channel upstream along a path marked by irregularly spaced poles—until the shoaling water stopped their westward progress. But the charted area stopped at their current location. It indicated nothing about the maze of winding waterways north and west. Gordon needed a map of Venezuela, not a chart, but understandably, he hadn't bought one for a voyage from Spain to Argentina.

"We will leave as soon as we are able," he told Strock, "but I can't promise you when that will be. I suggest you make yourself as comfortable as possible."

*　*　*

Unhappy, but resigned to an interminable wait before they proceeded to Buenos Aires, Strock went below deck to compose a wireless message to the man who had sent him on this expedition: Ernst Dussell. Dussell would not be pleased. Strock hoped he wouldn't be blamed for the abrupt halt to the journey.

Locking the door to his cabin, Strock wrote out his message in plain German and then pulled a copy of *Ulysses* from his suitcase. Dussell had decided to use an English novel for coding purposes. The novel would be a less obvious choice to an American codebreaker, not that they would be interested in a transmission from the Estrella Blanca. The illiterate Americans had probably never heard of an Irish writer, much less a novelist by the name of James Joyce.

The code was simple: he would go the page number representing the current day and month in digits, and then exchange every letter of his message with the letters on that page in the novel, starting with the second paragraph.

Strock looked at what he had written before encrypting it:

```
April 13, 1944. Damage to the steering caused the
captain to come into Orinoco River for safe harbor
until repaired. We are about 100 miles upstream from
the river mouth. Captain trying to obtain materials
needed. Uncertain of when we can leave. Please advise.
Strock.
```

Leaving his cabin, he ascended a set of metal stairs to the bridge deck, a space sitting atop the stack of cabins at the ship's stern. The enclosed portion of the bridge spanned the entire width of the structure with reverse sloping windows facing the bow. Open wing decks projected outward on both the port and starboard sides, allowing an unobstructed view of the deck below and the surrounding seas. A spoked wheel of dark wood was centered immediately aft of the windows, with the engine room telegraph on a nearby pedestal. Behind the wheel, several chairs were bolted to the deck, and two tables faced the back wall. A set of charts covered the surface of one table, and a radio transmitter was secured to the other.

Strock was not surprised to see the captain and the wireless operator, a shy fellow named Francis, seated at the table holding the radio transmitter. They were apparently expecting him. Strock approached the operator and handed him the coded message. "Transmit this immediately."

Looking at Gordon, Francis took the sheet of paper marked with random letters, but he made no motion to start tapping his key. When the captain nodded, the tap-tap-tap of Morse code filled the bridge.

"Let me know if you receive anything for me," Strock said sharply. He opened the stairway door and returned to his cabin.

Staring at the ceiling and sweating in the tropical heat, Strock tried unsuccessfully to sleep. Hours later, a seaman knocked on the door, handing him a flimsy paper with an unintelligible mass of letters filling the top half. Strock took it without expression, locked the door, and removed his copy of *Ulysses* from the suitcase. He flipped the book open to the same page that he had used to encrypt the first message and quickly deciphered the reply.

April 14, 1944. Vermeer in Maracaibo evaluating options. Stay in current location until contacted.

Strock knew that Dussell had contacts in the multiplying, expanding, semi-invisible web of Germans who sought relocation in South America. He didn't know who Vermeer was, or how he would be contacted. But Dussell had been clear: stay put.

What a hellhole to sit around in, he thought. Resigned, he returned to the bridge to see what the captain could tell him. Maybe the ship could get moving before anyone contacted him. The last few months had been bad enough without sitting on a mudbank in the jungle.

* * *

Strock thought back to an evening in late 1943, sleet coating the windows of the laboratory where he had worked with Dussell. The day ended and the other workers departed, leaving him alone with Dussell to make one last check of the gauges and fill the recorders with fresh paper. Dussell had invited him to sit in his office, an orderly space lined with file cabinets and bookcases. A picture of a pretty young blonde woman sat on the desk, the only personal effect visible.

Dussell pulled a bottle of schnapps out of a desk drawer and poured two glasses.

Strock was a technician, not a scientist, good with wrenches and welding torches and able to construct the strange-looking experimental apparatus precisely as directed. He had worked for Dussell for several years, always in a clearly defined role as a subordinate to the physicist who directed the activities of the laboratory. On previous visits to the office, he had stood before the desk to receive instructions on how to set up the equipment. Surprised and grateful for the unexpected courtesy and being invited to sit down as an equal, he relaxed in the chair next to the desk and lit a cigarette. Smoking was forbidden in the laboratory, but he assumed Dussell's generosity would extend to permission to smoke, although he had never seen Dussell use tobacco. A proffered ashtray confirmed his assumption.

"*Danke.*" Strock took the offered glass, sipping the schnapps. It was excellent. Dussell must have had good connections to get it in 1944.

"I have some news for you and an opportunity that you might want to consider," Dussell began. "This is the end of the nuclear program. The last few weeks have not been good to us." Speaking carefully, he described the events leading to the cancellation of their project and his thoughts about the future. It was the first time that he had shared anything about the politics of the secret work with Strock, who listened intently as Dussell continued speaking.

"Kurt Diebner, head of the Gottow laboratory where we work on the nuclear project, and Werner Becker recently outlined a path forward to the Nazi leadership telling them that a bomb will not be operational until 1947. When Hitler heard that, he ordered the program shut down and diverted resources to Werner von Braun's V-2 missile program. The stockpiled uranium will be utilized to manufacture armor-piercing antitank shells. Its density makes it capable of penetrating inch-thick steel. But it's a waste of material that has much more valuable potential."

Dussell paused and took a large sip of schnapps and looked closely at Strock, who realized that his supervisor was deciding whether to trust him.

"It is a tremendous waste," Strock agreed. "After all the progress we have made."

Apparently convinced, Dussell continued. "The end of the war is growing closer, and the defeat of Nazi Germany appears inevitable to those willing to entertain the notion. I've been thinking about how we might survive and make a living. Our knowledge about making a bomb with nuclear fission, potentially able to destroy entire armies, might earn us a welcome somewhere else in the world. But the knowledge is worthless without uranium to test and build an explosive. I thought about how to deliver both to a buyer willing to pay with money and a new life, and I remembered an acquaintance from the southernmost country of South America."

Strock nodded vigorously, his self-esteem inflated by Dussell's confidence.

Dussell continued. "When I visited Rome in 1941, I happened to meet a rising colonel in the Argentinian army, Juan Peron, at the Argentinian Embassy. We corresponded over the intervening years. Peron is fascinated by the new process of nuclear fission described in my letters. He is now vice president and secretary of war, overtly on the side of the Allies but sympathetic to the plight of the German refugees. Peron is eager to build Argentina's industrial and military capabilities as a counterweight to the North Americans. He has welcomed some escaping German scientists with their advanced technology."

Dussell refreshed both glasses with schnapps. "As a participant in the secret nuclear program, my status allows me access to the diplomatic pouch without scrutiny by the Gestapo's lower ranks. I sent a message to Peron and received an enthusiastic response. I would be welcome in Buenos Aires, especially if I can bring some of the technology and equipment with me. And an associate with expertise would also be welcome."

So, he's going to Argentina. And taking me. Out of this disaster falling around us. Strock was exultant.

"I need someone to help me take the uranium from the laboratory in Berlin, drive it to a ship docked in Spain, and accompany it to Buenos Aires. If you are interested, it will be a new future for you in a new country after the war," Dussell concluded.

"I am your man, as always. Tell me what I need to do," Strock replied.

Dussell visibly relaxed.

Strock did not hesitate; like most Germans, he was aware of the impending collapse of the Third Reich and desperate to avoid the misery certain to follow the end of the war. He was unaware—but would not have been surprised to know—that Dussell kept a Luger pistol in the same drawer that produced the schnapps bottle. A refusal to support Dussell's plan would have led the evening to a different end. It was easy to explain dead bodies with gunshot wounds in 1944 Berlin.

The agreement resulted in the uranium theft from the Berlin laboratory, a trip across Europe in the final throes of war, and the charter of the *Estrella Blanca*, destined for Buenos Aires, but now halted in a mudflat of the Orinoco delta.

CHAPTER TWO

Curacao, April 1944

THE HARBOR IN the Dutch colony of Curaçao was fronted by a
street lined with houses that looked as though they had been transported from the banks of an Amsterdam canal. Closely spaced, three or four
stories tall with small windows and steep roofs, they were better designed to
conserve warmth and shed snowfall than to deal with the tropical heat of a
Caribbean Island.

Occupied by several families each—refugees from occupied Holland
who had managed to escape to a Dutch colony in the Americas so far un-
touched by the Nazis—the buildings had a surrealistic look. Normally me-
ticulously scrubbed and painted, five years of wartime neglect was evident in
shabby exteriors bleached by intense sun and the steady twenty-knot trade
winds that blew incessantly across the island.

The island inhabitants were supplied by a constant stream of small boats
that brought vegetables and fruit from the Venezuelan mainland across the
clear indigo-blue tropical seas, cautiously steering around the coral reefs rim-
ming the shoreline.

Sitting at a waterfront table, Jerry MacDonald finished his coffee. Newly
appointed as the head of Pride Oil in Venezuela, he had arrived at the begin-

ning of the year. Six feet tall with light brown hair and a dark tan from tropical living, Jerry had grown up in the dust bowl of Oklahoma. He worked his way through the University of Oklahoma to obtain a geology degree which led to a job in downtown Manhattan with Pride Oil. He was a known favorite of Mike Woods, the president of Pride Oil, and moved up the company ranks quickly. But he seemed oblivious to his reputation, talking in a good-natured manner about life in Venezuela and the business of producing oil in Lake Maracaibo.

Bob Wright, his companion and the manager of Curaçao's Pride Refinery, was sweating profusely in the morning sunlight. "I'll plan on an extra ten thousand barrels a day starting next month."

"You'll have it." Jerry spoke with confidence. "That last well in the lake tested at five thousand a day. Shell tried to buy the production from us, but we got orders to send it to you."

Bob wiped his forehead with a napkin. "We need it. Standard Oil is sending all their production to Aruba or to the States. If we can't get more oil from the Pride concessions in the Lake, we'll have to shut down. I'm glad you're finding some new reserves. We've seen a steady decline since the start of the war shut down most of the drilling."

"It hasn't been easy," Jerry said. "Hard to find a working rig, much less pipe and drilling mud. But diesel fuel is incredibly cheap. We've scrounged around and found enough parts to keep two rigs going."

"What are the Germans doing in Maracaibo?" the refinery manager asked.

"They're around." Jerry replied. "The Venezuelan Nazi party has an office there, and we see some of the consulate staff at various receptions and parties. As long as Venezuela is neutral, they're entitled to be there as much as we are. But we're starting to see them get nervous. If Venezuela decides to throw in with the Allies, they'll be kicked out. And they don't want to go back to Europe. They can see the direction the war is going."

Bob lowered his voice. "By the way, I had a phone conversation with Alan Courtney in head office last night. He told me more about your last assignment as the field geologist for the Sunniland wildcat well in the Everglades. Said that a German U-Boat crew tried to take over the rig and seize the diesel, but the rig crew fought them off, with you leading them."

"Did he tell you the well discovered oil?" Jerry smiled. "That's what I'm happiest about, not being an amateur soldier."

"I already knew about the discovery. But it's an impressive story. I'd like to hear more sometime."

"We were told not to say anything at the time, but I guess it's okay now. I'll tell you about it next time I'm here," Jerry said. "But right now, I have to pack and catch the boat back to Maracaibo. Thanks for breakfast. It was good to see you again."

"Say hi to Maria for me."

* * *

Three days later, Jerry and Maria, his beautiful Italian wife from Queens, sat at their usual late afternoon table by the pool on the shore of Lake Maracaibo watching the shipping traffic move past. A body of water the size of Rhode Island and connected to the Gulf of Venezuela by a narrow passage, the lake was flanked on the western side by low hills near the Colombian border. To the south and east, the Andes Mountain chain separated the lake and its surrounding marshes from the capital city of Caracas. The city of Maracaibo, founded by the Spanish in 1574, was located on the western shore of the passageway. The waters of the lake, dotted with drilling platforms, oil tankers, fishing boats hauling nets, and small sailing craft, supported a scene of hectic activity.

The tall National Hotel profile blocked the five o'clock sun, creating a welcome shade in the tropical heat. A well-known spot with American and European expatriates, the hotel had been a popular destination for celebrities before the war. Signed photographs of American movie stars—including Humphrey Bogart, Clark Gable, Lauren Bacall, Bette Davis, and others— were displayed on the tunnel connecting the basement of the hotel to the bathing area. With three restaurants, a marina full of cabin cruisers and run-abouts, and an arcade of fine shops, the hotel was a quiet oasis in the busy city. Jerry and Maria had spent three weeks there when they arrived, waiting for the house they now rented to be readied and their belongings to arrive from their apartment in New York City.

"How was your tea with Paula yesterday?" Jerry asked.

The wife of a German businessman, Paula had introduced herself at a party hosted by Maracaibo's mayor. Still officially neutral, Venezuela was home to citizens of the Allies and the Axis, who usually maintained a polite but distant air when they encountered each other in neutral settings. Paula was an exception. Outgoing and seemingly oblivious to the diplomatic chasm between the Americans and herself, she had attached herself to Maria, chatting about the social scene in Maracaibo. Maria had agreed to meet her for tea the following week.

Jerry was certain that Paula's husband, Hans Diess, was sending any available information on Pride Oil activities back to Germany, and he had cautioned Maria about saying too much. But they were bound to see Paula and Hans when they were both invited to gatherings like the one hosted by the mayor. It would be impossible to avoid polite conversation and the occasional invitation to tea or a drink. And Jerry knew that Maria wanted female companionship.

Maria was drinking white wine, condensation covering the surface of the wineglass. She wore a white blouse and a flowered skirt, both purchased from the local market. "I like Paula. But I can tell she's trying to find out what she can. She seems to think that since my maiden name was Magianni, I have sympathies for the Axis. But it's nice to have someone to talk to."

Jerry poured more wine into Maria's glass. "I'm sure they are starting to believe the Americans will land in France any day, and Germany will lose the war. They may be trying to make friends and find a way to stay here instead of going back home. It's going to be a mess over there after the war."

They sat in silence for a moment, wondering what the world would be like when the war finally ended.

After a moment, Jerry changed to a more cheerful topic. "How's your Spanish coming along?"

"Really well, but I keep getting it mixed up with Italian." Maria laughed. "I have this list of non-English words in my head, and I pick one out, and sometimes it's the wrong language. But using it every day makes me learn it."

"You did hear more Italian than English in the neighborhood where I met you. Some of your cousins didn't seem to speak English at all."

Jerry had met Maria on a New York City subway, walked her home, and then showed up at the bar where she worked the next day. Raised in a poor neighborhood in Queens, Maria had spent her high school afternoons bartending in the establishment of her Uncle Ignatius. It was a rough patch in the city fabric, frequented by men who had served time in prison and would probably do so again.

Some of them were related to her, but Jerry knew she thought of all of them as cousins. The bar's clientele had looked after her. They listened to her banter with customers and quickly responded to obnoxious suitors. Maria could handle suggestive comments and proposals herself, brushing them off with a smile and an insult. But if a drunken customer reached over the bar to grab her arm and pull her closer, one or two "cousins" dragged him out to the sidewalk. A quick apology was sometimes sufficient to avoid a beating, but not always. Maria had never been overtly threatened. If anyone had lost their senses sufficiently to do so, her cousins would have shattered his skull.

Maria's caring and outgoing personality contrasted with her rough upbringing. She reminded Jerry of the women in the dusty countryside where he had been raised. They dealt as best they could with the challenges of life, including violent men, but always remained willing to help others.

Six months after meeting on the subway, Maria and Jerry were married, moving into a large apartment in Queens. After spending a few months in the Florida Everglades, Jerry returned to Pride's Manhattan headquarters and was assigned to the Venezuela office in Maracaibo. On learning of their impending move, Maria purchased a Spanish dictionary and began practicing.

The reality of Maracaibo was not what they had expected. The city was beautiful. But modern buildings, Spanish ruins, and slums with abject poverty were distributed haphazardly throughout the city. Masses of people with barely enough sustenance to stay alive lived close to a few with extreme wealth, and there were not a lot in between. The area where they lived and where the Pride offices were located was comfortable and modern, but a taxi ride from their house to the National Hotel passed through dense neighborhoods marked by hardship. Shoeless children, dogs, and chickens competed with cars and wagons for space on dusty dirt streets. Whenever the taxi stopped, beggars would knock on the windows, demanding money. The taxi drivers looked straight ahead, ignoring pleas and shouted threats, edging forward slowly.

"What time to you want to go to mass tomorrow?" Jerry asked Maria. Both Catholic, they were happy to be in an environment where their religion was embraced and commonplace, a contrast to what they had found in the deep South of the United States. Latin Mass in Maracaibo was celebrated with the same familiar words they had grown up with, although they couldn't understand the Spanish announcements and the homily. But Maria picked up more and more and translated for Jerry after each service.

"Let's go at eleven." Maria replied. "Gives us time for breakfast. Besides, that's when most of our friends go."

"That sounds good. I'm leaving for the Orinoco survey this week, so this is probably the last time I can make it. Tuesday, I have a new geologist coming in from the States, and I need to go to Caracas and pick her up at the airport."

"Her?" asked Maria. "I haven't met a woman geologist yet. Where is she from?"

"Penn State. Mike Woods recommended her. Not sure how he knows her. She's a PhD student, and he says she can take it in the boonies. We'll see. If she can't, I'll send her home."

"I just read an article by Margaret Meade in National Geographic. If she could get by in Samoa, then this lady should do just fine with a group of Pride Oil geologists. If she wants to. What's her name?"

"Debbie Borowski. I'll bring her by for dinner after we get back from

Caracas."

"Good. I want to meet her. I believe she'll do just fine in your field party if she wants to. But I'm not sure why she would want to spend weeks at a time with a group of men, living in a tent in the wilderness."

"She's a scientist, a geologist, like the man you married. We do it because we want to understand how the earth was formed, and how it looked in the past. Sometimes that means spending time in the middle of nowhere. And we want to see new parts of the world. Debbie is probably going to feel like an army nurse in a field hospital with a bunch of men. Busy, protected, but looked at a lot."

Jerry knew his wife wasn't jealous. He'd had plenty of opportunities with different women in New York City but gave them up immediately when he met Maria. Maracaibo was full of beautiful young women, on the streets, in stores, and at the hotel. They smiled at Jerry while giggling at his Spanish. He would smile back and touch Maria on the shoulder—obviously in love with his wife—and move on without responding.

* * *

The taxi drew up to a restaurant in downtown Maracaibo, a stone edifice originally constructed by conquistadors and more recently converted to the most sought-after dining room in the city. The driver opened the back door, offering a hand to Maria and a pretty brown-haired woman with curly hair, while Jerry got out of the front seat. Entering the restaurant, Jerry greeted the maitre'd by name in English, immediately supplemented by Maria's halting but understandable Spanish.

"*Esta es nuestra amiga* Debbie Borowski," Maria told the maitre'd.

"*Encantada de conocerte*," he replied, escorting them back into a room half filled with heavy wooden tables covered with white tablecloths, softly lit by chandeliers and candles on the tables. The maitre'd pulled out chairs for Maria and Debbie, and the waiter appeared. He took their orders for a gin and tonic and a bottle of white wine, holding a lighter for Debbie's cigarette.

Satisfied with the service, Jerry turned toward the two women. "We had to wait on a thunderstorm to take off from Caracas today. A bumpy flight. But we made it back in time for dinner."

Maria turned to Debbie. "Jerry told me something about you. I'm glad you're here. We're a long way from Pennsylvania and New York City, and it's nice to see another woman from the States."

"I'm happy to meet you. Jerry told me a lot about you. Said you met on a subway. That's a good story. I'm really grateful that he's letting me work on the survey."

"I'm sure you will earn your way," Jerry replied. "Mike Woods recommended you highly but didn't say where he had met you. What's the connection?"

"I met him after he gave a presentation for the geology department at Penn State. He stayed to speak with the students. I told him about my research, and that I really wanted to fill it in with some field work in South America. He offered me a summer job in New York last year, and I guess he was impressed enough to recommend me to you."

"How did you end up studying geology?" Maria asked.

"I took a lot of detours, but I am getting where I want to be," said Debbie. "Would you like to hear the story?"

"Very much," Jerry and Maria replied in unison. The waiter opened the wine bottle and offered Jerry a taste. Declining, Jerry motioned for him to let Maria taste wine. After the ritual of approval was complete, the waiter poured two glasses for the women and handed Jerry a gin and tonic. Debbie took a sip, then started telling her story. Jerry and Maria listened intently as she spoke.

* * *

A descendant of the Polish families that had immigrated to America in the nineteenth century and found work in the mines and steel mills of Pennsylvania, Debbie had grown up in the small town of Coal Run. She watched her father, brothers, and cousins descend into the darkness of the mines when they were old enough to work, seeing daylight only on Sundays for the rest of their lives. Glad to be spared the expectation of working a thousand feet below ground level, she rebelled against marrying one of the local men. Blue-eyed with curly brown hair and tall with her mother's slim physique, she was sought after by suitors she had no interest in. She didn't want to spend her life raising a family in a hollow that was cold and dark during the winter months and coated with black dust all year long.

Escape had come with a chance visit to State College while accompanying her mother to visit an elderly relative in nearby Bellefonte. She persuaded her mother to let her wander the campus, promising to be at the New College Diner at three for the trip home. Upon entering a brick building, she saw a hallway with glass cases full of rocks and minerals. The open door of a laboratory revealed a bearded young man looking through a microscope.

"Hello," he had said. "Are you looking for someone?"

"No, I just have an hour to see Penn State, and I saw the door open."

"Are you a new student?"

"No," she replied. "I'm still in high school. And I don't have money for college."

"You should move here and get a job," the microscopist said. "If you live here in town, you can meet people and maybe get a scholarship. Come by and see me if you end up in town."

"Are you a professor?" she asked. He seemed pretty young.

"No, I'm a graduate student. My name's Bill, and I'm working on my master's thesis, describing the Tuscarora Sandstone. The microscope lets me see things that tell me where the sand grains came from, and how strong the currents were when they were deposited. Want to take a look?"

He moved aside, and Debbie peered down the tube, squinching her left eye shut. Sand grains filled the field of view—white, brown, and speckled with black spaces in between. It was a look at another world that she did not know existed. The microscope revealed a fascinating level of detail and complexity. She had always regarded rocks as something like the coal piled up in heaps around the small mountain town where she had lived. Thanking her new acquaintance, she left the building, walking down a sidewalk shaded by elm trees to the street bordering the campus.

A week after graduation from high school, she moved to State College and became a waitress, serving the students and faculty who patronized the restaurant across the street from campus. They told her where she might apply for scholarships. She filled out an application almost every day until she was awarded a tuition waiver from the Mineral Conservation Agency.

After six years in State College, attending classes during the day and waitressing at night, she graduated in 1941 with a degree in geology. As the campus emptied of young men during the war, admission to graduate school was easy to obtain, along with a stipend to work on a research project. Her PhD dissertation studied the geology of rocks formed from clay. Three years later, after a summer working at Pride Oil, she found herself in South America ready to map the formations on the northern edge of the Orinoco River.

* * *

"That's how I got here," Debbie smiled. "Anything to stay out of those mines. And I love geology."

"That's a good story," Jerry said. "I started out wanting to study engineering, then became fascinated after I took my first geology course. I've never wanted to do anything else since."

Jerry noticed the waiter standing by. "Let's order," he said. "Then we can talk about life in Maracaibo and what we will be doing in the Orinoco Delta."

Two hours later, with dinner finished, a taxi dropped Debbie at the National Hotel before taking Jerry and Debbie to their rented house.

"The plane leaves at 7:00 a.m. tomorrow," Jerry said as they went to bed. "Glad you got to meet Debbie."

"I like her," Maria yawned, then reached over and hugged him. "She's doing what she wants to do. I want to see more of her when you get back."

* * *

A latecomer to Lake Maracaibo, Pride Oil's presence was considerably smaller than that of Standard Oil and Shell, the giant companies controlling most of the production. Before Jerry had arrived, Pride managed to obtain a concession on the southern end of the lake and drilled a successful wildcat. But future opportunity in Lake Maracaibo was limited by the large areas of the lake bottom already granted to Shell and Standard Oil by the Venezuelan government.

Wanting to expand the country's already huge production, the government promised new concessions would be granted in the fall of 1944. One promising area was located near the Orinoco River on the eastern side of Venezuela. The Orinoco was a huge stream, second only to the Amazon, and it drained into the Atlantic Ocean. Oil had been discovered there, but much of it was "heavy oil," a tar-like substance that oozed into wells at rates too low to be worth anything. But some wells north of the river produced lighter, less viscous oil at commercial rates.

Jerry believed that if Pride Oil had a future in Venezuela, it would be on the Orinoco River delta, not the waters of Lake Maracaibo. He had convinced the Pride Oil president, Mike Woods, to provide funds needed to obtain a land concession and acquire seismic data in the delta. The Orinoco River delta was a vast expanse of land and water. The river divided again and again, flowing through multiple passes to the Atlantic Ocean. Shooting a seismic survey in the marshy terrain would help determine if drilling a wildcat well was worth the investment. But before a seismic crew could move in, a geologic map of the delta was needed to design the survey. Drawing the map would require fieldwork to evaluate the rocks and the geologic structure of the area.

Jerry decided to lead the party himself rather than delegate it to Kevin, an American geologist who worked for Pride in the Venezuelan office. He told Maria that he didn't believe Kevin had the ability to lead an expedition in the wilderness and bring back the required information. He didn't have to tell her that nothing made him happier than sitting on a boulder and examining a chip of a rock that he had broken off with a hammer, learning about the earth in a new place and how it had formed.

He assembled a field party. In addition to Kevin, it included Pedro, a Venezuelan geologist assigned by the government in Caracas to keep track of the expedition; Jorge, a Venezuelan from the delta area who would serve as a guide; and now Debbie, the graduate student.

Their task would be to explore the terrain north of the river, recording the types of rock exposed and the angles at which they dipped into the earth. The information they gathered would provide insights into the underground geologic structures that could then be mapped in detail with a seismic survey.

CHAPTER THREE

The Orinoco Delta, April 1944

THE FLOATPLANE DESCENDED rapidly, the roar of its motor fading as it leveled off a hundred feet above the water. Jerry directed the pilot to the drop-off point for the first transect as Debbie pushed her face against the window, looking forward at the winding waterway below.

"Another mile downstream, Rulof. Then touch down and taxi into the bank."

"Okay. About thirty seconds to splash." Clad in a short-sleeved khaki shirt, his right arm bearing a tattoo showing a condor, the pilot reached to lower the flaps, cranking a control wheel with a scarred right hand. A Dutch expat who had arrived in Maracaibo with Shell after flying oilfield support around the globe, Rulof left the corporate world to pursue his own flying company. It consisted of one plane, a single engine pre-war Atlantic Fokker. The wheels had been replaced by pontoons to allow takeoff and landing from Lake Maracaibo and the bays and rivers of Venezuela.

Rulof had a reliable reputation for flying over uncharted mountains and jungles. Jerry hired him on the recommendation of another expatriate, a boat captain who transported men and supplies to the drilling and production platforms in the lake. Rulof also spoke excellent English, which was a plus for

Jerry as he struggled to learn the colloquial Spanish needed to communicate with the oilfield workforce.

"What the hell is that up ahead?" Rulof asked in a puzzled tone as they approached the landing spot. "Looks like a ship. Wonder what it's doing here? No port nearby, and farther upstream than they need to be for safe harbor from a storm."

The ship was an elderly freighter about three hundred feet long with a flat deck stretching aft from the bow to a stack of cabins topped by the bridge. It was pushed bow first onto the riverbank, immobilizing it while leaving the stern in deep water so that it could back off when ready to leave. A small group of men on the foredeck studied a piece of machinery. They saw the plane and waved, seemingly unperturbed at being discovered.

"They're right where we want to start," Jerry said. "Seem friendly enough. Land and taxi up to the beach a few hundred yards west of them while we unload."

"Okay," Rulof agreed. The plane dropped until the floats touched the water, sending up a wake of spray, and slowed abruptly. Steering with the rudder, Rulof directed the plane toward the riverbank near the freighter.

The name *Estrella Blanca* was painted on the stern above a home port designation of Buenos Aires.

"Argentina," the pilot muttered. "Undoubtedly smuggling something to be up here. Sure you want to get off?"

"We'll be okay," Jerry said. We've done a lot of work getting ready for this transect. They'll know we're here now, so moving it a few miles won't make any difference. Let's go ahead and get off."

Rulof nodded and pushed the throttle slightly forward, causing the plane to move slowly toward the mud strip bordering the river's edge. The floats comprising the plane's landing—narrow pointed tubes with a flat upper surface—pushed up onto the bank two hundred yards upstream from the *Estrella Blanca*. One by one, the four men and one woman gingerly stepped onto the float and then jumped to the shore. Their boots sank into the mud. Standing on the float, the pilot opened a small door in the rear of the plane and tossed pieces of luggage ashore. The five passengers each strapped on an enormous, heavy pack that rose a foot above their heads and caused their knees to momentarily buckle. When they stood upright again, the pilot handed each of them a metal suitcase or a duffel bag.

"We'll be monitoring the radio. Call if you need us. But it will take me five hours to get here from Maracaibo, so don't wait too long to call if you need help. I'll be coming back every three days with supplies and to take back your notes and maps," the pilot announced.

"Thanks, Rulof. We'll be in touch if we need you. Otherwise, see you Saturday." Jerry pushed the plane away from the bank, allowing Rulof to taxi toward the middle of the channel.

The landward border of the low, muddy riverbank was marked by a four-foot-high bluff, a natural levee of sand created by muddy floodwaters overtopping the riverbank during the rainy season. About three hundred feet wide, it separated the river from a savannah of cordgrass that stretched to the north. The savannah was low and marshy with patches of semi-dry land isolated by streams flowing south into the Orinoco. They would learn nothing in the savannah, where mud covered any rock formations they might be interested in. Small cliffs and exposed hilltops were visible in the distance where rocks comprising the subsurface oil fields to the south were exposed at the earth's surface.

"Let's get going," Jerry directed his small crew. "We need to set up a camp on dry ground. The we can unpack the equipment and make sure it works. We'll start mapping tomorrow. The Oficina Formation should outcrop in those hills. "

Struggling to climb the small escarpment with heavy packs, the group moved inland, grateful for firmer footing. They encountered a natural clearing where a change in the soil resulted in short, stunted vegetation.

"This is where we should set up for tonight." Jorge walked in front of the single file. His indigenous bloodlines were evident in jet-black hair, brown skin, and dark eyes. A mustache drooped down both sides of his mouth, resembling a Hollywood portrayal of a Mexican bandit. Jorge had grown up in the delta but now worked for Pride on one of the rigs in Lake Maracaibo. Jerry had recruited him as a guide to the delta region, as well as cook, mechanic, and overall handyman.

"Looks good to me, Jorge," Jerry said. "Dry and away from the river in case the water comes up. "

"Also farther away from crocodiles," Jorge replied. Camping at the water's edge overnight would definitely entail the risk of an unwelcome visitor.

They spent the afternoon setting up three tents, olive drab canvas structures identical to those used as company command centers for the U.S. Army. Debbie had refused Jerry's offer to bring her a separate tent, telling him that she was happy to sleep on a cot in the same tent with the other two Americans. Jerry suspected that she didn't yet trust any of her new acquaintances and would rather put up with snoring than awakening to find one of them sliding into bed beside her. A second tent was shared by Jorge and Pedro, who Jerry had met only a few days ago when he had shown up from Caracas. The third tent would serve as an office. Inside, they set up two folding tables on which rested metal cases of geologic instruments.

"Kevin, open those cases and let's check out the gear," Jerry said.

"Where's the key?" Kevin, a bearded man going bald early with brown hair and glasses, asked in a frustrated tone. He had insisted that the cases be locked, although the possibility of theft between takeoff and landing was miniscule. Searching through his briefcase, he fished out a cylindrical skeleton key, popping his lips in satisfaction. Kevin unlocked the metal cases, fussing as he noted their condition after being thrown into the small cargo compartment of the airplane. He spread the equipment on the table. A collection of tape measures, rock hammers, chisels, small magnifying glasses attached to neck cords, and folding compasses were unloaded. Jerry exhaled in relief as another case was opened. The transit and surveyor's rod had made the flight undamaged. Without the surveying instruments, they could not accomplish what they had set out to do.

The last equipment to be placed on the table was a case which Debbie had loaded onto the plane. Kevin tried to unlock it, but the key didn't fit.

"I locked it myself," Debbie said. "I'll unpack it later."

"What's is it?" asked Pedro.

"A Geiger counter," Debbie replied. "Different shale formations each have a characteristic radioactivity. Shale all looks the same with a hand lens, so this should help distinguish them when we find them in outcrop."

"Sounds pretty complicated. Are you sure you know how to use it?" Pedro spoke in a condescending tone, moving closer to Debbie.

"I'll teach you some day," Debbie matched his tone, irritated, and turned away.

Watching the interchange between Debbie and Pedro, Jerry spoke up and took control of the conversation. "Well, we haven't forgotten anything or broken anything getting here. It's getting to be time for dinner. Jorge, I understand you are an excellent cook. Is that right?"

"*Si*. But there isn't much to do except heat up these cans. All we brought was some surplus American C rations."

"That will do for the first few days," Jerry said. "Can you build a fire? I'm going to talk to someone on that freighter. At least let them know who we are and that we're not going to bother them."

* * *

The bow of the *Estrella Blanca* towered above the muddy shoreline, a wall of rusted steel that was out of place in the marshy environment of plants and water. "*Hola*," Jerry shouted, presuming that Spanish would be a language they both understood. "*Yo quiero hablar con el Capitan.*"

A man in dirty overalls leaned over the rail, his red hair showing beneath a greasy cap. He responded in clear English. "I'm the captain. My name is Gordon."

"Hi, I'm Jerry. We're geologists with Pride Oil from Maracaibo. We're doing some surveying, and this is where we plan to start our next transect. What are you doing here?"

"We're on our way to Buenos Aires but broke a rudder cable. Managed to jury-rig a repair to get us up here. We're going to sit here until we can get what we need to fix it and get back to sea. This is as far inland as the stakes marking the channel went, and I don't have a chart, so we stopped here yesterday. How far upstream is the nearest town?"

"Not much except villages until you get to Ciudad Bolivar in about another hundred miles. We flew over it on the way down here from Maracaibo, but I've never been there. We have an extra seat in the plane that's picking us up in a few days if you want to go back to Maracaibo with us. I'm sure you can get what you need there—it's an oilfield town. But I don't know how you can get it back here."

"Thanks for the offer. Let me think about it. It would at least be a start. Need any help setting up?"

"I don't think so," Jerry replied. "We set up camp and we're going spend the night. We'll head out in the morning and start mapping north toward the hills. Come on over in a couple of hours and have a beer. We brought plenty."

Gordon smiled. "I gladly will. Thanks for the invitation."

Jerry returned to the office tent and watched Debbie unpack the Geiger counter. She connected the battery pack and set it on the table serving as desk, workbench, and dining table for the group. The instrument sat in a green steel case. It had a series of black knobs and switches on top, centered around a large dial. One cable led to the battery pack, and another was connected to an instrument that resembled a small flashlight. Debbie flicked the on switch to test the device. A loud buzz sounded from a small speaker on the side, startling her. She looked at the dial and swore in a dialect that Jerry assumed was Polish.

"What's wrong?" Jerry asked.

"Not sure. Damn thing must have gotten some dirt in the probe. All the way here and no replacement." Dejected, she turned the machine off and studied the small cylinder at the end of the cable.

"Looks okay," she said to one in particular.

"Maybe it will show variation between the shales, even if the absolute values are off," Jerry offered.

"That's possible," Debbie replied, sounding slightly encouraged. She put the Geiger counter in her pack along with a raincoat and tightened the straps.

* * *

Jerry opened the mosquito netting flap, welcoming the tall man with thin reddish hair that he had met earlier. Close-up, he could see the man's dark suntan and a nose that had been broken more than once.

"Gordon, this is Debbie, one of our geological crew. Debbie, Gordon is the captain of the ship next to us."

Debbie nodded. Jerry had explained the predicament of the *Estrella Blanca* while they finished setting up camp and told his crew that he had invited the captain for a beer. "I'd ask him to dinner, but they probably have something better than C rations on their ship."

"Pleased to meet you," she said. "Jerry told us why you were here. I hope everything works out for you to get where you want."

Transfixed, Gordon stared at the pretty young woman and stuttered, "Thank you." Jerry rescued him by introducing him to Jorge and Kevin as they entered the tent, carrying the ice chest filled with bottled beer.

They ate Jorge's dinner after Gordon left. One they had their fill of spam, fruit cocktail, and Vienna sausage, the group gathered in the office tent where they were protected from mosquitoes and flies by the cloth netting.

"What do you think of the ship next to us?" Debbie asked.

"I wish they weren't here," Jerry replied. "Gordon seems like a nice enough guy, and he has a good story. But they are undoubtedly smuggling something. They probably won't give us any problems, but I don't trust them."

"Do you want to do anything differently?" asked Kevin.

"No, tomorrow we will run a transect due north from here," Jerry said. "The Oficina Formation should outcrop somewhere in the next ten miles."

They all knew that the Oficina was the reservoir rock in the heavy, viscous oil fields to the south, and the hope of finding where it formed new fields was the reason Pride Oil had sent them to the Orinoco delta.

Jerry continued, "We'll have breakfast at six, same menu as dinner to-night, and then head out."

Later that evening, the three Americans lay on cots in the heavy canvas tent surrounded by mosquito netting and unable to sleep.

Coughs, grunts, screeches, roars, and shrieks penetrated the darkness.

Jerry said helpfully," We need to get some sleep. Full day tomorrow."

"I've never heard so much noise," Debbie muttered in the darkness.

"Sounds like our farm in Oklahoma when a coyote got into the hen-house," Jerry said.

"I spent a lot of time camping in the west and heard everything from owls to mountain lions," Debbie said. "But nothing like this. I have no idea what might harm us, and which ones are trying to find a mate or establish their territory, like a bull moose."

Sleep finally came to all three, until a scream from Debbie, accompanied by the noise of an animal trying to root its way underneath the edge of the tent, jolted the two men awake. Jerry reached under his cot for an electric lantern, the light revealing a creature that resembled a large hog, but a hog with a long snout that curved down, somewhat resembling a short trunk. The strange-looking animal made a snuffling noise as it pushed at the canvas wall, about to collapse the tent on the sleeping party.

"Get out of here," Jerry cried, shining the lantern into the eyes of the beast. He struck a pan with a geopick, causing a loud bang. The combination of the light and noise caused the creature to retreat, leaving the wall of the tent torn loose from the ground but the canvas structure still standing.

The canvas flap opened, and Jorge stepped inside carrying a rifle. "It's a tapir. They don't eat meat, but it must have sensed something in here that it does want to eat. Where'd it go? That would be enough meat for a week."

"Forget it," Jerry said. "We don't need it, and we don't have any way to refrigerate it. But I'm glad you brought a rifle. What else is out here?"

"A lot of animals," replied Jorge. "But the only ones you need to worry about are crocodiles and jaguars. Nothing else is going to attack a man. But there are monkeys, snakes, and a lot of bugs that can hurt you if you get in their way."

*　*　*

The open tent flap revealed gray light downriver toward the east, signaling the beginning of a new day. A dense fog rose from the muddy river and covered the campsite, reducing visibility to a few feet and deadening the sounds of the riverside clearing. Within fifteen minutes, it was light enough to make out tent outlines, but there was no brighter globe to give a sense of direction.

"Don't walk away from the camp." Jerry crawled out of the tent and stood up. "You won't be able to find your way back if you go ten feet away."

"Turn around, everyone." Debbie stated in a stern voice. "I need to go to the bathroom, and I'm not walking out of sight to get lost or eaten."

Jerry smiled with approval. Debbie was obviously used to existing in the wilderness with a party of men and wouldn't let modesty prevent her from demanding what she needed. She wouldn't need coddling.

The rest of the party laughed and obeyed. Fifteen minutes later, they all sat on logs near a driftwood fire, waiting for hot water to boil and provide coffee. The fog was as dense as ever, turning the circle around the campfire into a room with a dreary ceiling and gray walls. Combined with the knowledge that they were hundreds of miles from any civilization, it created a sense of dismal isolation.

"We can't get started until the fog lifts," Jerry said. "But let's get the equipment set up. We'll start the transect as soon as we can see where we're going. I want one person to remain here. If the fog settles in again unexpectedly, we'll need someone to bang on a pot to bring us back in."

"I'll stay," Pedro offered. He seemed unnerved by the dense cloud enveloping them and appeared glad to spend the morning sitting on a log.

"Okay," Jerry told him. He was somewhat surprised that a native of Venezuela, and a geologist who presumably had spent some time outdoors, would be frightened by the fog. Evidently Pedro preferred his office and the nightlife of Caracas to the wilderness in which he now found himself. But someone had to stay, and Pedro would do fine.

Looking north, Jerry saw the shape of a tree emerging from the gloom. "If you can't see that tree, start hitting the cookpot with something every five seconds until we all return."

Jerry unpacked a metal stake about six feet in length and picked up a sledgehammer. "We'll drive this in on the bank, above the high-water mark. The government chart of the river shows us where this bend is located. We need to mark the stake well enough so the seismic crew can find it when they show up."

Suddenly the fog lifted. It disappeared in a matter of seconds, bathing their campsite in soft sunlight and revealing the riverbank where brown water flowed steadily east toward the Atlantic Ocean.

Jerry started walking toward the river, but Jorge grabbed his arm.

"Wait a second. Let's make sure nothing moves," Jorge said in an urgent tone. "One of these driftwood logs could be a crocodile."

Jerry assented and watched debris scatter over the band of mud between the sandy bluff and the flowing water. The driftwood stayed immobile. After a minute or so, he continued toward the bluff and pushed the first stake into the wet soil. It went in easily for a few inches, enough to hold it in a vertical position. A series of energetic blows with a sledgehammer sank it into the soil until just a foot remained above the surface.

"Bring the rod and transit over here," he commanded. "Let's get started."

Kevin brought the transit—an instrument resembling the combination of a nautical sextant and a telescope atop a triangular wooden stand—and he placed it directly above the stake. Fiddling with the wooden legs and instrument adjustment screws, he managed to place it so that a plumb bob suspended from a string hung at the center of the stake. Then he adjusted the telescope until it was level in every direction.

"Good," Jerry said. "Debbie, go due north with your compass and hold up the rod about three hundred yards out. We'll wave to move you to where we want it."

Debbie trudged north through grassy terrain holding a handheld compass, sinking almost to the top of her boots at times. About three hundred yards out, she turned to face the men again. Kevin waved her east. She shifted her position and held the rod vertically, facing Kevin. He waved toward the east again, and she marched toward the rising sun. When she next held the rod in front of her, Kevin held two hands above his head, signaling that she had found the position due north of the stake Jerry had pounded into the riverbank.

Kevin peered through the telescope. "That puts her 320 yards away," he told Jerry.

"Good enough," Jerry replied. "Jorge, go stake it."

Jorge moved through the grass toward the newly established position.

Ten miles is about seventeen-thousand yards, Jerry calculated. *That means we have to repeat this process fifty or sixty times.* The result would be a marked line due north from the riverbank through the savannah toward the uplands, divided into three-hundred-yard intervals. Additional parallel lines laid out in the coming days would allow outcropping rocks to be located precisely, and a map to be drawn for the seismic crew that would follow in their footsteps.

They repeated the process throughout the morning, progressing to a point two miles north of the riverbank. As Jorge was driving the stake, Jerry suggested, "Let's stop and eat something."

Tired but pleased with their progress, they sat on hammocks of tufted grass and opened the cans from their C rations with a folding can opener. It was a tasteless lunch but provided calories and didn't require refrigeration.

The brown cardboard boxes containing their C rations each included four cigarettes. "Anyone don't want their cigarettes?" Jorge inquired.

"You can have mine," Jerry offered. He handed over a small package with a brown camel logo on the front. Debbie, Jorge, and Kevin all struck matches and lit up, inhaling contentedly.

Debbie blew out a haze of smoke, then asked Kevin and Jerry, "How much further inland do you think the first outcrops are?"

Kevin stood up and removed his glasses. He took a small pair of binoculars from his shirt pocket and fiddled with the focus. He looked toward the north. "There's a change of vegetation about two miles ahead. And it looks like there are some small breaks in the ground level. That might be something. Let's walk up and check it out. No sense in all this measuring if we're just going to end up with a transect across a bunch of dirt."

Leaving the surveying equipment behind, they walked north, letting Debbie take the lead. She looked down at her compass, then ahead at a landmark to ensure they kept heading north. The ground gradually became firmer as they left the marshy terrain behind, and the knee-high grass was replaced by open spaces of pebbly soil and small, stunted trees. A vertical rock face marked the southern end of a gradual upward slope in the ground level.

"Here we are," Jerry exclaimed in a satisfied tone. He knelt by the exposed rock and chipped off a small piece with a rock hammer. Holding the broken shard with one hand, he examined the dark, almost black rock fragment with a small magnifying glass that was suspended from his neck by a cord.

"Graywacke," he said. "This should be the southern outcrop of the Oficina. If we continue surveying in the transect until dark, we should reach this point before we finish today."

Jerry watched as Debbie turned on the Geiger counter, prepared to hear loud buzzing and see the needle on the dial jump to a high value as it had earlier. However, the machine remained quiet.

"I guess it fixed itself," Debbie said. "Maybe there was some dirt in the probe. These values are about the same as the ones I measured on shales in the laboratory at Penn State." She jotted a few notes in a field notebook as Jerry and Kevin measured the inclination of the beds with a Brunton compass and struck off samples with a rock hammer.

The sun sank behind the western mountains as they returned to the camp, catching them unaware. When it vanished behind the hills, the dense fog returned, enveloping the river valley in less than five minutes. Still a mile north of the camp on the riverbank, they watched the world disappear into a gray mist. The sudden shrinking of their world to a ten-foot-wide circle was accompanied by rapid disorientation. They were uncertain which direction they were facing.

Suddenly, a series of clanging sounds, five seconds apart, reassured them. They were close to their campsite.

"Let's head due south," Jerry said. "We should be able to follow the transect, and that will put us close enough to walk in based on the noise Pedro is making."

Debbie took the lead again, occasionally using matches from the C rations to check the compass in the absence of moonlight or a flashlight. They hoped to stumble across one of the metal stakes they had driven down to firmly establish their position, but after walking a distance several times the three-hundred-yard interval between the stakes, they had not found one. The clanging noise continued, but its direction was impossible to detect in fog that became denser by the minute.

"Let's go to the left," Kevin said. "That's the direction the clanging is coming from."

"No, let's follow the compass," Jerry responded. If we don't, we'll end up going in a circle for sure."

"Does anyone have any more matches?" Debbie inquired. "I used up my last one."

Jorge handed her a matchbook, and she took another look at the compass. "We need to go to the right," she said. "We've been veering left since the last time I checked. The clanging is misleading us."

They continued on, changing course to their right and following Debbie's compass to walk directly south. They paused while she took a reading, then ducked their heads as a sudden rain squall extinguished her match and soaked them. Frustrated, Debbie tried to strike another flame but only produced a soggy rubbing noise.

"Does anyone have any dry matches?" she asked.

Jerry produced a pack from his pocket, but they were soaking wet like his trousers. Jorge reached into his shirt with a similar result. Unable to see the compass, they stood together in the downpour and the darkness.

The clanging continued.

"Let's head to the right of where the noise seems to be coming from," Jorge said. "That's where we seemed to be when we could see the compass and hear the noise at the same time."

"Agreed. Walk in single file. Debbie, you've been out front enough. Get behind Jorge." Jerry ordered.

Debbie started to protest, not wanting to be protected from whatever risk walking point might entail. But she shrugged and fell in behind Jerry as the group walked on, their boots sinking into the mud. Fifteen minutes of bringing them closer to the camp, Jerry estimated, and tried to determine if the clanging noise was any louder. Suddenly, the clanging stopped, and the stillness of the tropical night, broken only by the sound of moving animals, closed in on them.

"He must be taking a break," Kevin said. "He'll start again in a minute." The group stood still, hoping for a resumption of the noise that was their only guide. The fog settled in, making it difficult to discern the next person in the group.

"Let's tie ourselves together," Jerry directed the others. "We don't want to lose anybody in this soup. Use some of that line we used to lay out the transect."

Unraveling a ball of cotton string, the three men and the woman tied themselves in a line. As they wondered which direction to set out, the clanging noise resumed.

"Guess he had to take a leak," Jerry said. "HALLOOO," he cried out. "Bang faster if you hear me."

The rhythm of the clanging did not change, but they walked slowly and carefully in single file toward what they perceived as the direction of the clanging. The fog lifted slightly, and the three-quarter moon lit the ground enough to keep them from tripping on the irregular surface.

"What's this?" Debbie stopped abruptly and looked down a depression in the ground. It was a footprint, one of a series that led off in a direction perpendicular to their progress. "There's someone else out here. They're headed to the camp. Do you think it's someone from the ship?"

Jerry looked carefully at the footprint, then pushed his boot into the mud. Lifting it out, he pointed and said, "That's my boot print. We've gone in a circle. No telling where we are."

They huddled together in a small circle, boots sinking into the soft soil. Debbie held the arm of the man next to her, who she recognized as Jorge from his breathing and shorter height. Someone grabbed her upper arm fiercely, squeezing her painfully through the fabric of her shirt. She recognized Kevin, shaking with fright. "Relax," she demanded. "We have to hold onto each other to stay together. But you're hurting me."

"Okay. But what do we do now?" Kevin replied in a hoarse whisper.

"We need to stay here." Jerry said. "If we keep wandering around when we can't see, someone will get lost, and we may end up in a bad place. Everyone just sit down on top of your packs where you are and try and get some sleep."

Jerry watched Debbie place her backpack on top of a tuft of grass, keeping it above the mud, and then sit down on it. *She's doing okay. I'm sure that spending the night worrying about crocodiles isn't easy for her.* Barely making out the shadowy figures of his companions, he looked at the phosphorescent dial of his watch. It showed 9:00 p.m. Only about twelve hours to go.

The clanging stopped again. He wasn't surprised. Pedro wouldn't be able to keep it up all night.

The field party sat and talked, occasionally opening a leftover can from their C ration lunch. After the inevitability of having to wait until dawn sank in, their predicament seemed less frightening.

Just as Jerry started to doze off, he heard a large animal moving through the nearby grass. "What's that?" he cried, struggling to keep the panic from his voice.

"Crocodile," Jorge said. "It's probably going back to the river. Shouldn't bother a group of five people on dry land." He sounded more optimistic than certain.

"Stand up and make some noise." Jerry didn't know whether that was a good or a not-so-good thing to do, but felt they had to do something. "Let it know there's a group here that isn't its normal food, and there are more than one of us."

The group stood up and started shouting into the fog. Terrified, they listened for the noise of a crocodile slithering toward the riverbank on its short legs, its belly dragging on the grass. Not hearing anything, Jorge declared, "It's probably gone. We could follow it's track toward the river if we could see it. Then we could follow the bank to the camp."

"Forget it," Jerry said. "Just sit tight. We have about ten hours to go. Relax and we'll be all right."

The night passed agonizingly slow, but the cacophony of animal noises didn't include any suggestions of another crocodile nearing the camp. The fog turned from black to gray, and eventually they could make out their companions sitting in a circle. No one had slept.

The fog disappeared in the space of a second, seemingly whisked away by a heavenly fan. Looking southeast, Jerry spotted the river and the camp about five hundred yards in the distance. Relieved, the crew shouldered their packs and trudged the remaining distance to find Pedro fast asleep in a folding chair, a cooking pot and hammer resting in his lap.

"Good morning!" Jerry said loudly,

Pedro startled awake.

"I'm ready for a nap," Debbie said. Her happy expression vanished as the Geiger counter in her pack started buzzing.

"What happened?" Jerry asked.

"I must have bumped the 'on' switch," she said, pulling the device out of her pack. "Or maybe the probe is still malfunctioning. Or maybe it's not the probe at all. Maybe the battery is getting low." Her shoulders sagged.

"So what's happening?" Jorge asked.

"It's getting a false reading," Debbie replied. "The radiation level is higher than anything expected from shales, and that's the only source of radioactivity around. I changed the battery earlier and jiggled the probe, but it doesn't make any difference."

"I thought it was working fine yesterday," Jerry said.

"It was working when we got away from the river. I thought some dirt fell off the probe. But something else is wrong."

"How do you know there is nothing radioactive around the camp?" Jerry asked. "Maybe there's something in the supplies that we haven't unpacked yet. If so, we need to find it."

Debbie nodded. "The readings aren't high enough to pose any danger to humans, but I guess we should at least rule out the possibility of an unexpected radiation source. I don't know what it could be." She walked over to the pile of boxes and crates that had been unloaded from the plane. The sound level of the buzzer didn't change.

"Walk in a circle around the camp," Jerry suggested. "Maybe something fell off a boat and drifted ashore."

Debbie picked up the Geiger counter and walked one hundred yards upstream. The reading diminished slightly.

"It's going down," she called. She headed back toward the camp and the river. "It's going up again." She continued downstream toward the beached ship and stopped. She looked at the freighter, tilted her head, and began walking toward it. Then she motioned to Jerry.

"The levels are increasing toward the ship," she said as Jerry caught up with her. "There's something radioactive associated with it."

Jerry looked down at the needle. They both walked steadily toward the beached vessel, noting the increasing response of the detector. Stopping a few feet from the steel side of the freighter, they noted the needle reading: fifteen milliroentgens.

"I don't know what's in there," Jerry said. "It sure is above background. Next time I see Gordon, I'll ask him what it might be. But your Geiger counter is working fine."

CHAPTER FOUR

Maracaibo, May 1944

LOCATED ON A street in downtown Maracaibo about a mile from the lakefront, the Novella Cantina occupied a wooden framed house painted pink and built on pilings about three feet above street level. A former three-bedroom home, the interior contained a combined kitchen and a dining room created by knocking down the dividing walls. The large front porch, set only two feet back from the street, held chairs that were usually full of men leaning back against the clapboard front wall of the house. Beer and liquor were plentiful, but the wine selection was almost nonexistent—a source of irritation to Sergio, who usually brought his own bottle to refresh himself as he whiled away afternoons on the porch.

The porch was empty this afternoon as he sat down and handed his bottle of Barbera to the waiter, who took it inside and returned with a filled glass. "*Buenos tardes*," the waiter smiled, putting the glass on a small table with a napkin. "*Quiere usted a comer?*"

"*No, gracias*," Sergio replied. He was waiting for a contact he had not yet met, a woman who had made arrangements to meet him on the Cantina porch at 4:00 p.m. He looked forward to the interaction, curious to see what she looked like, as well as why she would want to do business with him.

* * *

Tall and thin with dark hair and an aquiline nose resembling Ancient Rome statues, Sergio was attracted to women, and they were attracted to him. He had been born south of Naples in a poor village controlled by the Mafia and the Roman Catholic Church. A combination of family direction, economic circumstances, and a lack of willpower had landed him in a seminary at the age of fifteen. Not particularly spiritual, Sergio had appreciated the quiet environment, plentiful food, and lack of physical labor. But passing his adolescent years without female companionship was more than he could bear, and he would spend hours looking out the window while he studied, waiting to see the occasional passing of one of the young village women. However, strictly supervised and with no chance to visit the town unescorted, he had no opportunity to speak with them, much less hold one by the hand.

That all changed with his graduation from the seminary at the age of twenty-one. After ordination, he was assigned as a junior priest to a large parish located in the Trastevere neighborhood of Rome. With many of the young men away fighting Mussolini's African wars or training in the rapidly growing Italian Army, Sergio met a number of young women who were beguiled by his youth and appearance. Most were outwardly practicing Catholics, but some were not averse to seducing a priest. As the Second World War engulfed Italy, Sergio congratulated himself on finding a safe refuge with little danger or toil and a never-ending chance to encounter and bed beautiful women. A natural agnostic, he was not concerned about breaking the spiritual vows he had taken at his ordination. The constant lying and duplicity to his fellow priests and superiors, however, produced a weariness and coarseness in his attitude. He started thinking about leaving the church and starting a new life—a life where he could speak and act as he truly thought. He spent hours trying to think of an exit from his role that would allow him to keep the creature comforts and security he enjoyed as a parish priest.

As the war raged on, even a young priest in Rome had access to the Vatican intelligence network through rumor and gossip if not formal involvement. The information relayed by a global network of priests and lay people, supplemented by contacts at the highest level of officialdom around the world, was second to none. The 1943 Allied landing, the subsequent armistice signing, and the dismissal of Mussolini were followed by the Germans taking control of Rome and the north. Information flowed from the Vatican to priests who lived and worked in the parishes to Bishops and Cardinals. It was conveyed through conversations at lunch and visits from aides, and convinced Sergio that Germany could not win the war. This encroaching reality became the subject of nightly discussions in the rectory and at dinner with parishioners, conversations with an underlying nervousness that reflected an awareness of their German occupiers. Sergio wondered what life under an Allied occupation would be like.

The growing threat of Bolshevism, a system dreaded by the Vatican more than the fascism of Hitler and Mussolini, permeated the network of Italian Catholicism. It ran from the huge cathedrals of Florence and Venice to small churches located in isolated Tuscan villages. Some members of the Vatican hierarchy chose fascism as the lesser of two evils, believing the church could find ways to co-exist with it rather be abolished by an atheistic regime. They began setting up a network to help some of the Reich's most heinous criminals escape and find safe refuge in South America.

As the network became more organized, sympathetic priests and monks were enlisted to provide documents, food, and shelter. They helped arrange passage on ships bound for Argentina, Paraguay, Brazil, and other countries sympathetic to the tenets and goals of the Nazis. The efforts were coordinated by Bishop Franz Erkurt, a bulwark against communism who was based in the Vatican and a proponent of a stronger tie between the Church and the Nazi regime.

Always looking for priests who were willing to aid the growing tide of escaping Germans, the bishop requested a meeting with Father Mario Sengi, the rector of the Trastevere church and Sergio's supervisor. The beginning of the Lent season, symbolized by ashes on the foreheads of the faithful in Rome, was approaching at the end of the month. But that evening, in the third week of February, was still a time to celebrate with the excellent food and wine found in Rome. Bishop Erkurt and Father Sengi had dinner in a restaurant near the Ponte Vittorio Emanuele over the Tiber River.

Called into the office of the rector the following day, Sergio listened to Father Segni recall his conversation with the bishop.

"He wanted to know more about you. I don't know why. He heard about you from someone, but not me," the rector related. "I told him the truth—that you are not a true man of God. You and I have discussed this many times. You see the Church as a safe place to live and work during these terrible times, but you are more interested in feathering your nest and enjoying yourself than serving Christ."

Sergio listened silently. He was familiar with Father Segni's opinion of him and didn't care what he thought. His only concern was that somehow the rector would arrange to have him transferred out of the city and away from the plush life he had built for himself.

"He asked your views on the Germans," Father Segni continued, "if you hated them for occupying our city."

Sergio did not reply. He had studiously avoided discussing the German occupation with the rector, worried that a positive or negative comment might equally result in an unwelcome change in his status.

"I told him that you don't have strong views on anything except pretty women," Father Segni said. "If a German was young, blonde, and female, you would be most sympathetic. Otherwise, you would probably do whatever profited you the most."

"So, what happens now?" Sergio asked nervously.

"He wants to talk to you tomorrow. Go to his office at one. He will be expecting you."

The following day, Sergio walked up the broad avenue to the Piazza San Pietro, nervously wondering why Bishop Erkurt had summoned him. He was aware of the bishop's pro-Nazi sympathies but could remember nothing he'd done over the past few years that would have put him in a position of disfavor. Perhaps the bishop just wanted a new clerk. Sergio didn't want to work in the

Vatican, aware that young priests were constantly on call for whatever tasks the bishops and cardinals had in mind at the moment. He greatly preferred the quiet life of an assistant priest in the Trastevere parish.

Familiar with the offices of the Vatican, a labyrinth of palatial rooms for the upper levels of the Roman Catholic hierarchy and windowless cubicles for laboring priests from around the world, Sergio entered a waiting room. He nodded to the older man who looked up with a questioning expression.

"I am Father Sergio," he said. "I have an appointment with Bishop Erkurt."

"He's expecting you. Knock on the door and wait for an answer. Then go in."

Sergio knocked and entered the offices overlooking the Piazza, ornately decorated with walls showing masterpieces from the Renaissance, known to be a favorite period of Erkurt. The bishop rose from behind his desk and came around it, looking at Sergio curiously.

"I understand you like the ladies," he said.

"I try to help them find God," Sergio replied.

"That's not what I'm talking about," the bishop said. "But I don't really care. I need some help on a project. Do what I require, and your pension will be supplemented with gold. In a year, it will be the only currency worth anything in Italy. Don't meet my expectations, and you will spend the rest of your life as the resident priest for a monastery, isolated from the world, and you won't need money for anything."

Sergio nodded, afraid to speak. He wasn't sure if this was a trap, a situation that he needed to somehow avoid without offending the bishop, or an offer that would actually interest him. "What would you want me to do?' he asked cautiously.

"The war will be over in a year," the bishop said. "The Germans cannot prevail against the Americans. For every tank the Germans destroy, the Americans build ten more and ship them over here. There are, of course, Germans who recognize the end of the Third Reich is imminent and fear the Allies revenge." He paused, looking for a reaction from Sergio. Seeing none, he continued. "Some of these Germans have done terrible things, but that is between them and God. They are fiercely anti-communist, which is what the Holy Church requires now. If the Bolshevik armies overrun Europe, the Church needs a sanctuary. These people can provide it—if they can escape to a place where they can gather and establish themselves."

Aware of the trickle of refugees to South America, Sergio nodded. "I understand that Argentina might be such a place."

Smiling, the bishop responded. "Exactly. They need help to get there before the Americans and British capture and execute them."

Sergio made his decision. "What can I do?"

"I will give your name to people we want to help. They will contact you at your parish church. You will receive money, documents, and directions for where to send them next."

Sergio nodded his assent. He really didn't care what the Germans might have done, although he had heard horrible stories of the Gestapo and seen executions in public squares. But that wasn't his responsibility. Some gold, a patron high in the Vatican who owed him a favor, and a chance to stay in his comfortable surroundings were all he needed to agree.

On the last day of February, early in the morning, a middle-aged, balding, and overweight man showed up at the rectory door asking for Sergio. He waited in the parlor, tired and worn from traveling but with a look of superiority and determination. When Sergio appeared, the man introduced himself as Frank.

"I was told to ask for you," he said stiffly. "That you might help me with documents and transport to Naples where I can board a freighter. Is that correct?" The man held himself stiffly, with an air of restrained violence.

"That's correct," Sergio replied. "Would you like a glass of wine?" He wanted to learn more about this individual, the first of what would be a steady stream of Nazi officials in the coming years.

"Yes," the refugee replied. "I haven't had anything to eat or drink in a day. I had to leave in a hurry. Stayed too long, and almost did not make it here."

"What did you do?" Sergio asked.

"Don't worry about that," his visitor said. "I'm here now."

Leaving the man to sleep in a walled-off bedroom, safe from the prying eyes of visitors and the other clergy, Sergio put together a package including a passport, boat and train tickets, and some cash. It would be sufficient to get the visitor to Naples, under control of the Allies, where he could book passage to Buenos Aires. Several stops along the way would be required, but transportation and secure places to stay had been arranged with fellow supporters. There was little likelihood that the fleeing individual would be detained or identified as a Nazi official. Sergio wondered what the man had done and why he decided to leave now, with the Germans still holding northern Italy. Months if not years of severe fighting lay ahead.

Somebody must want him safe in South America. A thought struck Sergio. How easy it would be to take this man's place. People supporting the escape routes were expecting someone they did not know. Anyone who showed up with the right passwords and documents would find assistance for a voyage to the New World. The war had made Italy a dismal place to live, and the future promised no improvement over the coming years. South America promised not only a life in a new country, but a chance to leave the church behind. Sergio hesitated and then woke the sleeping refugee and handed him the package.

But thoughts of fleeing Italy occupied his every waking hour afterwards, wondering if he should have been bold enough to take a desperate chance.

Six weeks passed, and Sergio was growing weary of the fasting and penitential rites of the Lenten season when a young family arrived at the rectory door. A blonde, tough-looking young man accompanied by a pretty woman and a young child. An SS sergeant stationed in Milan, the man had decided to escape before the Allies invaded Germany. He visited his parish priest, who had arranged a journey as far as Rome. After verifying that they were expected, Sergio brought out a package of documents.

"Before I hand this over, I need to know the passwords for the rest of your journey," he told the German. "The bishop has told us to double check to make sure we are not being infiltrated."

The man stiffened. "We were told not to tell the passwords to anyone. We have come this far on the instructions given to us. Why should we trust you?"

The woman interrupted. "Tell him or I will. I don't want to spend life in an American prison. We're not in any position to negotiate."

Sergio smiled at her. "I'm obviously not going anywhere. I don't blame you for not wanting to tell me. But if you don't, you're not going anywhere either. These are my orders."

Reluctantly, the escaping Nazi spoke quietly, struggling to control his anger and fear. "Partridge, Peanuts, Pascelli, and Poconos."

"That should do it," Sergio said. He led them to the hidden room and then went down the street to the Gestapo headquarters. An hour later, the woman and child sat in chairs, watching the police sergeant interrogate their husband and father.

"A deserter, eh?" the sergeant yelled. "There are good Germans dying just south of here. What makes you think you can just leave when you want?"

The SS Sergeant had no reply.

"I'm going to contact Captain Heidel. He can decide what to do with you." the police sergeant said. He opened the door to a cell and pushed the SS Sergeant inside. Looking at the woman and child, he added, "You can wait in here with him."

They entered the cell, all three of them sitting on the only bunk to keep off the floor. They would spend a week there before their husband and father was shot.

After removing his cassock and donning the peasant clothes he had purchased while awaiting such an opportunity, Sergio left the rectory. He started walking south along the coast highway. Tired of the priesthood, tired of Italy, and tired of pretending that he wasn't interested in seeing pretty women, he had been awaiting the arrival of someone he could impersonate and replace on the escape route. The absence of the woman and child might be a complication, but he felt confident in being able to describe their emotional decision to stay behind rather than leave their European homeland.

Sergio arrived in Buenos Aires in March of 1944 with a fabricated biography and story of escape from an American prison camp. But the German community viewed him with suspicion. Although his German was fluent, they questioned his accent. Sergio decided that someone would eventually betray him after the war, and he had no desire to live with the Germans in any case. He studied a map of South America, weighing alternative destinations.

Brazil was out. He did not know any Portuguese. He looked at the countries to the north—Colombia, Peru, and Venezuela. Venezuela was intriguing. Its huge oil production would foster spin off businesses and create some opportunities for a middleman. He had given up his identity as a Catholic priest after arriving in Argentina and had no intention of resuming it, but he was confident that the skills he had learned aiding escaping Nazis would be useful in a new setting.

That proved to be true in the lakeside city of Maracaibo. Sergio became an intermediary, a fixer, an arranger for the underground network that aided the growing swell of refugees from Europe looking for a new life. He provided contacts, documents, lodging and transportation for a fee and asked no questions.

✳ ✳ ✳

Today's meeting on the porch of the Novella Cantina had been arranged by an Italian acquaintance who worked at the Pride refinery in Curacao. Sergio was not told where the woman was from or what she wanted, but he would help her if she could pay. As he drank the light red wine, he watched someone who matched the description he had been given walking carefully along the broken sidewalk of the dusty street in downtown Maracaibo.

CHAPTER FIVE

THE BLONDE WOMAN looked out of place in the South American city, and she was. In her late twenties or early thirties, almost six feet tall with striking blue eyes, a full-bodied figure, and classic features, she bore a resemblance to Marlene Dietrich. She walked upright with a confident stride, although she kept her gaze focused downward to prevent tripping on the chunks of displaced pavement. Her original name, Mannheim, had been carefully discarded, and her Dutch passport stated that she was Gretel den Martigh.

* * *

The mistress of a Gestapo commander in Orleans, she had never been involved in the arrests, tortures, and murders employed by the Secret Police to keep their captive populace subdued. She wasn't worried about what triumphant Allies might do to her in any official proceeding. But she was known to the French resistance and knew they would come after her because of her association with the man they referred to as the Butcher. As the Allies pressed north through Italy at the beginning of 1944, she had foreseen the inevitable conquest of all of France and returned to Germany alone.

Adrift in Berlin, she met a former lover, Ernst Dussell, at a cocktail party and took up with him again. He seemed busy, preoccupied, and worried about some matter that he refused to discuss. His job must have held some importance to the Reich because he did not lack resources or access to high-ranking officials. In any event, it kept him off the eastern front and safe for the moment in Berlin. And that meant having a house that could provide shelter for a mistress.

Returning from dinner one evening, Ernst stopped her on the way upstairs to the bedroom they shared and asked her to sit with him in the parlor. Opening the discussion, he asked, "Do you think the war is going to end soon?"

"Yes," she replied carefully. Anyone could see that it would not last forever, and it would not end well for the German people. But saying so openly could get one shot, regardless of their position or friends.

"I agree," Dussell continued. "And those of us in positions of authority are going to be persecuted. I have friends who are planning a new life in South America, in Argentina. The vice president there, Juan Peron, appreciates what we can do. Are you interested?"

"Yes," she said again, still careful. She did not have much to offer him except physical companionship, and he owed her nothing. She wondered what he was going to propose.

"I want you to go now," he told her. "Everyone is trying to figure out how to get to Argentina, and it's going to be a crowded highway. I'm planning something, and I need a contact in South America. Getting you there now will be easier than waiting until the war is almost over."

"What will you want me to do?" she asked. Living in Orleans had been easy, with no work, but she was branded by her association with the Gestapo chief. She did not want to repeat the experience in Argentina.

"Set things up for us. You will be given contacts and instructions. I will be joining you in Buenos Aires after I make arrangements for a present to be delivered to Juan Peron."

"I can do that."

"Good. You will need a code name. Something Dutch would fit with your new identity."

Gretel thought for a minute. "How about Vermeer? I always liked his *View of Delft*."

Mayday of 1944 found her in the tropical climate of Maracaibo, Venezuela, rather than the fall weather of Buenos Aires. Dussell had arranged passage to Curacao for her with a Dutch passport and a story of meeting a husband who was a Shell refinery manager. The voyage on a tanker returning from Europe to load another cargo of aviation fuel from the refinery had been uneventful, but the next leg of the journey had not materialized. Arrangements for a flight to Buenos Aires fell through twice, forcing her to remain on the tropical island. Dussell had provided her with sufficient funds to live well in a good hotel, but she was impatient to arrive in Argentina and begin a new life.

Days passed in a monotonous succession, and she fell into a pattern of drinking tea on the hotel terrace every afternoon. A variety of potential suitors approached her, drawn to the glamorous young woman sitting alone, but she had refused them all. Then two days ago, bored and frustrated, she was about to accept an invitation for cocktails from an island restaurant owner when the waiter brought a telegram to her table. It was a message from Dussell, telling her to take the short trip to Maracaibo on board one of the small lake tankers carrying crude oil from Lake Maracaibo to the Pride refinery on Curacao. He gave her detailed instructions to meet with someone named Sergio and charter a boat. She was to use the name Vermeer as an alias.

* * *

Gretel stopped at a sign nailed to the porch railing of the pink house, which announced that the business within was known as the Novella Cantina. Looking at the handsome young man on the porch, she said *"Esta un hombre con el nombre Sergio aqui?"* Her Spanish was excellent, acquired during a stay in Spain during the Civil War with her Gestapo paramour.

"Si," the young man replied. "I am Sergio. Who are you?"

"They call me Vermeer. What is the shortest way to Sicily from here?"

"By boat," Sergio answered.

Gretel nodded, satisfied with the response she had been told to expect. "They told me you have connections to get things done. Is that true, or am I wasting my time?"

She could see that Sergio was distracted by her appearance, but her abrupt tone brought him back to the business at hand. "I can get things done for someone who is willing to pay," he said. "But it depends on what you want. I deal in favors and helping people, not in merchandise or enforcement."

Gretel nodded. "I need a boat that can take me from the Orinoco River to Buenos Aires. Right away. And I can pay. I have German marks."

"Those will be worthless pretty soon," Sergio replied." I want American dollars or gold. For me to arrange the contract, and for the owner of the boat if I can set it up."

"All right." Gretel was not surprised. No one wanted German marks for payment outside of the Reich anymore. Dussell would have to come up with some hard cash if he really wanted a boat. But that was his problem.

"Tell me a little more about what's involved," Sergio said. "How big a boat do you need? And what will it be carrying? Do we have to avoid the customs patrol? Getting past the coast of Brazil will require some payments to the Brazilian Coast Guard."

Gretel nodded. She understood that she would have to provide a certain amount of information to make anything happen, although it put Dussell's plan at some risk. "The boat has to carry one man and some crates weighing about two tons. The cargo is on a freighter in the Orinoco River."

"You didn't answer the second part of the question," Sergio stated, looking directly at her.

"Yes, we will have to avoid the authorities until we get to Buenos Aires," Gretel said. "The cargo can be inspected. It looks innocuous, but we don't want it to end up in a warehouse in Rio while someone decides what to do with it."

Sergio shrugged. "That will mean an uninterrupted voyage from the mouth of the Orinoco to the Rio de la Plata without visibility from the shore.

In good weather, a fifty-foot boat could make that journey and carry the required cargo. But it would have to be self-sufficient and not stop for fuel. A small vessel would require sails."

"Whatever it takes. I'm not a sailor. But it will have to get to Buenos Aires."

"I'll see what I can do. How can I find you again? Do you live in Maracaibo?"

"Let's meet here again tomorrow." Gretel ended the conversation and retraced her path up the street.

*　*　*

The following day, Gretel climbed the stairs to the front porch of the cantina, joining Sergio at a table in the corner. She waited for him to speak.

"I've found a boat for you," he reported, looking at Gretel intently.

"That's good," she replied non-committedly. "Tell me about it."

"It's an old fishing schooner that works the Gulf of Venezuela between the islands and Caracas. It should be able to get up the river to your cargo and make the trip to the River Platte in good weather. No motor, strictly a sailing vessel. I told them the shipment would be less than ten tons—is that right?"

"That should do it. It was described as wooden crates, all of them together about the size of an automobile. That shouldn't be more than a few thousand pounds."

"They won't have any trouble handling that. I assume the freighter has a crane that can lift it from the hold and into the boat. When do you want to do this?"

"As soon as possible," Gretel answered. "They want it in Buenos Aires before the end of the war, and that looks like it's not too far off."

"All right. Ten thousand U.S. dollars and the boat will arrive at the freighter's location. If you decide to abandon the voyage at that point for any reason, another ten thousand is due. Another twenty thousand is payable when the cargo is offloaded in Buenos Aires."

"That's a lot, but not my problem," Gretel said. "I'll contact the people who want the cargo moved, and let you know. Let's meet back here tomorrow."

"Fine. How about a drink to celebrate?"

Gretel looked at him appraisingly. He was very good looking, and she had lived a clandestine life for a long time. She nodded and watched him turn to the waiter and order.

"I'll have a gin and tonic." He turned to Gretel. "What would you like?"

"The same."

Two glasses garnished with lime wedges appeared, and she raised hers. "To a successful voyage."

After an exchange of cables that evening, Dussell agreed to the vessel price. He had no other options. He would wire the funds to a bank in Maracaibo.

* * *

Gretel returned the next afternoon to the now-familiar cantina to see Sergio seated at a table inside instead of on the porch, talking to a man wearing stained coveralls, a fisherman's cap and a deep-water tan.

Sergio stood up and introduced her. "This is Carlos, the captain of the *Oso Negro*."

That's a strange name for a fishing boat, Gretel thought, extending her hand. "Pleased to meet you. I am Gretel. Thank you for agreeing to serve us."

"I haven't agreed to anything," Carlos said rudely, ignoring her hand. "I understand you want some boxes picked up from a freighter in the Orinoco River and taken to Buenos Aires. What's in the boxes?"

"I don't know," said Gretel. "It's worth moving. And the principals want it kept secret, obviously, so that it doesn't get stolen. You can open a box when you get them on board for all I care."

"I will." Carlos took a small cigar from pocket on the bib of his overalls, lighting it with a kitchen match scratched on the wooden floor. "If it's weapons that can get me hung if we are stopped, it goes over the side, and you can hire another captain to retrieve it from the river bottom. I'm not transporting machine guns."

"I can't imagine that's what it is," Gretel said. "The world is awash in weapons right now. No one would pay forty thousand dollars to move boxes of guns to Buenos Aires."

"Forty thousand?" Carlos exclaimed in a surprised tone.

Sergio winced.

"I was told it would be twenty," Carlos said.

"I have to make something," Sergio muttered.

"Well, you've just made ten thousand less," Carlos said. "I want thirty, and you can have ten for your trouble. It took you all of an afternoon."

Sergio glared at Gretel. "Okay," he said resignedly to Carlos. "When can you be there?"

"Beating upwind against the trades from Maracaibo will take me about three weeks. I'll need a week to get ready for a voyage to Buenos Aires. Let's say a month from today."

"If that's the best you can do," Gretel said. She knew Strock would not be happy spending a month on board the freighter, but Dussell would insist after she informed him about the lengthy timeline.

"One more thing," Carlos said. "You have to come with us. I'm a fisherman, not a pirate. And I can navigate to Buenos Aires, but I want someone else to explain what the hell we are carrying."

Gretel looked at Sergio, then at Carlos. She surprised them both by saying, "I want to go to Buenos Aires. And if the only way I can get there is on your boat, so be it. I'll go. But I expect to be the only woman on a small ship with you and your men. So let me be clear. If I go missing, if I'm hurt in any way, or just unhappy with you, you will be killed when we dock in Buenos Aires. Understood?"

"*Si, Señorita,*" replied Carlos. "But you will actually not be the only woman. My wife sails with us. I will let you share our cabin with her, and I will bunk with the crew."

He has no intention of giving up his comfortable berth for a hammock in the forecastle, and his wife probably won't want to sail all the way to Buenos Aires and back. But he badly wants thirty thousand U.S. dollars, so he'll let the crew know that I'm off limits in every way. Gretel passed an envelope to Sergio. "This is the first installment as agreed. I'll let you and Carlos decide how to split it up. When and where do I get on this boat?"

"It's docked on the lake, south of the city. The name is on the stern. *Oso Negro.* I named it after a black bear in a fairy tale. This is Tuesday. Be there a week from today at six in the morning. And bring everything you will need for two months—we won't be stopping at the pharmacy."

"I'll be there." Gretel stood up and left the restaurant, wondering if the boat would really be at the dock ready to leave in a week, if there really was a boat, and if it would ever actually reach the freighter, much less Buenos Aires.

CHAPTER SIX

JERRY STOOD OVER a drafting table in his office studying a map
of the Orinoco delta. A series of pins placed in a line north of the river
showed the location of samples taken and measurements of the bedding an-
gle. After their misadventure in the fog, the remainder of the fieldwork had
gone relatively smoothly. Starting at midmorning and returning to camp by
4:00 p.m. to avoid the onset of fog reduced their field time, and he had considered lengthening the workdays after the fog failed to return. However, he
maintained the shortened schedule, chastened by the fear induced from sitting in the dark and hearing the movement of a large predator.

Debbie's Geiger counter continued to function well away from the ship,
but Gordon had offered no explanation for the increased signal near the *Estrella Blanca*.

"Maybe it's something in the steel when it was built. Who knows what
they used?" Gordon had told Jerry.

Glad to be back in Maracaibo for a week before returning to the delta,
Jerry accepted an invitation to a reception at the Governor's house that evening. He promised Maria he would be home by midafternoon to change and
have time for them to take a taxi. He knew his wife was looking forward to it
but felt ambivalent about the affair. When he had first arrived in Maracaibo,

attending official functions felt like a deserved recognition of his rise within Pride Oil. After weeks of isolation at the Everglades drilling site, the bright lights, the beautiful gowns of the women, and the animated conversation represented a glittering world that had admitted him at long last. Jerry still enjoyed the social life of the expat community in the lakeside city, but the novelty had worn off.

What had not worn off was the undercurrent of whispered conversations, covert deals, and informal arrangements between the invited guests: Americans, Germans, British, and a few Italians in addition to the Venezuelans. They were all in the intelligence gathering business—if not for a foreign government, then for a commercial enterprise or personal survival.

They entered the room an hour late, delayed by Maria's last-minute decision to wear a different dress. The Governor greeted them as the last of the guests in the receiving line moved into the ballroom.

"Jerry, how are you?" he asked in perfect English, learned at Stanford.

"We are very well, Governor Gonzalez. Thank you for your hospitality," Jerry answered.

"Maria, you look beautiful as always," the Governor said. "Let me introduce you to one of your countrymen and a new resident of our city." He turned to a short pale man with thinning gray hair and wearing a linen suit. "This is Jerry MacDonald, the head of Pride Oil here in Maracaibo, and his wife Maria. Jerry, Maria—this is George Morales."

"I'm glad to meet some fellow Americans," George said. "I'm with the State Department—a bureaucrat pushing paper in the consulate office. What you're doing sounds a lot more interesting. If you're around tomorrow, I'd like to come by your office and chat. I could use your perspective on life in Maracaibo."

"I'll be glad to see you," Jerry agreed. Mike Woods had told him that he would be contacted by Americans in Maracaibo who wanted information on a variety of war-related subjects, and that he should cooperate. Jerry was certain that George Morales was more important than he described himself and would want to talk about Venezuela's new oil contract terms. Pride Oil needed to stay on good terms with the State Department.

* * *

Jerry greeted the secretary in his Maracaibo office two weeks later, his first day back at Pride headquarters after another visit to the Orinoco delta. "*Buenos Dias*. It's good to be back in town."

"*Buenos Dias*, Señor MacDonald. I have put the most important paperwork on your desk. The drilling manager wants to see you right away. And there is a message from señor George Morales."

The message was a request to meet for a second time. The first visit had been non-consequential, mostly a discussion about the likelihood of Venezuela following in the path of Mexico to nationalize their oil resources. Jerry returned the call and agreed to meet for lunch at a café located on a small street near the Pride offices.

As Jerry approached the table, it was evident that George had something more specific in mind. They exchanged small talk as the waiter served them broiled fish from the lake over plantains. George had a focused and direct demeanor.

"I've been told to help you if I can. What are you interested in?" Jerry asked.

George sipped his coffee and then replied. "A lot of the higher-ranking Germans know that they're going to lose. There's no way they can hold on against the Russians and the Americans. They've started moving gold, U.S. currency, art, and other assets to Argentina, planning to relocate there after the war. There aren't a lot of people moving yet, but we expect a torrent after the war is over. They'll need money to pay for the trip and to live on when they get to South America, and they won't be able to get it out of Europe when the Allies and the Russians are controlling everything. So they're sending it now. Kind of like setting up a bank account in a town where're you're planning to move."

"Haven't seen anything like that," Jerry mused. "The only thing out of the ordinary is a freighter stranded in the Orinoco close to where we're doing a geologic survey. It's stuck on the bank near the starting point for one of our transects. Captain said they're waiting for a cable to repair the steering."

"That could be important. Where did it come from?"

"They said Spain. Not sure if that's true or not. But there's something unusual about it."

"Oh?"

"A graduate student with us has a Geiger counter used to measure shale radioactivity, and it went crazy near the ship. That means there's something radioactive on it. But the captain said he had no knowledge of anything that would set off the Geiger counter."

"Not sure if that means anything to us. But obviously, the ship could be carrying assets from the Reich to South America. I'll let Washington know, and they'll probably try and find a way to search the ship—unofficially of course. If you have some people in that area, are you willing to help?"

"Sure," Jerry answered. "I'm going back next week for about six days to map another transect."

*　*　*

The next morning, Jerry sifted through a pile of paperwork. Invoices, cables from New York, and purchase orders were a constant source of irritation to him. It came with his promotion to the managerial ranks, but he found it an unwelcome distraction from planning the next step of the Orinoco Delta geological survey. A ringing telephone interrupted his task. Picking up the phone, he answered brusquely. "Hello."

"This is George. Can I come over right away?"

"Now is fine, "Jerry replied, welcoming the distraction. Thirty minutes later, George sat across from his desk.

"I was interrupted at dinner last night by a messenger from the consulate. Said there was a cable for me. Here it is." George pushed across a flimsy paper with the decoded message.

May 16, 1944. Imperative to understand source of
radiation on stranded freighter. Will send expertise.
Await contact and arrange for participation in
geologic party.

"I'm going back in a few days," Jerry told George. "If you have somebody you want to send along, we have room on the plane."

* * *

Five days later, a young man carrying a metal suitcase stood on the lake-shore dock that served as a base for Rulof's flying service. He was a book-ish-looking individual sporting a crewcut, rimless glasses, and the field clothes Jerry had instructed him to wear. He had arrived at the National Hotel the evening before, accompanied by George Morales, and introduced himself to Jerry as Sam. He offered no last name.

"I've got an instrument that can measure the frequency of the gamma rays emitted from that ship," Sam explained to Jerry. "It's been developed by some professors from the University of Manitoba, and they provided us a prototype. Uranium, thorium, and potassium all have different frequencies. We want to determine what the source is. Then we can decide if it's worth doing anything about it."

"I'm glad to have you along," Jerry said. "The reading from Debbie's Geiger counter is somewhat unsettling. I'd like to know what's in the ship, for my own reasons as well as whatever you are here for. Debbie and I are flying out to meet the rest of the crew and map another transect. I already told Debbie that you're from Livermore Lab and here to follow up on the radiation in the ship and make sure it isn't hazardous. There's some truth to that, in fact."

Boarding the plane and fastening his harness, Sam behaved like someone who was accustomed to small aircraft in out-of-the-way places, showing interest but no concern as the pilot started the single engine and taxied out into the lake. Shouting over the engine noise, Sam introduced himself to Debbie.

He described the details of the instrumentation that he carried, and how it enhanced the data obtained from a Geiger counter.

Five hours later, after a fuel stop at a remote jungle airstrip, the plane coasted to the riverbank near the rusted hulk of the beached freighter.

"This is where we started the first transect," Jerry said. "The one we're mapping now is five miles downstream. But we can stall around here until you can get a reading next to the ship and then take off for our current location."

"Can you pretend to be doing something scientific while I get the readings?" Sam requested. "I don't want to alert them that I'm particularly interested in whatever is in the ship."

"No problem," Jerry replied. "Debbie and I will drive some stakes to mark the transect near the river. It will be useful for the geophysical crew when they arrive, anyway."

Sam nodded and climbed out of the plane carrying the large suitcase. He waded ashore, then ascended the muddy bank to the edge of the grass that lined the river. Setting the suitcase carefully on the ground, he opened it and assembled a complicated instrument. It was a gray metal box about six inches in length with a tube extending from one end. A dial was mounted to the end of the tube, and a cord connected a detachable wand about six inches long to the box. A battery pack was connected to the instrument that provided power when a switch on the metal box was flipped.

Grunting satisfaction that all of the parts had survived the journey from northern New Mexico undamaged, Sam turned on the scintillation counter and read the dial. Looking at Jerry, he said, "That's all I need. It's reading point oh four eight million electron volts. That's uranium. There's a stash of uranium in that ship, and enough of it to be detectable through the steel hull."

"What are you going to do now?" Jerry knew there was radiation in the ship, and detecting uranium wasn't surprising. He didn't expect Sam to tell him much more than that.

"I'm going to go back to Maracaibo on the plane," Sam replied, "and then get back to Los Alamos as fast as I can. They'll want to know about this. And so will Washington. I don't expect to be back—any follow-up is out of my area of expertise. I'm just the guy who knows how to analyze radiation."

"That'll be fine," Jerry said. "The pilot's going to drop us off downriver and then head back to Maracaibo while there is still light. I hope to see you someday and talk about what all this means."

* * *

George Morales sat in Jerry's office a week later, smoking a small cigar. Since their introduction at the Governor's reception, Jerry had met George a few times in restaurants or in the Pride Oil offices. Other than the request to take Sam to the site of the *Estrella Blanca*, their conversations had been casual discussions about oil production in Venezuela and the social scene in Maracaibo. Jerry could tell from George's attention that he was being evaluated. But this meeting had a different atmosphere. George shifted in his seat, obviously uncomfortable.

"Thanks for taking Sam with you to the Orinoco," George began. "I got a report back on what he found."

"And?" Jerry didn't like guessing games. If George wanted something, he needed to say so.

"The ship contains uranium. We don't know how much or in what form. But his report is unequivocal." George looked at Jerry expectantly, waiting for a reaction.

"I knew that," Jerry replied. "Sam showed me the readings on his detector and explained it to me. I guess it's important for someone to have sent him all the way here to make the measurements. We already knew there was radioactivity in the ship from our Geiger counter. What do you intend to do about it? It's stuck on the riverbank until the freighter can get a new steering cable— which could take some time. They're not very high on anyone's priority list."

"We want that uranium. I told you there's a lot of stuff being smuggled out of Europe these days. We're not sure how uranium fits into that. It's heavy, has limited uses, and doesn't have much of a market. But we have a use for it. And we don't want it getting loose and unaccounted for in South America after the war ends."

"What do you need from me?" The ask was coming, and the sooner Jerry found out what it was, the sooner he could agree or start justifying a refusal.

"Before I tell you, I need to say that this is strictly between us. You can't talk to your superiors at Pride Oil about it, or to anyone else. The penalties for revealing top secret information are severe, as you can imagine. I won't try to scare you with them, but trust me, you wouldn't want to find out."

Jerry hesitated. He didn't like the sound of this but didn't see a way to back out now. There was a war going on, and his government was asking for assistance.

"Okay. I'll keep it confidential. What do you want?"

"Venezuela knows we would take over in a minute if the oil was jeopardized, but it's a neutral country, at least in theory. So we really can't send a destroyer up the Orinoco to seize the uranium. What's your next step in your work out there?"

"We have one more transect to run. I'm headed back out there tomorrow." Jerry waved at the cases of equipment piled in a corner. "Then we have a couple of weeks of office work to map out what we find and send it to New York. They'll design a geophysical survey. After that, the seismic field crew will arrive, probably from Trinidad, and start shooting."

"What does shooting have to do with a geophysical survey?" George was clearly perplexed.

"We shoot or explode dynamite to create sound waves below the surface. Measuring how they bounce off layers of rock tells us something about the geology miles below."

"That could work," mused George. "How does the seismic crew get up the Orinoco?

"Pride has boats under contract," Jerry replied. "We've got to send about thirty men plus sound detectors, dynamite, cables—things like that. The terrain is pretty open, so we don't need anything to clear the land other than some men with machetes."

"Where do these people come from?" George asked.

"The guy in charge is a geophysicist coming from New York. Jan Boer. He's done these kinds of surveys all over the world. He'll bring some experienced people from the Trinidad office and some unskilled labor to clear a path to set up the survey. And I plan to be there."

"We might want to add a couple of people to your crew. Can you come up with a cover story and tell us what they need to know?"

"Probably," Jerry said. "We need some men to set out jugs—that's what they call the sound detectors. Not much to it—just push a spike into the ground in a straight line. They'll look more like they fit in if they're South American—not from the U.S."

"They'll be from Virginia. FBI headquarters. Can you spin a story that they're working for Pride on a training assignment?"

"That might work. We can say they're new geophysicists learning how we acquire data. It doesn't just appear on a paper seismic line."

"And does the boat go back to Trinidad when the survey's done?" George asked.

"I'm not in charge of the boat," Jerry replied. "But I expect that'll be the plan."

"It will have some extra cargo on it. Is it big enough to carry a few thousand pounds? I'm not sure what form it will be in—boxes, pallets, sacks."

"That won't be a problem," Jerry said. We usually carry more heavy equipment than this survey will require. There should be room. And we have a small crane to lift tractors and swamp buggies ashore."

"Thanks," George said. "Let me work on the details. When will you be back in Maracaibo?"

"In about a week," Jerry said. "I'll have my secretary call you when I'm back in the office."

CHAPTER SEVEN

T HE SUN REFLECTED off the gray lake as dawn broke on the Maracaibo waterfront. Gretel boarded the *Oso Negro* carrying a canvas suitcase and wearing unfashionable leather boots.

The old sailboat had a crew of six, four fewer than when it was actively
fishing, but sufficient to sail the craft around the east coast of South America.
Tanned to a dark brown with black hair tucked under cloth caps, the crew
spoke softly in Spanish as they cast off the last two lines that secured the boat
to a wooden wharf. Built alongside a dirt road south of the city, the dock was
the closest thing to a home port that the vessel could claim.

A ketch with two masts stepped in front of the wheel, both rigged fore
and aft, the *Oso Negro* also carried a jib on the mainmast. The only sail hoisted for the undocking maneuver was the mainsail, which pushed the bow of
the boat east in a steady motion. The vessel was underway before Gretel had
placed her bag on deck and started looking around for Carlos.

Focused on navigating the boat through the shifting maze of stationary
and moving obstacles, Carlos acknowledged Gretel with a quick nod. "Put
your gear in the main cabin. When we get out of the lake, I'll help you get
settled."

Irritated that she wasn't shown more respect as the one financing the voyage, she left her bag on deck and walked to the bow around a raised cabin with

open windows. Gretel never got seasick and liked boats—or so she thought. This one was changing her mind, as a fishy stench rose from the hold and permeated the air. She started to regret her decision to accompany Carlos and the *Oso Negro* to Argentina, but at least she was finally moving to her destination, leaving behind the virtual imprisonment of Curacao.

Gretel overheard Carlos order the remaining sails hoisted, and the boat picked up speed. Slowed by the weed and barnacles attached to its bottom, it still made about six knots.

Gretel had estimated the distance to Buenos Aires the night before on a globe she found in the lobby of the Maracaibo hotel. It looked to be about forty-five hundred miles sailing around the hump of Brazil. She translated that to kilometers. Farther than Spain to New York. About a two-month voyage.

She wondered what she had let herself in for, and cursed Dussell for not arranging air transport from Curacao as he had originally promised. But it was better than what the French Resistance would do to her if they caught her in post-war Europe. When American soldiers had liberated Sicily, freed townspeople shaved the heads of girls accused of sleeping with the occupying German soldiers. The French would do far worse to the mistress of a Gestapo commander.

As the *Oso Negro* reached the northern end of Lake Maracaibo, the marshy western shoreline was replaced with docks and city buildings. Gretel saw the lakeside hotel swimming pool, an expanse of blue surrounded by umbrellas and a poolside bar. The lake narrowed as they entered the passage to the Gulf of Venezuela, and they swerved hard to port to avoid a southbound tanker. Gretel wondered about steering without a motor, but the crew handled the sailboat effortlessly, hugging the eastern bank of the passageway as they continued north.

Glad to be underway, Gretel returned to the suitcase she had dropped on deck near the helm. Picking it up, she asked Carlos, "Where is the cabin I will share with your wife?"

"It's at the stern," Carlos said. "But she decided she didn't want to go to

Buenos Aires. So, it's all yours. I'll sleep with the crew in the forecastle."

"Yes, you will," Gretel told him. Perturbed but not surprised by the announced change in plans, she wondered if Carlos really intended to spend the nights in a hammock for the next two months or hoped to reclaim his normal berth. But she realized that she had the best accommodations on the boat. She carried her bag down the aft companionway, passing through an open area with a table in the middle and hammocks lashed to the bulkheads. A door led into the stern cabin, a spacious room that spread across the beam of the boat and had two portholes on the stern. Gretel opened them both, grateful for the fresh air that diluted the smell of fish.

She opened her suitcase on the berth and removed a length of chain fastened to a padlock. She passed the chain around the doorlatch lever and then secured it to a grab rail at the top of the cabin, making it impossible to open the door from outside. Satisfied that she would be able to sleep uninterrupted, she looked around for a place to store her clothes. A single chest rested on the deck, apparently utilized by the captain's wife. Resigned to keeping her clothes in the suitcase for the duration of the voyage, she unpacked clean sheets and replaced the ones on the berth. After locking her suitcase, she carried Carlos' bed linen to the main cabin. One of the crew sat at the table eating a melon with a spoon. He laughed when he saw the linen, pointing toward a space on the deck below one of the hammocks. Gretel unceremoniously dumped the sheets on the wooden floor and then climbed the ladder to the open air.

*　*　*

The *Oso Negro* heeled over so steeply that the lee rail was submerged in the blue water, the old sailboat driven north by the perpetual trade winds, taking the seas on the starboard bow. Spray soaked the deck in a continuous shower of warm salt water. The sails were trimmed fore and aft, putting enormous pressure on the hemp cables securing the masts and straining the network of wood and rope. It appeared to Gretel that a single line parting would cause the entire structure to collapse. She wondered where the safest place to stand would be if something snapped and moved to the stern of the boat, standing between the taffrail and the helmsman. Accustomed to sailing on the North Sea, the weather did not intimidate her. But she was used to more substantial and better maintained vessels.

After sailing slowly and carefully through the channel linking Lake Maracaibo to the Gulf of Venezuela and passing the city of Maracaibo on the west with low, swampy marshland to the east, they were on the third day of their voyage. The Isla de Zapara fell astern. They sailed northeast with the Dutch island of Aruba visible to starboard and the helmsman holding the boat as close to the wind as possible. As they reached the open Caribbean Sea, the trade winds blew uninterrupted at full force from the western coast of Africa creating ten-foot waves that crested white on top.

On the first day of sailing, Carlos had described the course to Gretel, showing her the northern coast of South America on a map ripped from an atlas, not a nautical chart.

"The water is deep everywhere so we don't need to worry about soundings," Carlos explained. "The wind will blow due east continuously, which is the direction we want to go, so we have to tack into it. We're going to make Trinidad in two tacks, sailing northeast until we can turn southeast and clear Trinidad. We'll probably sail almost to Puerto Rico before we tack. It looks farther, but we would travel just as far making a lot of fifty-mile tacks and staying closer to the coast. And this is easier on the crew—no one has to work except the helmsman. Once we pass Trinidad, we change course and head south for the mouth of the Orinoco."

Gretel would have indeed preferred to stay closer to the South American coast, passing near the string of islands that stretched from Curacao to Trinidad. If the old boat sank, they might be close to a fishing boat that could rescue them. But at least they shouldn't encounter any government vessels on the route Carlos had described. Soaked through by the warm spray, she considered going below, but with all the portholes dogged shut, she wanted to avoid the pitching cabin. In spite of her immunity to motion sickness so far, she suspected she would succumb from the violent heaving in a closed space. So she leaned back against the taffrail at the stern, enjoying the tropical sun and ducking occasionally when a sheet of spray blew over the quarterdeck.

At least we're moving quickly, she thought, and indeed the boat sliced through the water at nine knots—although not in a straight line to their destination.

Gretel wondered about the man named Strock she was being sent to deliver to Buenos Aires with the uranium. She had never met him but knew that he was connected to the secret program Dussell had worked on. Dussell's telegram—the one that had sent her to Maracaibo and on this voyage to Argentina—hadn't said much about him, other than to ensure that both Strock and the boxed-up cargo arrived in Buenos Aires. She hoped Strock would be good company on the second half of the voyage.

"Look! Whales!" the helmsman shouted, pointing to a stream of water rising twenty feet above the surface before the wind blew it apart. A large animal broached the surface and moved across their path, swimming with a porpoising motion. It appeared to be a creature from another world and reminded Greta of biblical stories from her childhood, tales of encounters between men and Leviathan.

"Fall off!" Carlos yelled, and the helmsman turned downwind to avoid collision. The bow of the *Oso Negro* turned to port, causing the boat to sail parallel to the whale's path. A huge creature, fifty feet in length, swam closer to the starboard side of the boat, raising a head with a long lower jaw exhibiting rows of sharp teeth and a monstrous eye. Gretel watched it swim parallel to the sailboat, her sense of wonder replaced by dread at the close approach of the huge beast.

"Sperm whale!" Carlos shouted at the crew. "Keep going straight and hope he doesn't get mad." The whale moved closer, matching the speed of the *Oso Negro*, its huge eye only feet from the rail. Then it disappeared, sinking below the surface as an enormous tail towered above the deck of the vessel.

"Turn back to starboard," ordered Carlos. "It's gone. Unless it comes back." The boat resumed its previous course, beating to the east against the trade wind, when the boat shook violently as a huge blow struck the port side amidships.

"It rammed us." Carlos grabbed a backstay to stay upright and turned to a seaman. "Miguel, go below and see if we're taking on water."

Constantly wearing an apron of faded blue canvas that carried a hammer, screws, nails, twine, and a marlinspike, Miguel seemed to have the role of carpenter and sailmaker. He didn't participate in the work of steering and sail trimming but repaired whatever the hard driving of the old sailboat caused to fail.

Gretel saw him rush down the companionway, then reappear a few minutes later, standing on the ladder. He reported in a scared and excited voice, "We had a strake caved in about two feet below the deck. It's taking water now but won't be when we go on the other tack."

Terrified of being stranded in the water if the boat sank, waiting to be devoured by a huge mouth lined with sharp teeth opening below her, Gretel watched the crew respond to the imminent sinking. Instinctively, she moved to the highest point on the deck near the taffrail. It would make no difference if the sailboat didn't stay afloat, but for now she was as far from the monster as possible.

"Come about," Carlos ordered. Spinning the wheel, the helmsman turned the boat ninety degrees to starboard, the boom of the mainsail flung across the deck, narrowly missing Gretel's head. As the sails filled again with the trade wind, the boat heeled to the right, exposing the damaged side where the forehead of the sperm whale had dealt a massive blow to the old wooden timbers. Miguel disappeared down the companionway again to inspect the damage.

"How does it look now?" Carlos shouted to him.

"Water's stopped coming in," Miguel shouted back from below. "Two strakes missing. We can fix it, but it will mean putting a man over the side."

"That will be you," Carlos said. "We need a patch. How big is the hole?"

"About six feet long and a foot wide. But I can't swim."

"No one said anything about swimming. Take up enough of the floor in the main cabin to patch it. That's the only lumber we have that's not keeping us afloat."

Miguel descended again into the main cabin, and Gretel heard him shove aside the chests and duffel bags of the crew to expose a section of the cabin sole. A screeching noise and several loud pops preceded Miguel passing several boards and a bag of nails up to a crewman waiting at the head of the companionway. Raising his head above the deck, he told Carlos, "I can try and put some oakum between the patch and the hull, but I don't think it will do any good. I can't hold the board, hammer in the nails, and keep the oakum in place."

"Just nail on the boards," Carlos said. "We'll have to pump on the port tack until we get to a place where we can do it right. Keeping out the waves will have to do for now."

Gretel watched Miguel tie a rope around his waist, then carefully walk backwards down the sloping side of the sailboat, a hammer and the sack of nails tied around his neck. She was glad she didn't have to go in the water. She had no fear of the ocean but wouldn't want to get any closer to the enraged whale.

"Pass me the first board," Miguel called after he descended to the level of the staved in hull. Carefully placing it over the lower section of the damaged hull, he started to nail it to the wooden hull. The nails went in easily, and he called up to Gretel, who had moved to the rail above the suspended carpenter. "The wood is really soft. This old boat is about to fall apart. I'm not sure this is going to hold."

"He says the wood is too soft to hold the nails." Gretel turned to Carlos, who was still at the wheel.

"Put in more nails." Carlos moved to the rail next to Gretel and leaned over. "We'll screw it on when we get to a place where you can stand up."

Miguel nodded and continued hammering. A shriek from Gretel made him start violently, dropping the hammer into the blue water as the whale surfaced one hundred feet from the boat, again swimming slowly on a course parallel to the *Oso Negro*.

"Pull me in!" he yelled. "It's going to eat me."

"Stay put," Carlos commanded. "It won't do any good to pull you in if it sinks the boat. It will eat you anyway. Keep hammering."

"*Hijo de puta*," Gretel heard Miguel say under his breath. Then in a louder voice, "Pass me another hammer." Grabbing the proffered tool, he continued to nail the first plank over the gaping hole, followed by two more.

"It's done," he said. "Pull me up." Gretel felt her panic subside as Miguel climbed over the rail. At least they weren't going into the water with their tormentor right away. She noticed Carlos with a rifle, aiming it at the whale still swimming thirty feet from the boat. "What good is that going to do?" she asked. "It won't even feel it."

"If it attacks us again, it's all we can do," Carlos said. "Maybe it will scare it."

The whale moved closer to the rail, then its head disappeared below the water, the tail rising in the air as the creature dove into the sea. Looking at the empty surface of the ocean, Carlos hoped that it was gone. "Come about, and let's see how that patch holds."

The boat turned into the wind, the sails shivering, then continued turning to the northeast. The boom swept across the deck again, Gretel ducking beneath the swinging wooden pole, and the sails filled as the port side submerged under the water. Miguel descended into the cabin, and called out, "It's holding, but probably leaking a gallon a minute."

"We can handle that," Carlos said. He ordered two crewmen to rig the portable pump and lowered the intake hose into the bilge where the cabin sole had been ripped up. Chugging rapidly, the pump removed the accumulated seawater that had flowed in, which was replaced in a few minutes as the patch continued to leak.

"Stand by the pump," Carlos ordered the two sailors, "Keep it dry. We'll have to rotate every watch, but if we can keep on this tack another day, we'll have enough northing to come about and make Trinidad. We can beach it there and put on a proper patch."

Gretel leaned over the side, looking at the makeshift repair. Relieved that the boat was not in imminent danger of sinking, she was still shaken by the huge creature's assault on the vessel and the possibility that it could again return.

The *Oso Negro* sailed on through the day and into nightfall without another sighting. Too frightened to go below and sleep, she wondered what else might happen before they reached Argentina.

CHAPTER EIGHT

Maracaibo, June 1944

JERRY EXAMINED A map of the Orinoco delta that showed the river's twisting path as it flowed east toward the Atlantic Ocean. Crudely drawn without the topographic contours that would have required a professional surveyor, it depicted the ground elevation in colored bands. A transparent sheet of plastic overlayed the map, fastened to the table with stickpins. A series of purple lines were drawn on top in a north-south direction, terminating at the river on the southern ends and in the hills to the north. Another series of lines, created with an orange marker, ran perpendicular to the purple markings, and were annotated with arrows, numbers, and labels. Surface mapping showed a series of beds above the oil-bearing Oficina Formation dipping south underneath the river. The next step, seismic profiling that could see thousands of feet below the earth, might detect the structure of a possible oil field.

A man bent over the drafting table across from Jerry, studying the map in detail. Tall and white haired, he spoke perfect but accented English, a result of his Dutch ancestry and a lifetime of working in the wildernesses of the world. A former Shell geophysicist, Jan Boer had been hired away by Pride Oil to superintend the Orinoco survey. Jerry had arrived at the office that morning, tired after six days in the field, to find Jan impatiently waiting with his secretary.

Jan pointed to an orange line near the top of the map. "Is this the outcrop of the Oficina?"

Jerry nodded.

"How certain are you?" Jan asked.

"It matched the lithology of the cores from the subsurface wells in the heavy oil belt," Jerry said. "And it is overlain by a shale that our graduate student calibrated with her Geiger counter. I'd say we are about 80 percent sure."

Jan nodded. "You've measured the dip at five degrees to the south. Confident of that?"

"That's a good number," Jerry replied. Using a field instrument called a Brunton Compass, he had carefully measured the inclination of the contact between the Oficina sandstone and the overlying shale. It was sloping due south at five degrees from horizontal. An easy measurement if the rocks were exposed, which they had found to be the case at the northern extent of each of their transects.

"We'll run two lines in a north south direction," Jan decided. "We'll put them on top of these two transects—the one in the middle and the one five miles east of that. We should be able to image the top of the Oficina with no problem if it's overlain by a softer shale. And we can see if there's a fault trap somewhere between the river and where it outcrops."

"That's what I was thinking when we drew the map," Jerry said. "Are two lines enough? Be hard to come up with a drill-site location from a map drawn from only two lines."

"Let's shoot two, process the data, then see where to shoot more," Jan replied. "Without more information, we could just get ten lines that all looked alike."

Jerry reluctantly agreed. Although he was anxious to pick a location and move a rig to spud a wildcat well, he understood the reasoning. But it would add months to the timeline as the seismic data was acquired and processed.

"There's something else we need to discuss," he informed Jan. "The government wants to add two men to the field crew. They aren't geophysicists, but they can help with setting the jugs. But their reason for being there isn't to collect seismic data."

"I'm not surprised," Jan said. "Seismic crews are often a way for governments around the world to send people into remote areas for a variety of reasons. As long as they stay out of my way, I have had no problem—but I'm not paying and feeding them from my budget."

"We can take care of that. They'll meet you at the boat in Trinidad and tell you what their plans are when they get on board."

"And when will I see you again?" Jan asked. "Are you coming to the field with us?"

"I'm not going to ride the boat from Trinidad. Too much going on. I'll fly out and meet you for a few days after you get to the site."

Jerry thought about the request he had agreed to with George and how it might get carried out. Adding a couple of men to the survey party would not be a problem. The uranium could easily be transferred from the freighter to the *Osprey* as long as the packaging could be lifted with a crane. Jerry wondered what it looked like—gold bars, metal dust in jars, rods packed in barrels full of sawdust? In any case, the logistics would be straightforward. But he wasn't sure how the two men George was sending were going to convince the captain and crew of the freighter to give up the cargo. That part would be essentially piracy. Except that they were part of the U.S. military. Or maybe not. And in a neutral country. He resolved to stay out of that part of the operation. He hoped that Mike Woods would approve when he eventually learned how his geophysical operation had been hijacked.

*　*　*

FBI headquarters in downtown Washington, DC was not only the home of special agents capturing bank robbers and kidnappers, but also the offices of the counterintelligence effort in South America. Frustrated by competition and infighting, an impatient President Roosevelt had divided the wartime spying effort, assigning Europe to Bill Donavan's newly formed OSS and the southern hemisphere to J. Edgar Hoover's FBI. The G-men of the FBI did not see the gathering of intelligence as the fastest pathway to promotion and recognition and tried hard to avoid involvement in the effort.

Tom Barber had been assigned to South American intel because he spoke fluent Spanish. A slender man who carried himself with a military bearing, he had grown up in Zapata, Texas, the son of an American rancher and a Mexican woman. Finishing high school without prospects, law enforcement looked like a promising way to earn a living, and he had joined a division of the Texas Rangers. By the time Ma Ferguson had been elected governor of Texas and disbanded the legendary Rangers, he had gained enough experience to join the FBI. A Special Agent he had worked with on a bank extortion case gave him a reference, which led to an interview in Houston. He was offered a job with the comment that the Bureau needed some hard-assed lawmen to back up the newly hired college graduates who were filling their ranks.

Three months later, finished with training at the academy, Tom was a Special Agent assigned to the San Antonio office. When the Bureau expanded its intelligence gathering efforts in Latin America, he had been abruptly transferred to Washington.

Tom shared a windowless cubicle with another agent who had introduced himself as Matt Richards, a heavyset man sporting a mustache who had been studying and intervening in southern hemisphere shipping traffic. Hours of boring deskwork led to occasional conversations between the two men, and Tom learned that his coworker had been a river pilot in Savannah, guiding ships from the mouth of the river to the upstream loading docks. When the war started, Matt had volunteered for the Merchant Marine, but an FBI recruiter had persuaded him that he could contribute more by analyzing the movement of cargo in Latin America. His days were spent poring through reports sent in from dockside observers from Panama to Argentina.

Tom liked country music and kept the radio turned to a station that played the Grand Ole Opry. The twangy vocals reminded him of his home in south Texas. Matt had grudgingly tolerated the music when Tom had first set up the radio but was tapping his foot when the music was interrupted by the excited voice of a radio announcer.

We are interrupting this program to announce that the Allied invasion of France has begun. Hundreds of ships and thousands of troops are landing on the beaches of Normandy. This morning, June 6, 1944, will be remembered as the beginning of the end of the war.

"Well, I guess that's it. We've been expecting it." Tom turned up the radio as the feverish chatter continued. They were immersed in the broadcast when a secretary opened the door, saying, "You've been summoned to the corner office."

"Which one of us?" Tom asked.

"Both of you," she replied. "They're looking for someone who speaks Spanish and someone who knows something about ships."

* * *

A few days later, Tom Barber and Matt Richards walked up to the freshly painted boat tied to a wharf in the Port of Spain harbor. A converted fishing trawler, the masts that had formerly been strung with nets were now bare, and the holds had been emptied and scrubbed with turpentine. The ancient engine had been replaced with a new GM diesel, and the size of the fuel tanks had been doubled. A flagpole displayed a banner with the word *PRIDE* in yellow letters on a dark blue background, and a thicket of radio antennas rose above the pilot house. The name *Osprey* was painted across the stern.

A truck backed up to the stern of the boat was unloading reels of cable, wooden spools five feet in diameter strung with thick wire. A gang of workmen wrested the reels over a wooden gangplank to the deck, already crowded with crates that were being carefully lowered into the hold with a block and tackle.

"Is Jan Boer around?" Tom asked one of the laboring stevedores.

"*Sí, Señor.* He is in the cabin. Do you want me to call him?"

"*No, gracias,*" Tom replied. "I'll find him."

He turned to Matt. "Wait here and watch the bags while I talk to him.

I'll come get you."

He crossed over the gangplank, stepping down onto the deck before turning toward the stern. A trunk cabin with portholes on both sides, freshly painted dark blue with yellow trim, was positioned directly aft of the pilothouse and extended halfway to the stern of the vessel. The open door of a companionway revealed steps down to a gloomy cabin with walls and bulkheads of dark wood. Ducking his head at the base of the steps, Tom entered the cabin and saw a white-haired man sitting at a desk, scribbling notes in the light of an open porthole. The notetaker looked up as Tom introduced himself.

"Jan? I'm Tom Barber. My associate—Matt Richards—is topside. I understand that someone from Pride has talked to you about joining your crew for this project."

"I've been expecting you," Jan said. "I've had government people tag along from Oman to Malaysia. But I usually get more of a story than I've gotten about you. What the hell do you want?"

"We're both with the FBI. There's a freighter on the bank of the Orinoco where you're going to start your survey. There's something on board that our government wants. We're going to get it and load it onto your boat, then return to Trinidad with it."

Jan stared without speaking, waiting for more details. With none forthcoming, he said, "Do you expect the people on the freighter to just give it to you? Just two of you? If not, what do you propose to do? You know Venezuela is a neutral country, right?"

"We'll deal with that when we have to," Tom said. "They may be neutral, but there is a war happening, and we'll take the goods from them if they don't hand them over. Be prepared to load a cargo of about two tons and leave immediately for Trinidad when it comes on board."

"We're going to shoot a seismic survey," Jan protested angrily. "I was told to include some men in the crew who could help with setting jugs. Nothing was said about armed robbery and fleeing in the middle of the night. I'll end up with half a survey."

A valid point, Tom thought. He had been told to try and keep on good terms with Pride Oil. "We'll work out the timing so that you can finish before we seize the cargo. Maybe they'll hand it over gladly, especially if we pass out some Bolivars. I will tell you that Pride Oil and the State Department are behind us. Now as soon as we get our gear on board, we're ready to leave when you are."

"It will be a few more days," Jan said. "We are waiting for some instruments being sent from south Florida, where they just finished a shoot in the Everglades. As soon as they get here, we'll get underway. It will take us a day to get to the mouth of the Orinoco, then another day to get upstream where we are planning to lay out the first line."

"How long will the survey take?" Tom asked.

"About two weeks. We are going to shoot two lines. It will take us about five days to lay out each line, a day to shoot and record the data, and a day to pick up the jugs."

"Have one of your men tell us what to do. If anyone is watching, we want to look like we're part of the exercise. Tell your crew that we're new hires from the States sent down to learn how to do this. We'll be back with our gear in a minute." Tom went above deck and returned to the dock to help Matt to pick up the luggage and carry it up the gangplank. They each carried a pack and a duffel bag that looked much heavier than clothes and personal effects.

"Put your bags in the small cabin to port," Jan said when they stepped onto the deck of the *Osprey*. "You will be by yourselves. I'll tell the captain that you get special treatment because Pride sent you, even if you are expected to do the same work as the rest of the crew."

The two men carried their belongings into the small cabin, squeezing through the narrow doorway into a room with four bunks, stacked two high on opposite walls. Tom looked around approvingly. There was only a single door to the cabin, and it had no portholes or other openings. Closing the door would cut off any source of daylight but prevent anyone from seeing the contents of the cabin.

"Put the weapons under the bunks, and the transmitter on the extra bunk," he told Matt as soon as they were alone. "Pick a place to sleep and stow your personal gear." He opened one of the packs and withdrew a chain and padlock. "We keep this locked unless someone is inside. We each have a key. Make sure that no one sees inside when you leave."

The duffel bags thunked as the muffled heavy metal objects within hit the wooden deck. Matt pushed them under the bunks. A radio transmitter was set up on one of the middle bunks at waist level, and a key placed next to the gray box. Matt pulled out the light socket from the overhead lamp and attached a wire from the radio to the ground, turning the boat's electrical system into an antenna. He put on earphones, then tapped out a short message. After a few seconds, he nodded and took off the earphones. "They got the message. They know we've arrived."

"All right," Tom said. "We have less than a week in port, two days of travel, and two weeks of seismic surveying. That means we'll be loading the uranium in about three weeks."

CHAPTER NINE

The Orinoco Delta, June 1944

WITH ITS PADDLEWHEELS spraying a curtain of water, the steamboat slowed as it approached the riverbank adjacent to the *Estrella Blanca*. Painted white with streaks of rust, equipped with paddlewheels to navigate the shallow water of the river and driven by a steam boiler, the old boat made the trip on a bi-monthly basis, traveling the Orinoco River from Ciudad Bolivar to the Atlantic. When it had passed the stranded freighter three weeks ago, Gordon dispatched Liam to Ciudad Bolivar with instructions to inquire about steel cable and fresh supplies of food.

The bow of the steamboat pushed onto the muddy shore and Liam stepped off, carrying heavy bags in each arm. The paddlewheels reversed as soon as Liam landed on the bank, pulling the steamboat back into the channel to resume its trip downstream.

"I see you got some vegetables," Gordon said when Liam boarded the freighter. "Any meat?"

"Nothing I could keep fresh," Liam replied. "But I did get some canned stew. Give us a break from capybara and crocodile."

"Any cable?"

"Not this trip, but I ordered some. They'll have to send it overland from

Caracas. By donkey cart, it looks like. I thought I'd return to Ciudad Bolivar when the steamboat comes back on the upstream trip and pick it up. Should have it here in about two weeks."

"I can imagine you'd rather wait there than here," Gordon said sarcastically. "But all right. Plan to board the steamboat when it comes back, and we'll expect you to show up with the cable on the next trip. But that means the rest of us will have to sit on this goddamn mud bank until you get back."

Liam nodded and carried the groceries below, leaving Gordon alone on the main deck.

Looking over the rail of the grounded ship, Gordon noticed a swirl in the muddy water—eddies pushing upstream against the current. The turbulence was accompanied by the sound of a diesel engine, its exhaust sending black smoke up into the clear blue sky. Gordon moved to the other side of the *Estrella Blanca* to see a large boat backing into the bank, paying off a cable secured to an anchor in the river bottom. The stern of the new arrival, displaying the name *Osprey* in white letters, was ten feet from the grassy bank when it halted abruptly as the cable was snugged up around a bow cleat.

Dressed in ragged pants without a shirt or shoes, a man dropped into the water carrying a rope, hammer, and a steel stake. Standing in water up to his shoulders, he waded ashore and then proceeded to a point ten yards inland from the water to drive the stake into the muddy soil. The man drew the rope right and secured the stern of the boat from drifting downstream, an accomplishment recognized by the boat captain shutting down the engine. A wooden gangway was rolled from the afterdeck to the bank, providing a dry path for men and equipment to reach the shore.

More boat traffic than we've seen in a month, Gordon thought. He climbed down the ladder secured to the bow and walked over to where the *Osprey* had backed into the bank. He called out to a tall, white-haired man who was obviously in charge. "Hi. I'm Gordon, the captain of the *Estrella Blanca*. You must be the Pride Oil seismic crew. Jerry MacDonald told me you were coming."

"Yes. I'm Jan Boer, the crew chief. Jerry will be here in a couple of days. Excuse me for not stopping to chat right now, but we need to get set up."

"I understand. We'll be here for a while. Maybe we can talk later." Gordon returned to the *Estrella Blanca*. He stood at the bow and watched the unloading of equipment from the *Osprey*. He recognized Jorge from the geological survey, but the rest of the men were unfamiliar. Gordon remembered Jerry saying that he had assigned Jorge to the seismic survey to again fill the role of guide, troubleshooter, and chief mechanic, but that Kevin and Pedro would not be returning to the delta.

Gordon watched Jan stride down the gangway, stepping off and assessing the condition of the ground. Evidently satisfied, Jan called out, "You can roll off the tractors and wagons. Don't fall off the edge. We can set up a base camp on that bluff." His voice carried clearly across the water.

The seismic crew manhandled the heavy equipment onto the bank. Jorge stood by Jan at the edge of the water, waiting for the tractors to be brought ashore.

"Start those tractors, Jorge," Jan ordered as soon as the tractors were on the riverbank. "We can pull the wagons up to the campsite."

Jorge pushed a button on one of the machines which coughed to life with a cloud of white smoke. He motioned to one of the crew to move it over to the nearest wagon and walked to the next tractor. Pushing the button resulted in no visible or audible result, and he swore in frustration. "Battery's dead. Lost its charge. Probably need a new one."

Raising a cover over the engine, Jorge wrapped a rope around the flywheel and motioned to a large man to pull on it while he tweaked a lever. The engine spun with no effect.

"Try again," Jorge demanded. "Faster."

The man braced himself, placing a foot on the front tire of the tractor, and pulled with his arms and back, falling backward into the mud. The extra effort was rewarded by a sputter, and a brief revolution of the flywheel.

"One more time," Jorge said. "It's trying to start."

The man stood up, ignoring the mud staining the back of his white shirt, and repeated the exercise. The third pull was rewarded by the engine coughing twice and then settling into a sustained putter. Jorge swung his leg aboard and settled onto the seat behind the green metal steering wheel, shifted the tractor into reverse, and backed toward the tongue of another wagon.

By late afternoon, four wagons had been pulled up the embankment, tents were set up, and a kerosene stove was heating water for coffee. Jan and Jorge stood together, evidently planning their next steps, as Gordon descended to the riverbank again to offer his assistance.

"Is there anything I can do for you?" he asked as he approached the two men.

"The equipment made it in good shape," Jan said. "Now we need to find a stake that Jerry left here to lay out our survey."

"Is it a pole with a green pennant? If so, I can see it from the bridge," Gordon replied. "It's inland from here, about five hundred feet north."

"Thanks," Jan said. "That will be the southern end of their first transect. We want to run the seismic line as close to the transect as we can without doing a whole lot of clearing." Gordon accompanied Jan and Jorge as they trod inland through the marsh soil, the green pennant becoming visible as soon as they passed a clump of low bushes.

"This is the stake that we drove in," Jorge yelled. Jan walked up to it, then turned back to look at the boat moored stern to a few hundred feet upstream. "This is the starting point," he told Jorge. "We'll put the first jug here. Jerry said their transect ran due north. Let's walk keep walking and see if we can find a couple more stakes."

"I'll go with you," Gordon volunteered, interested to learn more about how the survey was going to be executed. Several conversations with Jerry had educated him on how the geologists mapped the rocks outcropping at the earth's surface but surveying below the ground was a novel concept to him. He was looking forward to seeing how it would be done.

A half-hour walk later, Gordon saw another green pennant waving above the underbrush.

"Over to the left, Jorge," he told the shorter man. Pushing aside the tall, thick weeds, they came upon a small, cleared area where Jerry's group had planted a second stake. Jan took a compass from his pocket and oriented himself to look due south. The stake on the riverbank was concealed by the tall weeds, but he could see the bridge of the *Estrella Blanca* and the radio antenna of the seismic boat slightly to the left

"That's pretty close to a north-south traverse," Jan informed Jorge. "We'll start at their first stake, and survey in the line going due north. We should be within fifty feet of this stake. It's more important that the line is straight than exactly following their transect. Let's go back to the boat and we'll start in the morning."

"Can you explain to me what you are going to do?" Gordon inquired as they walked back to the river.

Jan looked at him, assuming the demeanor of a professor instructing an interested student. "We're going to shoot two seismic lines. That requires laying out a set of sensors that we call jugs and pushing them into the soil. They're connected by wires and can detect sound waves created by shooting off explosive charges. The waves reflect off underground layers of rock, and the data collected can be interpreted to create a map of the subsurface geologic structure. The map might show high and low areas, subterranean cliffs formed by breaks in the earth called faults, and tilted layers of earth. The right configuration could provide a target for drilling an exploratory well."

"And what does that have to do with the stakes we just located?" Gordon asked.

Jan resumed his lecture in perfect but formal English. "The jugs have to be in a straight line. Setting them out that way can be very simple in an open meadow, or it can require clearing trees and underbrush in a dense forest. This survey will be fairly straightforward. Some underbrush will have to be cleared, and further north some trees will probably have to be felled. But the area is relatively clear and will require a relatively low amount of slashing. The biggest obstacle is that the men setting out the jugs will have to lug them through this marshy soil."

"I see," Gordon said. "Thanks for the explanation. I'm looking forward to watching how you do it."

* * *

After a breakfast of canned sausage and fresh guava the next morning, Gordon watched two of the seamen chipping paint on a rusted winch, sweating in the hot, damp air. He had left the wardroom to avoid further conversation with Strock, walking around the ship to supervise the ongoing maintenance. Looking north, he could see a group of about ten men swinging machetes, clearing brush in a straight line north from the stake they had found yesterday. Eight of the men looked like natives of the delta or the islands north of the coast. But two were obviously North Americans with white skin turning red after only a few hours of exposure to the tropic sun. Gordon wondered what they were doing there. Perhaps it was some sort of training exercise for new employees of Pride Oil. Or maybe a disciplinary matter for unruly workers who were told that they had one last chance before being fired.

CHAPTER TEN

Maracaibo, June 1944

A **FLOATPLANE TAXIED** across the lake surface on pontoons suspended from the wings. Accelerating upwind while avoiding the shipping traffic and scattered oil platforms, the plane lifted from the water and bounced twice before it gained enough altitude to clear the choppy waves and rise toward the clouds.

The open front windows of Maria's cabana at the National Hotel looked across the pool to the lake, affording a view of the maritime traffic that reminded her of the East River. The ships were less varied, however—all tankers carrying crude oil north to the refineries on the Dutch islands and to the U.S. mainland. With the U-Boat threat greatly reduced, convoys had been suspended and the ships kept to their own schedules, creating a continuous stream of laden tankers moving north and empty ones riding high as they returned to Lake Maracaibo.

"Hi, Paula." Maria smiled at the young woman who entered the cabana wearing a bathing suit with a ruffled skirt that showed off her slim body. Paula never went in the pool and avoided the sun but dressed in a bathing suit like the other women lying poolside on chaise lounges. Maria knew Paula badly wanted to fit into the expatriate society of Maracaibo, an endeavor that was becoming more difficult every week. As the Allies advanced through Normandy, the Germans in Maracaibo were beginning to be viewed with the contempt assigned to losers everywhere. Stares and questioning glances that were hidden a year ago had become obvious.

Maria had grown up in a world where women often ended up in bad situations that they had no role in creating. A husband sent to prison marked the wife as a criminal, regardless of how much they had been aware of the loan-sharking, extortion and worse. Maria saw Paula now being tarred by association in the same way—identified with the men who were now losing the war.

Jerry had warned Maria again about talking too much, but she convinced him that conversations limited to social events and the goings on in the Maracaibo expat community were harmless, and she continued welcoming Paula to the poolside cabana.

"Good morning," Paula replied.

She's not her usual smiling, chattering self this morning, Maria thought.

Paula removed a cigarette from a package of Lucky Strikes and lit it with a Zippo lighter. "One benefit of being here is good cigarettes. I've forgotten how bad the ones we rolled in Germany were. But I guess I'm going to find out again."

"Are you going home?" Maria asked.

"No. Hans has no place to go back to. The office he worked in has been bombed to rubble, and the staff has disappeared. But at some point, I guess we'll have to return, unless there is a way to remain in Venezuela. He's looking for some other line of work."

"Europe is not going to be a pleasant place for a few years," Maria commented. "I'd want to stay here too. But I don't know what it would take. Venezuela's neutral now, but I understand that they're close to declaring war on Germany."

"If they do declare war, I guess we'd be interned as enemy aliens," Paula replied. "But I don't know how enthusiastic they would really be about doing that. They don't have a place to put us, and Hans has some connections very high in the government. But it certainly won't be an improvement for us if that happens."

Maria looked out at the lake. The wind had picked up, and whitecaps rolled over the green water as a thunderstorm formed to the south. She wondered what she would do in Paula's situation. Returning to a country about to be ruled by two conquering armies wouldn't be a choice anyone would make. Staying in Venezuela would require money, and a lot of it, especially if war was declared on Germany.

"Hans wants to go to Argentina," Paula said. "We hear that they're welcoming Germans there. But we don't have money for a plane ticket, and that's the only way to get there. Please don't tell anyone," she added. "We need everyone to think we're happy where we are and staying put. If war is declared, maybe everyone will pretend to forget that we're German."

Maria wondered what kind of business Hans actually took part in. He reminded her of the men she encountered on the avenues of Manhattan—office workers, well dressed, with soft hands that did not show the bruises of physical labor, and an attitude that whatever they did was vitally important. Hans worked in an office that sold pumps to the oil companies, but Jerry didn't think that he could get a pump from anywhere to sell these days. He told Maria that he suspected Hans' real job was to acquire information about oil production from the lake for the Germans.

Paula was silent for a moment, obviously struggling about what to say next. She spoke softly and hesitantly. "I met a man named Sergio. He seems to have some connections and said he could get me two tickets on a Pan Am flight to Buenos Aires. He wants my jewelry." Paula paused and looked sad. "And he wants to sleep with me."

Maria said nothing. The choice was Paula's to make. Do nothing, and perhaps get sent back to Germany before the end of the war. The Soviet Army was sweeping toward Berlin, burning with rage toward anything and anyone German. If she and Hans returned to Germany now, they would have little control over their lives, and could easily end up dead or worse. Or give Sergio what he wanted and live keeping a secret from Hans for the rest of her life.

Maria wondered what she would do. She had known women faced with similar choices from her upbringing in the rough neighborhood in Queens. A man who was late on a payment on a lost wager—or who spoke disrespectfully to a powerful gangster or cop as a result of too much whiskey—could face jail, a beating, or worse. The women they lived with knew that perhaps sex might be traded for forgiveness. Some decided one way, some the other. She knew that if Jerry was in danger, she would do anything to save him.

Paula looked at her expectantly, unburdened and not speaking, but clearly expecting advice. Maria shifted her gaze from the lake to Paula before replying.

"I can't tell you what to do. But I guess I wouldn't do anything yet. Nothing is going to be settled right away, and I wouldn't make a decision until you have to."

Disappointed, Paula looked away. "Well, I guess that's good advice," she said. "I'm glad that at least you weren't surprised that I even thought about it." Waving at a poolside attendant, Paula ordered a screwdriver and relaxed on the chaise lounge, carefully staying in the shade.

Maria watched her through the dark sunglasses that she had purchased during their time in Florida. Paula's jaw set. Maria realized the woman had reached a decision and would do what she had to in order to get the tickets. Returning to war-ravaged Germany, internment in a tropical hellhole, or a life of wheedling, pleading, and pretending were all unacceptable.

* * *

The next morning, Maria looked up as Paula entered the cabana, greeting her with a single word: "Well?"

"I actually enjoyed going to bed with him," Paula replied. "Sergio's a good-looking man, and obviously likes women. He took my jewelry and gave me the tickets, but there's one detail he didn't tell me about until he was headed out the door. The Pan Am flight leaves from Caracas, not here. We have to take a small plane to Caracas to get on it. And the only plane available is evidently chartered to Pride Oil, which means I need a favor."

"That must be the floatplane that Jerry is taking to the geophysical survey site. I'll ask him for you. They're planning to go tomorrow. Is that too soon?"

"Tomorrow is perfect. The Pan Am flight takes off in two days. We'll stay in a hotel in Caracas."

"Okay. I'll ask Jerry tonight."

"Please don't tell him what I had to do to get the Pan Am tickets," Paula said. "I like Jerry. Don't want him to think badly of me."

Maria didn't respond. Jerry might agree to take the two Germans to Caracas but would want to know the details. She wasn't going to lie to him. And he would enjoy hearing the story. Paula had made a habit of flirting with him at the Government House parties, and he probably wouldn't be surprised.

*　*　*

Maria was right.

After she shared the story at dinner, Jerry chuckled. "What would you do?"

Then he got serious. "Well, I don't see any reason why we can't take them. We have room for five, and Debbie and I are the only ones flying out tomorrow. But the survey crew will be waiting for me to give them some direction, and we need to get there first. So we'll go straight to the site, and the pilot can drop them in Caracas on the way back. There's a floatplane dock at the Terminal, and they can take a taxi into the city."

"Debbie's going back with you?" Maria asked. "I thought she was only along for the geologic survey, not the seismic part."

"That was the original plan," Jerry said. "But she needs more data for her dissertation. I told her yesterday she could come with me and collect more samples while we're shooting the seismic."

"Can I come too?" Maria asked. "There's one empty seat. I'd like to see something of this country besides Maracaibo. I can return with the pilot after he drops off Paula and Hans in Caracas."

"I don't see why not. You can see something of the Andes and the Orinoco, and the country around Caracas, from the air. I'm going to tell Rulof to just land and drop off Hans and Paula, then come straight back to Maracaibo. But you and I can take a trip together to Caracas soon."

CHAPTER ELEVEN

The Orinoco Delta, June 1944

STROCK AWOKE TO someone pounding on the door, his tiny cabin stifling in the heat even with the ship's engine shut down. The single porthole was closed to keep out the ravenous insects and occasional bat, which allowed stench from the bilge to permeate the room. Without moving, he shouted, "Come in, damn you, if it's so important!"

The door opened to reveal the face of the wireless operator. "I have a message for you," Francis said. "It was marked urgent. But the rest is in code. I wrote it down for you." He offered Strock the flimsy sheet of paper.

"Uh, okay. Thanks," Strock managed to say. He grasped the paper and nodded, waiting for the operator to leave. Shutting the door, he picked up the copy of James Joyce's classic work and decoded the message.

```
June 22, 1944. Vermeer arranging alternate
transportation via water to Buenos Aires. Remain with
the cargo. Dussell.
```

Strock shredded the message and angrily threw the pieces into the wastebasket. The instructions meant that he would probably spend more weeks on the *Estrella Blanca* and then take a journey in whatever kind of craft to Buenos Aires. He had envisioned being in Argentina by now, entertained by a grateful Juan Peron after delivering the uranium.

Life on the *Estrella Blanca* had settled into a steamy but uneventful routine. Gordon did not maintain the series of watches that were required to man the ship on an offshore voyage but kept one man as a lookout throughout the night, a precaution against theft from the avaricious native boatmen. The remainder of the crew were awakened at dawn and served breakfast cooked on an oil stove in the galley. The challenge of maintaining a fifty-year-old ship in semi-seaworthy condition provided the crew with an unlimited list of potential chores, chipping and painting, greasing machinery, and repairing dry rot on the wooden decking. Two more meals were served, at mid-day and at dusk, before the crew retired to their bunks in a cabin dimly lit with kerosene lamps. The only appliance that required electricity was the wireless, and Gordon ordered the steam engine started on a weekly basis, turning a magneto that recharged the battery bank.

We could exist here for years, Strock thought dejectedly, *or at least until we run out of canned beans.* He had made a few trips inland across the grassy savannah, mainly for exercise, but there wasn't much to see. He had thought about asking the geological party that was encamped next to the freighter if he could join them on their excursions but didn't want to draw attention to himself. But boredom overcame him, and the next morning he waved to one of the native boats, motioning toward a ladder that hung from the ship's side. The man paddling the dugout canoe—wearing nothing but a string around his loins and hair bundled above his ears—came closer and held onto the bottom rung.

A conversation in broken Spanish on both sides, accompanied by hand gestures and the offer of a coin, resulted in Strock boarding the boat for a trip into one of the winding streams that branched off from the main waterway. He had seen canoes come and go from the narrow tributary and imagined that there was some sort of village bordering it.

The canoe moved slowly, paddled on alternate sides by the native boatman.

Rounding a bend, Strock lowered his hand into the water, wanting to wipe his brow in the intense heat. He was shocked and angered when the boatman struck his hand with the paddle, knocking it upward out of the water. Turning with irritation, he yelled in German, "What the hell are you doing?"

The boatman pointed over the side, motioning to a large school of small fish, about a foot long. "Piranha," he said in Spanish.

"Are they good to eat?" Strock asked. They looked pretty easy to catch. He could almost scoop them out of the water with his hand.

"I will show you about what they might bite," the boatman said. "But I want another coin to pay for the bait."

"Okay." Strock gave the man a worthless brass coin.

The boatman nodded and reached into a cloth bag at the stern of the canoe, removing a small, live rodent-like animal with its feet bound together by twine. He tossed the animal into the school of fish, which erupted into a frenzied attack as razor sharp teeth devoured it to the bones in seconds.

The boatman watched Strock's shock at the savage attack. "They can eat a cow or a person in a minute. Or your hand in the time it took them to eat that rat."

Convinced, Strock put his hands in his lap, careful not to tip the canoe. It had seemed sturdy enough, but now it rocked slightly, and he wondered what it would take to overturn it. If he fell into the water, he would not be able to get back in the canoe.

Looking up, he saw a village of small huts raised above the muddy soil on the riverbank. The structures were built with a log framework that supported a rough planked floor under a thatched roof. Walls of thatch looked like they would provide some shelter from the constant precipitation during the rainy season but do nothing to keep out the hordes of mosquitoes. Fires burning in stone-lined pits appeared to be a source of heat for cooking, and smoke rose to dry racks of fish. The only inhabitants visible in the mid-day heat were a few women and children clad in scraps of cloth who tended a small garden at the edge of the encampment.

"*Adonde estas les hombres?*" Strock asked his guide.

"They are fishing," the man replied in Spanish. "Tending to traps they have set in the water. Do you want to go ashore?"

Strock looked at the primitive village. There didn't seem much to see, but he was here, so he decided he might as well take a look. He nodded, and the boatman pushed the bow of the canoe onto the bank, a series of grooves in the sediment showing where a number of similar craft had recently been beached. Strock climbed out carefully onto dry land, wondering how deep the water had to be for a piranha to swim up and take off part of his foot, encased in leather though it was.

He trod toward the nearest hut, his interest piqued by a woman wearing only a small skirt, sitting on the top step. She was young and somewhat attractive, especially to someone who had not been with a woman since the *Estrella Blanca* had left Spain. He approached, wondering if she spoke any Spanish, and if she might be interested in earning a coin.

Seeing him approach, the woman rose and entered the hut, waving to him as she stepped inside. Intrigued, Strock followed her through the door. Inside was a room without furniture, half covered with piles of pelts and cloth blankets that were obviously intended for sleeping, dimly lit by sunlight filtering through the hatched roof and walls. The woman turned and offered him a pot filled with a dough-like substance, taking some with her fingers and placing them in her mouth. Strock took the offering and pushed his thumb into the opening of the pot, scooping some of the dough and placing it on his tongue. It tasted like some form of yams, saturated with the fish odor that permeated the village.

"*Gracias,*" he said. "*Se habla Espanol?*"

She looked at him blankly and shook her head. Clearly anticipating that he would eat more from the pot and give her something for the meal, her face showed disappointment as he handed the pot back to her. Silently, she returned to the entry and resumed her position on the steps.

Strock followed her outside, looking at the river to see his guide paddling downstream, leaving him stranded. The man was paddling briskly away, evidently going to resume his fishing chores with his companions.

"*Hola!*" Strock shouted. "Come back." He was sure that the boatman could hear him, but the man continued to paddle back in the direction they had come, ignoring Strock's shouted commands to return. Frightened at being abandoned in the tropical wilderness, Strock turned toward the hut to see the woman had also vanished, presumably to continue her chores in the vegetable garden.

Strock was a creature of cities and parks, and the voyage up the Orinoco River his first experience in a true wilderness. The place was not silent but filled with the noise of insects, birds, splashes, and the breeze rustling through thatched huts. Fighting down panic, he climbed the steps to the hut, sitting down where the woman had been a few minutes earlier. Sitting above the ground in a man-made shelter where he had recently been offered food reduced his sense of helplessness. He remembered leaving the *Estrella Blanca* without a word to anyone else. Accustomed to the German spending hours alone in his cabin, none of the crew would miss him or bother to look for him.

Looking at the sun directly overhead, Strock decided that the guide would return by nightfall, or at least if he did not, someone else with a canoe could and would take him back to the *Estrella Blanca*. He couldn't imagine spending the night in the hut—assuming that the inhabitants would invite him to do so—much less sleeping on the open ground. From the safety of the *Estrella Blanca's* steel deck, Strock had seen crocodiles floating like logs in the water. He wondered if a crocodile could climb the steps up to the hut. Pulling out a pack of cigarettes, he tried to strike a flame, but the matchbook had gotten soaked in the canoe. Climbing down the steps, he walked over to the nearest fire, placed the tip of the cigarette on a red coal, put it in his mouth, and inhaled deeply before returning to the hut. The nicotine calmed him, but he realized that he only had four cigarettes left and cursed himself for setting off on this expedition believing it would only be a brief canoe ride.

Sitting six feet above the ground, Strock could see over the grassy plains that were dissected by the tributaries feeding the Orinoco. Small clumps of trees interrupted the savannah, and hills rose in the distance to the north. A group of animals in the distance that looked like pigs were rooting in the ground. Closer to where he sat, Strock saw a man's head rise above the grass, then disappear, then reappear a short distance away. This was repeated several times. He decided that the man must be tending nets, standing up in the precarious canoe to pull in trapped fish, then sitting down to paddle to the next location.

Several hours later, three canoes appeared around the bend downstream, each paddled by a single native man. Strock watched them pull the small boats onto the bank and start tossing a variety of fish and turtles into wooden tubs. The men looked curiously at the white man, dressed in khakis and a pith helmet, who walked down to greet them.

"Can you take me back to the ship?" he asked in Spanish. "I can pay you in Bolivars. One Bolivar?"

The natives looked at him blankly, either not understanding or not caring to understand. In either case, no one offered Strock a passage back to the *Estrella Blanca*. Discouraged, he picked up a paddle and stepped into one of the beached canoes, tossing a coin onto the bank. "I will leave it at the ship," he said. "I'll paddle myself back."

The men stood motionless and watched him leave. One stooped to pick up the coin, putting it into a small pouch suspended from a string around his neck. Another went up the beach to one of the huts, returning with a bow and arrow. He settled into another canoe and pushed off into the muddy stream. Picking up a paddle, the native man followed Strock's course, his familiarity with the boat moving him quickly along the German's path through the water. As he passed the bend downstream, he was within a few hundred yards of Strock's canoe, gaining rapidly. When he was within one hundred feet, he slowed to match the pace of the boat ahead, dipping his paddle quietly into the water.

Oblivious to the pursuit, Strock paddled vigorously, confident that he could retrace his journey earlier in the day from the *Estrella Blanca*. He didn't believe that the natives would interfere with a white man taking one of their canoes but was still relieved when they stood by as he departed the village. Unaware of his pursuer, he punched his paddle into the water, soaking himself. Seated only a few inches above the water, all he could see was grass several feet high lining the banks and the hills in the distance. If he could have seen the river from above, he would have noticed a side channel that went nowhere, a dead end that was the result of the river's path during a long-ago flood. But moving downstream, he only saw a fork in the river, with no indication of which waterway would lead to the main channel of the Orinoco and the Estrella Blanca. Picking up the paddle, he drifted slowly, still unaware of his pursuer.

The fork to the right was wider, and reasoning that it must be the stream that led to the Orinoco, Strock resumed his efforts and continued into the mouth of the dead-end channel. After about one hundred yards, his paddle struck the muddy bottom when he pushed backward on it. Looking ahead, he could see nothing but grass, as the waterway ended in a small open lake. Cursing, he realized his error and turned the boat around, almost falling overboard as he realized that there was another canoe only a few yards behind him. It was occupied by a native with a painted face, dressed only in a breechcloth, sitting with the paddle athwart the gunnels and holding a bow and arrow. The man stared at Strock impassively, not reacting to shouted questions in Spanish as the German demanded to be led to the main channel of the river.

Overcoming his initial surprise, Strock noted that the native was small, only about five feet tall, and looked malnourished. The bow and arrow he carried resembled a child's toy, the arrow about two feet long with a carved wooden point. Strock reasoned that the man couldn't hurt him, and his fear diminished. Waving the man aside, he started to paddle back to the fork of the river, planning to take the other passage.

He bumped the other boat as he passed. The small man with the bow grabbed the side of the canoe to steady himself. Although he didn't make any threatening gestures, Strock's nervousness increased. He couldn't understand why the man would follow him and not help him, unless to rob him, but he didn't think that the native was physically capable of harming him. Paddling harder, he drew away from the other canoe.

The arrow pierced his kidney, the point burying in his lower back. The initial pain was shocking. Enraged, he turned around, determined to ram the other boat and drown his pursuer with his bare hands. But his arms wouldn't move to pull the canoe through the water. Paralysis set in quickly, as the curare poison, capable of killing any large mammal, destroyed his nervous system. The native man paddled up and pushed Strock into the water, future food for piranhas or crocodiles. He tied the empty craft to his own canoe and began paddling back to the village.

CHAPTER TWELVE

A HAPPY AND excited group of passengers made their way down the seaplane dock to Rulof's floatplane. Hans and Paula each carried a heavy suitcase, all that Jerry had told them the plane could carry. Jerry wondered about how they had decided which of their worldly possessions to bring to their new life. Debbie had a duffel bag with field clothes and carried her Geiger Counter suspended by a shoulder strap. Along for a day's ride, Maria had brought only a purse.

Anticipation of a new life, adventure in a new country, a chance to learn more about the Orinoco delta, and sheer exuberance were reflected in their faces. They handed Rulof their luggage to store in the compartment aft of the seats, boarded the plane, its engine idling at a low roar, and strapped themselves in. Satisfied that everyone was secure, Rulof closed the door that he had left open for ventilation and taxied toward the open water.

With George Morales' warning about top secret information still on his mind, Jerry had not told Maria about the plan to seize the uranium from the *Estrella Blanca* or the potential for violence if the ship's crew did not surrender it. It was something that kept him awake at night.

Maria would be back in Maracaibo later that day, safely out of the way. Keeping Jan and the survey crew out of the way would be enough of a challenge, and Debbie's presence would add to the danger and the complexity. But she was the one responsible for finding the cargo of radioactive metal in the first place. And he admired her dedication to completing her research. In the end, he decided to let her accompany him, but resolved to find a way to send her back before the FBI agents boarded the freighter.

After leaving Maracaibo, they flew over the mountains separating the lake from the plains to the east. The pilot had flown between the snow-covered peaks, winding through valleys with rocky walls, and then losing altitude to follow the Orinoco River downstream.

Seated in the co-pilot's seat with Maria directly behind him, Jerry leaned sideways so that his wife could see out of the windscreen over his shoulder. The meandering ribbon of the river, a strip of light brown dividing a canvas of green, turned into a runway of small waves. Most of the flight had been at a height of two thousand feet or less as the pilot strove to save gasoline, only climbing to cross the Andes.

Seated in the second row of the cramped cabin of the airplane, Debbie and Maria peered out the side windows. They looked down on a country that was unaware of being watched, and the low altitude let them see native villages perched on stilts, small herds of the giant rodents called capybara, crocodiles, dugout canoes paddled by a single person, and narrow creeks meandering through a grassy plain.

As the plane swept around a bend, a large ship came into view at the edge of the river near a smaller vessel moored a few hundred feet away. To their left, a group of men in the distance awkwardly swung large knives to hack away at dense underbrush. They had created a linear clearing starting at a stake on the riverbank and extending inland about half a mile. Next to the stake, an auger was being drilled into the earth by an engine mounted on the back of a wagon, creating a four-inch hole that Jerry knew would be about twenty feet deep when completed.

Another group of men was surveying in the middle of the clearing, setting stakes so that a straight line would be easy to follow. A tall white-haired man looked back toward the river as he supervised the work.

"That's Jan Boer, the crew chief," Jerry shouted to Maria over the engine noise. "We had dinner with him when he was visiting the office in Maracaibo. And that boat is the *Osprey,* that brought the crew and equipment from Trinidad."

The plane slowed, the nose lifted upward, and the pontoons splashed into the water.

"Spectacular," Maria told Jerry. "Now I know what I want to do. Learn to fly one of these."

"No reason not to. We'll look up a flight school when we get back to the States. I'd love to have a pilot in the family to fly me around," Jerry replied, smiling.

The plane taxied to the bank next to the *Estrella Blanca*. "I wondered what the boat would look like," Maria said. "You've been telling me about it. Doesn't look like much but a big pile of rust."

"That's not too far off," Jerry said. "They're still stuck here, evidently. That's the captain, Gordon, walking this way. He doesn't look happy."

"Hi, Jerry," Gordon said abruptly as he drew nearer to the disembarking group. "I appear to have lost Strock, my only passenger. He was seen boarding a native canoe two days ago but hasn't been back since. Can your pilot fly me around a little to see if he's stuck somewhere?"

Jerry didn't see a way to decline the request. A European lost in the wilderness wasn't likely to be alive after two days, but an attempt had to be made to find him. Jerry had described Strock to Maria after meeting him on the *Estrella Blanca* a few weeks ago, visiting the ship at Gordon's invitation. A reclusive and sullen-looking fellow who had offered only a perfunctory greeting. Jerry wondered what he was doing on the ship, but Gordon hadn't volunteered anything. A wandering German trying to get to Argentina was not unusual in the summer of 1944.

"Okay," Jerry decided. "There are two more passengers on the plane. I'll tell them to get off, and then Rulof can fly you in a five-mile square. If he's gone further than that, we'll never find him."

"Thanks," Gordon replied. "I don't think there's much chance we'll find him either. But it will help a lot if I can tell the people who chartered me that I made an aerial search."

Jerry stepped back on the float, talking to Rulof through the open window. The pilot turned to Paula and Hans. "A slight change in plans. We are going to search for one of the crew of that ship who is missing. You need to wait on the riverbank for thirty minutes. We'll be twisting and turning, and it won't be comfortable. After we finish, you can get back on and we're off to Caracas."

Paula and Hans climbed awkwardly through the small door, stepping onto the float and then the muddy riverbank. Expecting to spend the day in Caracas, they both wore city clothes with expensive leather shoes that sank quickly into the soft mud. Looking irritated, Hans started to say something to Jerry, then held his breath.

Gordon pushed Hans aside to enter the plane, crouching as he moved forward to occupy the copilot's seat next to Rulof. The floatplane taxied to the center of the river, turning into the wind for takeoff. The plane accelerated and the pontoons rose from the water. They sank to touch the water briefly, and then the airplane slammed to a halt as the port float struck a submerged log. It twisted violently to the left, the nose sinking and the propeller beating the water, stalling the engine as the plane settled back on the pontoons. The port pontoon settled lower in the water, evidently taking water after the impact.

Watching from the bank, Jerry saw Rulof open the door and step onto the float, which was filling with water. The pilot waved energetically at the group watching on the riverbank, motioning them toward the crippled plane.

"Send out a lifeboat to tow them in," Jerry ordered the watching crew of the *Estrella Blanca*. Seeing blank stares, he asked Maria to repeat the order in Spanish.

Nodding comprehension, one of the lifeboats set off from the *Estrella Blanca*, two men rowing and a third steering from the stern. Approaching the drifting floatplane, they tossed a rope through the open doorway to the pilot, who wrapped the end around a strut.

Ten minutes later the floatplane was pulled onto the bank adjacent to the stranded freighter, the engine cowling pulled off as Rulof assessed the damage.

"We're lucky the blades didn't come apart and through the windscreen. We broke a blade, but the hub seems okay," he said. "Probably also damaged the crankshaft but can't tell about that until we take the engine apart. I've got a spare blade, and I can patch the pontoon and ferry it back to Caracas. But it will be tricky, so I'll need to go alone. The engine might stop, and I'll have to put it down quick."

Things just got more complicated. Jerry thought. *Now I've got four people to get out of here before the FBI boards the freighter. Well, I'm going to take care of Maria and Debbie first and at least get them off this ship, then see what to do with Hans and Paula.*

He turned to Gordon. "We're setting up a camp five miles downstream, where we're going to start shooting the second transect. If you can put us up for the night, Debbie, my wife, and I will move there on the *Osprey* in the morning. But we don't have space for our two passengers in the camp. Can they stay on the *Estrella Blanca* for a few days until we see how we're going to get out of here?"

"Sure," Gordon said. "I feel responsible for the plane. I guess Strock is just gone. I need to contact his company with the wireless and let them know. But your passengers can have his cabin. You and your wife can have mine. Debbie can sleep on the bunk in the bridge for the night."

"Thanks," Jerry looked at Maria, who was ashen and shaking. After watching the accident, her infatuation with airplanes had apparently vanished. "You'll finally get a chance to see what life is like in the field."

Reassured by his calm, Maria regained some of her composure. "Any idea how we're going to get out of here?"

"We have another week of shooting and need the *Osprey* for support. I'll radio Maracaibo and see if they can send another plane. Otherwise, we'll go back to Trinidad on the *Osprey* and fly back to Maracaibo from there."

* * *

The wardroom of the *Estrella Blanca* was a rectangular space, enclosed by a floor, walls, and ceiling of painted steel with a liberal amount of rust showing through. A steel table was welded to the deck and surrounded by a collection of wooden chairs. The long dimension of the cabin was perpendicular to the length of the ship, and four portholes faced the bow overlooking the hatches that covered the hold. The room was now crowded with the plane passengers, Gordon, and Francis seated at the table. The rest of the crew ate in the galley a deck below. The table was covered with plates and dishes containing the remnants of their dinner.

"Thanks for the meal," Gordon said. "We haven't had fresh vegetables or meat since the last steamboat from Ciudad Bolivar."

"You're welcome," Jerry replied. He had shared the food they had brought on the plane with Gordon and the crew of the *Estrella Blanca*. It would mean that the survey crew on the *Osprey* would have to be satisfied with canned goods after a few days, but he wanted to leave Gordon feeling satisfied, if not happy, about Jerry unloading the two passengers on him.

"When can you fix the plane?" Paula asked Rulof. "You should have seen that log in the river. We have tickets on the Pan Am flight in two days." She huffed and turned to Jerry, "You should have dropped us off on the way here," she added with a glare. "If we miss that flight, we're stuck. We can't get to Buenos Aires, and we have nothing left in Maracaibo."

"You won't make that flight," Jerry said bluntly. "You wanted to come, and I let you, but there were no guarantees. You're here for a few days until we get another plane."

"Maybe you can change them for a later flight," Maria said, trying to inject some optimism into the conversation.

"Impossible. Sergio told me that they were for this flight only. He had to bribe someone to get them, and if we aren't on that plane, they're worthless." Dejected, Paula looked down at her food, tears dripping from her nose. She got up from the table and returned to the small cabin that Gordon had assigned her to share with Hans.

Hans looked at Maria, his face turning red and his head moving forward in a jerky motion as he spoke. "You misled us. We spent all our money on those tickets, and you said the floatplane was going to take us to Caracas. You need to pay us the money we spent for the tickets."

Jerry started to speak, but Maria waved him to keep silent. "I did you a favor," she said. "I didn't guarantee anything. I'm sorry you're stuck here, but you can't expect perfection when you travel."

"The tickets were five hundred U.S. dollars," Hans said. "I'll expect payment whenever we get back to Maracaibo. Or I will have to take other actions. And you won't like them."

Hans had always been distant but courteous to her, but now his desperation had resulted in a threat of physical harm. Jerry's impulse was to beat the man senseless, but he remembered Maria telling him about the advice she had received as a teenager from her oldest cousin: *Never take any crap from anyone.* He knew she would want to respond to Hans herself, so he sat silently as she spoke in Italian, her words cold and flat.

"You can use those tickets for toilet paper. And if you talk to me like that again, I'll cut you where Paula won't have anything to do with you."

Hans flinched, evidently understanding enough Italian to translate Maria's words. He glanced up to see Maria staring at him, her face conveying contempt, and he left the wardroom without replying. Jerry glanced around at the others sitting at the table, the corner of his mouth twitching as he struggled not to smile.

Gordon and Francis were looking down at their empty plates, their faces expressionless. Debbie blinked and stared at Maria, surprised at the sudden change in her tone and expression. *She hasn't seen Maria's tough streak,* Jerry thought. *Most people never see that and don't expect it in such a beautiful and outgoing woman.* He could see that Debbie hadn't understood Maria's response to Hans, but it was obvious that the Italian words had conveyed both derision and a threat sufficient to send Hans back to his cabin.

Debbie swallowed, then looked at Maria with a smirk. "Ran him out of here, didn't you? Good for you."

"Well." Jerry broke the silence. "They're stuck here for a few days. Gordon, thanks for letting us leave those two on your ship."

"Sure." Gordon replied. "We can use the company," he added sarcastically. "Can't be more of a pain in the ass than Strock."

"What's your status now?"

"I sent a wireless to the contact that Strock had been using. Francis said they'd been using a code, but I told him to just send it in plain English. Said Strock had been missing for a couple of days and we think he's dead, and what did they want us to do. Haven't received a reply yet."

"We'll be here a few more days," Jerry said. "Maria will go back on the plane if we can get a new one. Debbie and I are going to stay with the survey crew for the next week. If we can't arrange another plane, we'll all go back to Trinidad on the *Osprey*. Any news on a new steering cable yet?"

"Liam's in Ciudad Bolivar and should be returning on the steamboat day after tomorrow. Should have a piece of cable that we can use to repair our steering. If so, we could be out of here in a few days," Gordon replied.

Jerry picked up a spoon and began tapping it on the table, the nervous motion drawing Maria's attention. He knew that if the ship's departure became imminent, Tom Barber and Matt Richards would board it to seize the uranium. It might happen before the geophysical survey was finished and before the *Osprey* was ready to leave the delta. He wondered when Gordon's curiosity about the cargo would be sufficient to pry open a box and see what was there, or if he already had. He had been assured by Sam, the young scientist who had measured the radiation, that it was not hazardous. But he would still be glad to get Maria off the ship. And he didn't know how Tom was going to intercept a moving freighter. The problem would become much more complex after the *Estrella Blanca* pushed off the muddy riverbank.

"Well, if you leave before a plane comes to take them back, you can drop off Paula and Hans with us. We'll take them back to Trinidad."

* * *

Jerry stood next to Jan on the riverbank the next morning, watching as

Debbie and Maria walked up the gangplank to the *Osprey*. Debbie carried a duffel bag with her clothes and the case containing the Geiger counter. Marie had only her purse, all she had needed for a day trip on the airplane.

"You can borrow some of my clothes," Debbie offered. "I'm a little taller, but other than that we're the same size. And I have three extra sets. Should be fine if we can find a way to do some washing."

"Thanks. I haven't seen you the last few weeks in Maracaibo. What have you been doing?"

"Jerry let me work in the Pride office, compiling my notes and starting to draw maps of the Orinoco delta shale formations," Debbie replied. "I still need more data on the eastern side of the survey. If I can fill in that gap, I can draw some definite conclusions about the occurrence of shale beds in the vicinity of the Oficina Formation. So I convinced Jerry to let me return to the delta and make more measurements."

"Are you going to be working with the seismic crew?" Maria asked.

"No. I'll be on my own this time, spending nights on the *Osprey* but working in an area miles from the seismic crew. Being alone on the savannah is a little scary, especially after being lost in the fog the first night we were here, but I'm determined to get the information I need to complete my research.

Maria stepped onto the deck and turned toward Jerry. "When will we see you?" she asked.

"The boat will take you down to the camp and then come back up here until Jan finishes this seismic line later today. I'm going to stay here with Jan." Jerry responded. "We should be back at the camp by dark."

"I'll stay at the camp for today," Debbie offered. "We'll make sure someone is cooking dinner. I'll start my fieldwork tomorrow."

Grateful that Maria would have some companionship her first day at the camp, and that he could focus on the work of shooting the seismic survey, Jerry waited as the captain of the *Osprey* started the engines and backed away from the bank. When the bow of the boat turned downstream, he walked with Jan toward the group of men clustered around the auger, eager to see the explosion that would complete the seismic line.

CHAPTER THIRTEEN

Germany, June 1944

DUSSELL LOOKED AT the wireless message that he had translated from the dots and dashes of Morse code, crushed it in his hand, and threw it into a wastebasket. Transmitted in uncoded English, it told the entire world that someone named Strock was missing from the *Estrella Blanca*. Fortunately, it did not say anything more about the location of the *Estrella Blanca*, where the ship was going, or what cargo it was carrying. Unfortunately, it said nothing about the condition of the ship or when it might be seaworthy again. And he had no way to contact Gretel. The boat she had chartered had a radio capable of reaching nearby ships but not bouncing electromagnetic waves off the ionosphere to send transmissions across the globe.

He walked over to the wireless set that he had installed in the laboratory and learned how to use. His skill with the key was perfunctory and slow but adequate. He tapped out a message:

June 25, 1944. Estrella Blanca, wait for a contact from Vermeer. Will arrive in a few days. Have Vermeer send message to us. Vermeer will give further instructions.

He wondered if he should still tell Gretel to transfer the uranium to the *Oso Negro* or have her board the *Estrella Blanca* and proceed to Buenos Aires in Strock's place. The freighter was faster and far more capable in the open ocean than the smaller boat, but it had been proven to be unreliable mechanically. If it foundered in the open sea, the entire project would be a failure. But it would arrive in Buenos Aires weeks ahead of the *Oso Negro* and would preclude a risky transfer of the uranium to the smaller boat.

He decided to wait until Gretel arrived at the *Estrella Blanca* and contacted him. The decision really depended on the condition of both vessels. The one that was the most likely to reach Buenos Aires with the cargo—regardless of the time the voyage took—was the ship that should take the cargo. If the uranium was loaded onto the *Oso Negro*, he would tell Gordon not to expect payment for a cargo that was not delivered. If it remained on the *Estrella Blanca*, he would instruct Gretel to pay off the *Oso Negro* captain and tell him the charter was cancelled.

He resumed taking notebooks from the laboratory shelves and placing them in wooden trunks, stacking several notebooks in layers at the bottom of the containers. A variety of clothes obtained from bombed-out houses and stores then filled the trunks, concealing the notebooks from a casual search. The notebooks were the result of years of nuclear fission research by both Dussell and the famous physicist, Becker. In addition to the uranium, they would be his passport to acceptance and a new life in Argentina. He had arranged transport with Bishop Erkurt by lorry to Naples, and then on a coastal fishing boat to Spain where passage had been arranged on a ship headed to Buenos Aires. The ship left port in three weeks.

Aside from the trunks, Dussell had no plans to take any of the laboratory equipment or furnishings with him. If the Argentinians wanted to set up a new research facility, they could buy what was needed after the war. The radio was too bulky and heavy to transport and would require too much time and effort to set up in a new location. After making a decision with Gretel on which vessel to entrust with the uranium, he intended to leave Germany immediately.

CHAPTER FOURTEEN

The Orinoco delta, July 1944

GORDON HEARD PAULA and Hans arguing bitterly, unhappy at being left on the *Estrella Blanca* when Jerry, Debbie, and Maria had departed on the *Osprey*. He was pleasantly distracted when smoke from the steamboat exhaust rose above the grassy plains, revealing the vessel's position while it was still hidden by the trees lining the riverbank. As it rounded the upstream bend, Gordon saw Liam waving from the bow and pointing to a large spool wound with wire rope. The steamboat pulled alongside the ship, metal gunwales scraping the steel side of the freighter.

"We got one hundred feet," Liam shouted. "That's the only way they would sell it. More than we need. But the price wasn't bad."

"Good. Sitting here isn't making any money, for sure." Gordon waved to a crewman, who maneuvered a crane over the steamboat deck. Ten minutes later, the spool was resting on the deck of the *Estrella Blanca*.

Esteban inspected it with satisfaction. "This will do," he told Gordon. "It's more than we need but will let us replace the entire section around the helm."

"How long to rig it up?" Gordon asked.

"A day. While we've been sitting here waiting, I welded up some blocks to splice it together. Most of the work will be cutting out the old cable and threading this one through the channel in the hull."

"Okay." Gordon turned to see Paula approaching him. Hans had been avoiding the crew since the incident with Maria in the wardroom, appearing only at mealtimes and spending solitary hours on the bow watching the river. But Paula had established a congenial relationship with Gordon and the other officers, apologizing for Hans but making it clear she no longer wanted anything to do with him.

"What does this mean?" she asked.

"It means we can finally get out of here. Day after tomorrow. We've been waiting for this to replace our broken rudder cable." Gordon had told Paula they were awaiting orders from the company that had chartered the ship to determine their next destination. After sending the first wireless, they had received instructions to wait for someone referred to as Vermeer who would relay further direction.

"Do you know where you're going to go yet?" Paula asked.

"I don't. It will take us a day to get back to the mouth of the river after we start the engine. I doubt they'll want us to take their cargo back to Spain, so I imagine we'll continue to Buenos Aires like we originally intended."

"Buenos Aires?" Paula paused for a second. She moved closer to Gordon, putting her hand on his upper arm and pressing her thigh against him. "That's where we're going. Can you take us?"

"Well, maybe," Gordon said. He wondered what might happen on the voyage. *Why not*, he thought. "Okay," he answered, putting his hand on her back. She didn't flinch but pressed closer. "You can stay in the cabin you're in now." He didn't mention her husband. If she wanted to let him share the cabin, that would be up to her. If she didn't, he could sleep with the crew.

Paula kissed him on the cheek. "Thank you so much," she said. "I'll try and repay you somehow."

✳ ✳ ✳

Removing the rusty wire rope from the sheaves and passageways in the ship's interior and replacing it with the new steering cable had left Esteban with deep scratches and a bruise on the top of his head. He wore coveralls stained with rust and drank water from a glass offered to him by a seaman before he spat some out. It had taken two days to cut the steering cable and splice on the new piece that would allow the rudder to respond to the helm on the bridge. The hardest part had been threading the new cable through the small openings that led from the rudder post at the stern to the wheel, requiring Esteban to push the inch-thick cable to a man waiting on the other side, who then pulled the bulky wire through to the next compartment. The conduit for the steering was designed to accommodate a cable, not a human, and the spaces were cramped and hot.

He looked up to see Gordon approach and answered his question before he could speak. "It's done. We can go whenever you get the engine started and back off the bank. It isn't like new but should do until we get to a proper shipyard and can replace the whole cable."

"That's all we need," Gordon said. He had silently watched the repair, not wanting to slow it down by asking questions. Anticipating a successful outcome, he had told Liam to raise steam in preparation for starting the engine and notified Paula and Hans that they would be leaving shortly. He wished they could have stocked more fresh groceries before pushing off, but he was not going to delay two weeks until the steamboat returned from Ciudad Bolivar.

Two hours later, Gordon shifted the engine telegraph to full astern, signaling the engine room crew to go to full power and put the gears in reverse. The propeller kicked up mud, pulling the stern of the ship away from the bank and into the middle of the channel, overcoming the suction of mud that had settled in around the bow over the last weeks. As the ship was caught by the current, it drifted sideways, then turned with the bow pointed downstream as the newly repaired steering cable moved the rudder to pull the stern around. Gordon shifted the telegraph to slow ahead, and the *Estrella Blanca* started to retrace the path that it taken weeks earlier.

"Turn the wheel hard to port, then hard to starboard immediately. Make sure you stay in the channel. But we need to make sure that the repair holds before we get too far," Gordon ordered. The helmsman nodded and the ship zigzagged in the channel, the rudder turning as soon as the wheel was moved.

"Looks good so far," Liam said.

"Yes. I'm going to head downstream just fast enough to maintain steerage way. Now that we're able to move, I don't want to hit anything. But we should be at the mouth of the river by nightfall. We're supposed to wait there for this Vermeer person. I guess he's coming from Trinidad in a boat."

"Too bad," Liam said. "Now that we can move, I'd like to keep going. Watching this river go by was getting pretty boring."

"True. But we don't know where to go yet. I guess we'll get to Buenos Aires sooner or later, but it might be later."

"There's Jerry's crew," Gordon pointed out as the *Estrella Blanca* passed the camp. The *Osprey* was moored stern first to the riverbank, and a collection of tents, tractors, and boxes full of equipment littered the higher ground away from the river. He saw Maria stand and wave and he waved back.

The *Estrella Blanca* continued its downstream voyage, following the Orinoco as it meandered through the grassy plain. It entered the mangroves bordering the stream as water from the Atlantic Ocean mixed with the fresh river, creating a brackish environment that the low, green trees could thrive in.

Paula appeared on the bridge, ducking as she passed through the oval door opening at the top of the stairway. "We're on our way," she said happily. "How long to Buenos Aires?"

"Remember, we're going to have to stop at the mouth of the river and wait for someone to contact us," Gordon replied. "It should only be a day or two. I told Jerry you were going with us if we're going to Buenos Aires. If we don't for some reason, he'll send the *Osprey* to come pick you up, and you can go back to Trinidad with them."

Gordon recalled an afternoon in bed the day before. Paula had knocked on his cabin door while Hans sulked alone in the cabin they shared. It had been an enjoyable but not a memorable experience, and she promised to provide an encore in the middle of the voyage. Gordon could see that Hans's attitude was making the journey even more difficult for her than it had to be, starting with his outburst when the floatplane was damaged. He wouldn't be surprised if she divorced him after they reached Buenos Aires. He suspected that there were probably a lot of wealthy, attractive German men who had escaped Europe without their wives or girlfriends and would be looking for female companionship.

The ship approached the mouth of the river, following the channel marked by wooden stakes. Gordon had recorded the passage on the way upstream and navigated the ship to a location where the open Atlantic was separated from the river by a mangrove island. The anchor winch had been repaired as part of Gordon's determination to keep the crew occupied, and now the chain rattled as the kedge descended to the river bottom, swinging the bow to point upstream as the rumble of the engine stopped. The bridge was high enough to see over the mangrove island, and the ocean was now visible on the port side.

"Liam, have someone keep a watch on the channel coming in," Gordon ordered. "We don't know how this Vermeer individual is going to get here, or in what. But let me know of any approaching boats."

Gordon thought that Vermeer would most likely be arriving from Trinidad, probably in one of the small coastal trading boats that brought fresh produce to the island from the farms upriver in exchange for oil from the refineries located on the island. However, the wireless message had conveyed no information, just instructions to wait. So, Vermeer could have travelled overland and would approach the *Estrella Blanca* from Ciudad Bolivar or could be arriving from Europe in a large ship. He would have to wait and see.

CHAPTER FIFTEEN

Off the Coast of South America, July 1944

MIGUEL HAD BUILT a seat for Gretel immediately forward of the taffrail, a place where she could watch the ocean and the working of the boat but stay out of the way. The bilge kept dry by constant pumping, the *Oso Negro* reached Trinidad and Carlos drove her into shallow water at high tide. Miguel attached a line to the top of the mainmast, and Gretel heaved on it with the rest of the crew to turn the sailboat on its starboard side as the water receded. Low tide left the side of the hull high and dry, allowing the carpenter to replace and caulk the broken planks. The repair had delayed them for three weeks, but now the *Oso Negro* was on a starboard tack, cruising southeast and paralleling the coast of South America as it approached the mouth of the Orinoco River.

Gretel debated trying to raise the *Estrella Blanca* on the small radio that Carlos kept locked in a cabinet but decided against it. Strock would be expecting her and would follow the orders she had received from Dussell. Better not to start a conversation that might confuse things. She wondered how long it would take Carlos to navigate the *Oso Negro* upstream to the stranded freighter. He would have to work the boat upriver against the current, which would slow their progress to only a few miles a day.

Gretel's time at sea had taught her to not worry about events that she could not control, and she focused on the brilliant blue of the tropical ocean, putting the *Estrella Blanca* and Strock out of her mind until she actually saw them. The trade winds pushed the sea surface into steep rollers, white capping as the wind blew off the tops of the cresting waves. Looking sideways into the water as the waves approached, she could see schools of small fish that sometimes flew from the water like birds. Occasionally a larger fish, some with a bill that resembled a sword, would surf the downwind side of the seas, devouring the smaller prey.

Carlos came on deck, ignoring her momentarily as he raised a sextant and measured the inclination of the noon sun. He pointed the telescope of the instrument directly at the sun, his eyes protected by the dark shades that he placed between the tube and the eyepiece. Standing effortlessly on the swaying deck, he altered the inclination of the tube until the sun bisected the horizon, noted the reading on the curved dial, then wrote it on a scrap of paper to be copied into the log at a later time.

"Change course twenty degrees to starboard," Carlos instructed the helmsman. As the boat altered course, now traveling due south and perpendicular to the brisk wind, the deck heeled further and the *Oso Negro* assumed a rolling motion, running with the seas on the beam rather than taking them on the bow.

Gretel had become accustomed to the movement of the boat in any sea weeks ago and quickly adjusted to the change, grabbing the rail next to her bench. "What does this mean?" she asked Carlos.

"We're getting close to the mouth of the Orinoco," Carlos replied, moving along the rail to her seat. "We're looking for a tall buoy about five miles out. We'll go in closer to shore, sail along the coast and look for it. When we see it, there should be a set of markers leading into the river."

"What if we don't see it? What if we pass it in the night?"

"Well, then we'll turn around and come back north. But it should be about twenty miles ahead. We should see it this afternoon. We have light until about seven."

Gretel and Carlos had discussed approaching the *Estrella Blanca*, contacting Strock, and transferring the cargo until they were both tired of the topic. Nothing more needed to be said. They would take care of it when they found the ship.

A shout from the masthead interrupted Gretel's thoughts. "Buoy dead ahead! About ten miles. And I see the top of a ship right inside the mouth of the river!"

"Is the ship coming out or going upstream?" Carlos yelled back. Entering the mouth of the river would be tricky in a relatively small sailboat. Cresting waves on the bar would require careful maneuvering to avoid broaching. If a ship was coming out and blocking the channel, the *Oso Negro* could be forced into shallow water where the steep waves could capsize the boat.

"Neither," the lookout replied. "It looks like it must be anchored. Not moving."

Carlos grunted, then picked up his telescope from a shelf near the wheel and focused it on the approaching buoy.

Gretel saw a line of smaller, floating markers leading away from the buoy toward the shoreline, presumably marking the channel that entered the river. The *Oso Negro* approached the buoy and altered course to starboard, putting the wind behind it and surfing on the following sea. The deep water in the marked channel prevented the waves from steepening into breakers, and the boat rose and fell smoothly as it approached the shoreline. The entrance to the river became visible, a break in the beach with surf on either side. The river evidently curved to the right beyond the mouth, sheltering the freighter where it lay anchored.

"That's Isla Tercera," Carlos told Gretel. "Once we're past that, we should see some stakes marking the right channel. There are a lot of forks, some shallows, and dead ends. But there's enough river traffic to make maintaining the channel markers worthwhile, so we'll trust them. Not that we have any choice."

Gretel ignored him, looking at the freighter as the *Oso Negro* turned and the stern of the ship became visible. "That's the *Estrella Blanca*!" she exclaimed. "What the hell is it doing here?"

Carlos shrugged. He had been hired to bring Gretel to the ship, and there it was. Happy not be headed up a shallow, twisting river against the current, he asked, "What do you want to do now?"

"Anchor, then take me over in the dinghy. I want to go see Strock and find out what's going on. And find out what we're supposed to do now."

Carlos nodded and turned toward the *Estrella Blanca*, ordering the sails lowered and the anchor readied. As the *Oso Negro* approached, he ordered the anchor lowered and turned the bow into the current so that the boat drifted down closer to the motionless freighter. Ten minutes later, Gretel stood in the stern of the dinghy, addressing a tall, red-haired man at the top of the freighter's boarding ladder.

"I need to talk to Strock," she shouted. "Can I come aboard and see him?"

"He's not here," Gordon replied. "Who are you?"

"You can call me Vermeer," Gretel responded. "Where is he?"

"Dead," was the reply. Gordon stared at her, obviously surprised that Vermeer turned out to be a woman.

"Tie up to the ladder and come on aboard," he shouted down. A few minutes later, Gretel stood next to him on the bridge deck, listening to the story of Strock's demise and the message that she was to contact Dussell on the wireless.

"Can you reach Germany from where we are?" she asked Gordon.

"Yes. But in Morse code, not voice."

"I need to code a message. Can you give me a table and some privacy?"

Gordon pointed toward a table covered with navigation charts and offered her a chair, then moved to the other end of the bridge. Gretel pulled a paperback copy of *Ulysses* from her pocket, composing a transmission:

July 7, 1944. Arrived at Estrella Blanca. Steering repaired and anchored at mouth of Orinoco. Understand that Strock is dead. Awaiting instruction.

The wireless operator took the scribbled sheet and started tapping on the key, sending rapid Morse code into the atmosphere. He finished and turned toward Gretel, handing her back the sheet and standing up.

"Do you want to wait for a response?" Gordon asked. "If so, do you want something to drink?"

"Yes. I might as well stay here as on the *Oso Negro*. And tea if you have it."

Gordon nodded, gave instructions in Spanish to a crewman who seemed to double as a steward, and disappeared through the bridge door. A minute later, a young woman with European features and creamy white skin started to enter the bridge, obviously curious about the new visitor and what it meant for her future.

"Paula, you'll have to wait outside," Gordon said politely. "Our visitor is waiting for a wireless."

Disappointed, Paula left the bridge, replaced in a short time by the seaman bringing a pitcher of tea with two cups, and a bowl of sugar. Gordon poured and handed a cup to Gretel.

"Sorry, but we haven't had milk for months."

"I haven't had tea since I left Maracaibo. This is wonderful. Thank you." Gretel stirred in a spoonful of sugar and sipped the hot liquid. *Good English black tea. God knows how they got it.*

The wireless key started to tap, and the operator wrote down a series of letters that meant nothing, then handed the yellow paper to Gretel. After she returned to her table, Gretel opened the James Joyce novel and translated the jumbled letters:

July 7, 1944. What is the condition of the Oso Negro and the Estrella Blanca? Which is more likely to be capable of reaching Buenos Aires?"

Looking at Gordon, she asked, "They want to know the condition of your ship. With the repair, can it reach Argentina?"

"Yes," he replied. "We have a fix for the steering cable that will hold. It will have to be replaced in a shipyard someday, but we can steer with no problem. The steering cable is the only reason we're here—the rest of the ship and the machinery are working fine."

"How long will it take?" She knew that Dussell would want that information.

"About two weeks. Once we're out of the river, we'll follow the coast about twenty miles offshore. We've got to get around Brazil, then head in southwest to the mouth of the Rio del Plata."

She looked around the rusted freighter noticing the peeling paint, grease-stained decks and machinery that looked like it would never be put in motion again. Her mechanical background was largely limited to learning how to drive an automobile. Gretel realized that she could do nothing more than relay her impressions to Dussell, but the ship didn't seem very seaworthy. It looked like one large wave could break it in two.

Then she looked down at the *Oso Negro*, floating alongside. The patched hull had held up after the makeshift repair in Trinidad, and she knew it could cope with heavy seas. But it looked very small compared to the freighter. Carlos had told her it would take a month to sail from the Orinoco to the Platte. And that was with favorable winds. "It could take twice as long," he had admitted.

"I need to write another cable," she told Gordon. He motioned to the table, and moved away, watching her pull out the copy of *Ulysses* and start to transcribe a message.

July 7, 1944. Captain says Estrella Blanca is seaworthy and will take two weeks to reach Buenos Aires. Looks dilapidated, but he assures me it can make the voyage. Oso Negro is seaworthy, but small for an ocean voyage this length. Time depends on weather, but at least four weeks. Recommend staying with Estrella Blanca.

"Send this" she directed the radio operator. "I should get a response soon. I will wait."

Francis took the handwritten sheet and began to tap the meaningless letters in Morse code, his eyes focused on the writing as his wrist rapidly punched the dots and dashes that were transmitted to the receiver in Germany. Finished, he handed back the cable to Gretel and leaned back in the chair.

Gretel looked out the windows of the bridge deck at the muddy river, watching the crew of the *Oso Negro* washing the sails. Carlos was directing them to rig a pump and rinse the canvas with the river water, and the crew took advantage of the unlimited supply of fresh water, stripping off their clothes and taking turns standing under the hose. She wondered what the accommodations would be like on the *Estrella Blanca* compared to the small cabin on the *Oso Negro*. There was evidently another woman on board. It would be good to have some female companionship.

The telegraph key began to chatter, and the operator put on headphones and began transcribing the incoming message. Handing the paper to Gretel, he asked, "Do you intend to send a response?"

"Wait and let me read it," she said impatiently. She pulled out the copy of *Ulysses*, and after substituting the letters on the incoming message, she read:

July 7, 1944. Continue on Estrella Blanca. Pay off the Oso Negro and send them on their way. Confirm.

Gretel nodded, expecting the instructions. She had already coded a response and directed the radio operator to send the coded translation:

July 7, 1944. Confirmed. Expect to depart tomorrow.

She stood up and faced Gordon. "We are going to continue your voyage, and I am going with you. I need you to send someone over to the *Oso Negro* and transfer my luggage. I will go with them to inform the captain. I need a cabin. A good one. I'm replacing Strock as the representative of your charter."

As she expected, Carlos accepted the news without protesting. He had agreed to the long ocean voyage to Buenos Aires, but Gretel knew he wasn't really looking forward to it. It would take months to return to his lucrative trade between Maracaibo and the Dutch Islands. Taking the envelope from Gretel, he opened it and pulled out the bank draft.

"How do I know this is good?" he challenged. "I could get back to Maracaibo and find out this is worthless. I thought you said you would pay cash."

"If I'd brought cash, I would have fallen in the ocean weeks ago, and it would be in your pocket. I know you searched my cabin. This is good. And you would have had to accept an even larger draft if we had gone all the way to Buenos Aires."

She knew that Carlos had thoroughly searched her possessions the day they had left Lake Maracaibo and discovered that she had not brought the promised currency. Gretel surmised that he had decided to continue the voyage, thinking that if he wasn't satisfied with the payment when they reached Buenos Aires, he would hold her hostage until he somehow got paid. Her transfer to the *Estrella Blanca* would leave him with little recourse if the bank draft was a fraud, but he had no alternative but to accept it. He shrugged and put the draft in his pocket.

"Good-bye," Gretel told him. The voyage to the Orinoco had been more of an adventure than she had anticipated. She knew that without Carlos' knowledge and seamanship they would have drowned. He was a brigand, but a relatively honest one. She hoped that Gordon would do as well captaining the *Estrella Blanca*.

"I will see you someday in Maracaibo," he replied, watching as the two seamen lowered her trunk into the boat and prepared to row her across to the freighter. Gretel boarded the small craft and waved once more as she reached the deck of the *Estrella Blanca* minutes later.

"You can have my cabin, and I will take Liam's. He can bunk with Francis." Gordon told her. "We have two more passengers going to Buenos Aires in the guest cabin, the one that was occupied by Strock. They happen to be German, so that will give you some company."

"Thank you," she said graciously, following him through a door into the stack of cabins on the aft end of the ship. He opened a door to starboard, motioning her through to a small room containing a single bunk, a desk, and a comfortable chair. Two portholes looked out onto the water, and there was a private commode separated by a door. The accommodations were the best on the ship, she knew, and a huge improvement over the *Oso Negro*. They would certainly suffice for the two-week voyage to Buenos Aires.

"I'll let you unpack. We're going to wait until dawn tomorrow to leave. I don't want to navigate out of the river in the dark, and it's already three o'clock. I'm going to make sure we are prepared to go," Gordon said and left. Once alone, she began removing clothes from the suitcase she had lived out of for a month and hanging them in the small locker.

CHAPTER SIXTEEN

The Orinoco Delta, July 1944

THE CLEARING CREW rose at dawn, ate a cold breakfast, and picked up machetes, axes, and brush hooks to hack away at the high, thick grass and small trees. They were followed by four men placing the detectors—orange jugs that would detect the reflected sound waves bouncing off the subterranean layers of the earth. They planted them in the earth by pushing down on a steel stake and connected them with a black wire. A third team used an auger to drill four-inch holes at intervals about half a mile apart, planting charges of dynamite within the earth.

Jerry was satisfied with the work and pleased with the faster pace that the crew was able to achieve on the second line. They would finish shooting this line today and return to Trinidad on the *Osprey*, sending the data back to the Pride Oil office in New York. After the data was processed and the results used to construct a preliminary map of the Oficina Formation, he could determine the location of additional lines, probably four or five. The final product of the seismic shoot would be a detailed map of the subsurface structure, hopefully indicating a location where it would be worth the risk to drill a wildcat well.

Jan was supervising the emplacement of a dynamite charge as Jerry approached, walking with Maria. Debbie was pulling cable off a spool, handing it off to a man who lowered the charge down a hole in the earth.

"Morning," Jerry greeted Debbie. "Glad to see you helping out. But I thought you were off somewhere working on your research project."

"I finished," she replied. "Got all the data I need. Thought I'd help with the survey as long as I'm here."

Jerry turned toward Jan. "I need to talk to Tom Barber. Is he close by?"

"He's setting jugs," Jan replied. "I moved him and his companion up from clearing brush. They're about half a mile north of here."

"I'll find him." Jerry set off on the cleared path, leaving Maria behind with Jan. He had told Maria about the uranium cargo and Tom's plan to seize it when it became evident that she would not be returning to Maracaibo on the plane, and that the unanticipated movement of the *Estrella Blanca* might precipitate the event while she was still in the camp.

"Why didn't you tell me sooner that you were involved in all this?" she had asked, irritated by the revelation of something he had known for weeks.

"I was told it is top secret, and I couldn't. I shouldn't even be telling you now. But I'm not going to put your life at risk, and I think you need to know so you can stay out of trouble."

"You mean out of the way. I can take care of myself. You'd better do the same. Are you going to tell Debbie?"

"I can't. Top secret is top secret. She'll just have to wonder what's going on when it happens. But I'll make sure she's out of the way."

That had been the end of the conversation, but the passage of the freighter that morning, even earlier than he had expected, lent some urgency to the situation. He didn't know what Tom Barber had planned, but he probably didn't intend to follow the ship out into the open ocean. He saw the man now, bent under coils of cable and a basket of orange sonic detectors, slogging along the path.

"Tom! We need to talk."

Turning around, the FBI agent set down the detectors and walked back toward Jerry.

"The *Estrella Blanca* just passed. They're going to anchor at the mouth of the river and wait for someone to give them instructions. I don't know how long they'll be there, but they could leave for Buenos Aires any time."

Tom grimaced. "I need the boat," he told Jerry. "I'll leave you here with the crew to finish up. We'll go to the freighter, load the uranium, come back here and load the survey crew, then head for Trinidad. We're going to have to go tonight and board the *Estrella Blanca* before dawn tomorrow."

Jerry hesitated. He hadn't told Mike Woods about what he had committed to, and if the *Osprey* was damaged, the survey crew, instruments, and the recorded data would be marooned on the shoreline of the Orinoco. He wondered if he was going to be fired when it all came out.

"I'm going with you," he said. "I know the captain, and I can talk him into transferring the cargo without a fuss. I assume you're going to pay for it."

"We hadn't thought about that. I don't know what the going price for uranium is. And we don't want to tell him that's what it is. Has he opened it yet?"

"Don't know. Anyhow, it's not Gordon's cargo. Whoever is going to contact him at the mouth of the river owns it. Offer a price based on silver. That won't make it piracy."

"I'll need to get approval, but that won't be a problem," Tom said. "I'll send a message as soon as we get back to the boat. In the meantime, we have time to finish laying out this last line."

"You're going to need to take the captain of the *Osprey*. Someone's got to run the boat."

"Matt has a master's license. Used to be a river pilot in Savannah. He can get us downstream. I don't want to involve the captain. It'll just be the three of us."

*   *   *

Dusk was settling over the river and the green plains of the savannah when the final detector and charge of dynamite had been placed. Jerry stood at the southern end near the bank, watching one of the technicians wire the detectors to a series of recording devices and the explosive charges to an electric detonator. The man finished his task and looked up at Jan, saying, "We're ready."

"Set it off," Jan replied, watching the cleared path. The man pushed down on the detonator handle, setting off the buried explosives and causing showers of muddy water to erupt from the ground. The recorder needle bounced continuously as the sound waves bounced off the subterranean layers back to the detectors, creating a picture of the earth miles deep below the surface. The entire event lasted less than a minute, the recorder needles settling as the sound waves dissipated into the earth.

"That's it," Jan ordered. "Start packing up. We'll finish loading the boat tomorrow, and head back to Trinidad in two days."

"There's something you need to know about," Jerry told him quietly. Not wanting to distract Jan from the final stage of the geophysical survey, he had waited to tell Jan about the upcoming trip to the *Estrella Blanca*.

Jan listened to Jerry's story, clearly irritated, before replying, "Well, at least we finished the second line before those two cowboys start something that's likely to end badly. There are records on the *Osprey* that I'm going to bring onshore tonight in case they end up sunk—or shot. We can wait here for another boat if we have too. I think we'll also unload some food and water. And set up some more tents to spend the night in."

* * *

Moonlight made the low banks of the river barely visible as the *Osprey* headed downstream, Matt steering while Jerry peered at a crude chart with a flashlight. The stakes marking the channel could only be seen a few feet away, so he read off the magnetic heading to the next stake, hoping they would see it before running aground.

"Steer one hundred three degrees," he said, the course that should put them on the marker at the next bend in the river.

"One hundred three degrees," Matt repeated. They had left at moonrise, anticipating that it would give them sufficient light to navigate downriver and arrive at the *Estrella Blanca* before dawn. Seated behind them in the pilot-house, Tom removed a Thompson submachine gun from its case, placing the circular magazine in the receiver after filling it with bullets.

Jerry recalled Tom's advice: *If we start shooting, just fall flat and crawl behind something solid.* He didn't plan to participate if shooting did start. It was a different situation than the assault by the German U-Boat sailors on the Everglades drill site last year. His original purpose, making sure that Pride Oil didn't get involved in an international incident, seemed pointless now. Two armed men were on a boat under contract to Pride Oil, intending to take something that belonged to another group that was possibly armed. The only mitigating factor was that the U.S. government was authorizing the raid. He hoped that would be sufficient excuse if something went wrong.

CHAPTER SEVENTEEN

A **FAINT BREEZE** came through the open porthole of the wardroom, providing some welcome relief from the oven like temperatures. Gordon had invited Gretel to dinner after she had settled in his cabin, asking her to be in the wardroom at 18:00 hours. She stepped through the oval doorway to see Gordon, two other men, and a European couple seated at the steel table. Gordon stood up and made the introductions.

"This is Miss Vermeer, who is replacing Strock as the representative of our charter. And this is Liam, our first mate; Francis, our radio operator who you have already met; and your fellow passengers, Paula and Hans."

"Cheers," Liam said. "Glad to have you aboard."

Francis looked down and avoided her gaze, shyness overcoming him.

"I am very happy you are here," Paula said. "It will be wonderful to have another German woman to talk to on the voyage."

"I expect we will have a lot to discuss," Hans said. "Please let me know if I can help you understand what is happening on the ship, and ensure you are accommodated as you expect."

"I am glad to be here, but I regret the unfortunate disappearance of Herr Strock." Gretel sat down in an empty chair. "What are we having for dinner?"

"Liam brought back some groceries from Ciudad Bolivar along with the cable that allowed us to make the repair. We have no refrigeration, so we will be subsisting on canned food and dried rice for the remainder of the voyage. But tonight, we have grilled pork chops and fresh vegetables, so we'll eat very well." Gordon passed Gretel a plate and the platter of pork chops as he spoke.

Gretel enjoyed the dinner, happy to have tea served after the meal, and she made small talk with her new companions. Darkness fell on the river, and Paula, Gordon, Francis, and Liam went to their cabins, leaving Gretel and Hans alone in the wardroom.

Gretel heard Hans speaking but paid little attention, thinking about the voyage ahead. Hans was talking about his connections in Buenos Aires and the importance of his work to the Argentinian government. According to Hans, his work as an intelligence agent in Maracaibo, collecting and transmitting information on the Americans and the Lake Maracaibo oilfields, was of immense interest to Juan Peron. In addition, he had made a fortune on the side that he was transferring to a bank in Buenos Aires.

"And you," Hans continued, trying to keep eye contact with Gretel, "you have come a long way. I understand from Gordon that you are the representative of the company that has chartered our ship, replacing the unfortunate Strock. I never met him. He disappeared before we got stuck on this vessel by our airplane pilot."

He stopped talking and looked at Gretel as though he were waiting for a response that would shed some light on her plans. Gretel nodded pleasantly, waiting for him to resume his dissertation on his wealth and importance. She tolerated the boasting, wanting to maintain good relations with the German couple during the voyage, but she wasn't about to enlighten him.

Hans paused for another moment and then started talking about who he knew in Juan Peron's government.

Paula reappeared in the wardroom and interrupted him, looking at Gretel. "Thanks for the transport. We wouldn't be going to Buenos Aires if your company hadn't chartered the ship. We can't thank you enough."

"I'm glad for the company," Gretel replied. "It's good to speak German again. Are you going to stay permanently in Argentina?"

"Yes," Hans interjected. "We know a lot of people there who have been trying to convince us to move. Germany isn't going to be a very pleasant place for a long time. Especially in the east where the Russians are going to be in control."

"What are your plans after we arrive?" Paula spoke directly to Gretel, ignoring Hans.

"I'm going to be there for a while," Gretel said vaguely. She didn't say that she had no intention of ever returning to Germany and didn't offer to keep in touch when they reached Argentina. Dussell should be coming soon via the transport he had arranged through the Vatican ratlines, and whatever his plans were, she was sure they wouldn't involve these two.

Gordon stepped into the wardroom, closing the door quickly against the tropical mosquitoes. "We'll be leaving at first light. We need daylight to navigate the river out to the open ocean. As soon as we can see, we'll pull the anchor and head out to sea. Wanted to let you know to expect a lot of noise late tonight when we start the engine and pull up the anchor."

"I think I'll turn in," Hans said. "See you in the morning." He paused, expecting Paula to precede him. She stayed seated at the wardroom table, continuing her conversation with Gretel. Irritated, Hans shrugged and entered the stairway.

"Can you tell me what is important enough for your company to charter a ship to carry it to Argentina?" Paula asked. "I can't imagine. I've heard most of the Germans who are making it out have only their clothes and a few gold coins."

"I don't really know myself," Gretel said. It was true, in a sense. Dussell had never discussed his work with her, but she had overheard him conversing with colleagues about a bomb that could be made from uranium. Once, she had gone through his briefcase while he slept and discovered a notebook filled with numbers and equations that were incomprehensible to her. She was sure that the cargo packed in the hold of the *Estrella Blanca* was uranium, Dussell's present to Juan Peron.

"Well, I'm glad that it's big enough to need a ship. Gordon told us that he was waiting for you and instructions on whether to continue the voyage.

Having the cargo on board seems to be the reason to go to Buenos Aires. I hope someday you can tell me what it is."

Gretel shrugged, not wanting to continue the conversation. They would be together for at least two more weeks, and it was good to have another woman, especially another German, to talk with. But she didn't want to be quizzed anymore about her plans or the shipment in the hold.

"I'm going to sleep too," she told Paula. "I hope we're out to sea when we meet for breakfast."

* * *

The clanking of the anchor chain, the exhaust of the steam engine, and the sounds of the ship coming alive awakened Gretel at four in the morning by her watch. She turned in her bunk, pulling the pillow around her ears. About to fall asleep again, she heard the noise of a collision on the side of the freighter, near the boarding ladder, followed by booted footsteps on the steel stairway. She heard Gordon shouting, and other men responding, all in English. The door to her cabin opened, and she saw Liam standing in the doorway, speaking without an apology for the intrusion.

"The captain wants you on the bridge. We have been boarded by pirates. There's a discussion about the cargo. Since it's yours, he thinks you should get a chance to say something." Liam closed the door, leaving her in darkness.

Pulling on an overcoat and boots, Gretel arrived on the bridge to see two men with Thompson submachine guns standing against the bulkheads, holding Gordon, Liam, and the helmsman captive. Another American-looking man was talking to Gordon.

"This is the representative of the company who chartered us," Gordon told the intruders. Turning to Gretel, he said, "These people want to buy your cargo."

"It's not for sale," Gretel said.

"My name is Jerry," said the man who had been talking to Gordon. "This man is Tom, and this is Matt. These men are sent by the U.S. government.

They're going to take the cargo in any case but want to pay you for it. "

"I'm not authorized to sell it," Gretel said. "If you take it, it's piracy. They hang people for that."

"It's wartime, and the cargo is considered contraband," said the man called Tom. "But to do this peacefully, we're willing to pay you the price of silver. That's forty-five cents per ounce. I am authorized to write you a bank draft after we load the cargo and can estimate how much there is."

Gretel hesitated. She could start a new life in Argentina with that much money. But Dussell and his associates would track her down and kill her. She had been sent to deliver the uranium to Argentina and absconding with the money would mean death.

"Let me go down to my cabin," she said. "I have a bill of lading that states the weight. You can calculate the price from that."

Without waiting for a response, she left the bridge, entering her cabin and locking the door. Opening her trunk, she removed a machine pistol and three magazines of ammunition. She hesitated, then pulled up a false bottom and took out a Luger pistol with two more magazines. She left the cabin but did not return to the bridge. Instead, she banged on the door to Paula's and Hans' room.

The door opened a crack, revealing Paula's face. "What's going on?" Paula said. "I heard all the clomping about and the shouting. What's happening?"

"We've been boarded by pirates, and they intend to steal my cargo," Gretel told her. "If they do, there's no reason for this ship to go to Buenos Aires. If you want to continue the voyage, you have to help me stop them."

Paula opened the door, revealing Hans on the bed. Still dressed in the clothes she had been wearing in the wardroom, she stepped into the narrow passageway. "I will do anything to get there. I'm not going back to Europe. Tell me what to do."

"Do you have any weapons?" Gretel asked. Seeing a negative response, she handed the Luger to Paula. "Do you know how to use it?"

"No," Paula replied. "I've never shot a gun."

"Let me do that talking—and shooting, if it comes to that. Just point it at them. That will make an impression at least. What about him?" She pointed to Hans. He was snoring loudly. A tipped-over bottle of rum lay on the small night shelf next to him.

"He's worthless," Paula said. "Talks a lot but doesn't do anything. Leave him here."

"All right," Gretel agreed. "Follow me. We'll have to surprise them on the bridge. They look like hard men and won't scare easy. Remember, if they get the cargo, we're not going to Buenos Aires."

"Wait a minute," Paula said. "Let me distract them." She returned to the cabin and reappeared quickly wearing a thin nightgown showing the outline of her body. She pointed to the Luger hidden behind her back, secured with a belt.

"Good idea," Gretel said.

Paula stepped through the door from the staircase to enter the bridge and walked to the opposite side. The six men stared at the young woman wearing a filmy gown and obviously nothing else, momentarily distracted from their surroundings. The door opened again, and Gretel entered, pointing the machine pistol at the group and saying, "Put down the guns or you are dead."

Tom moved sideways, creating a gap between himself and Matt that made it impossible for Gretel to cover them both. Gretel pointed the machine pistol at Tom's stomach with a steady hand, preparing to fire, when he dropped the Thompson and raised his hands. Matt hesitated, watching Gretel aiming at Tom, and twitched as though he was about to risk lunging at her.

Paula pulled the Luger from under her nightgown and aimed the barrel at his head. "You heard her!" she shouted. "Put down your guns."

Matt held the barrel of the submachine gun and carefully placed it on the floor, raising his hands as he backed away from Gretel. She held the machine pistol with familiarity, a skill learned on outings with her Gestapo paramour. He had enjoyed shooting and had taught her to share in his passion during weekends in the French countryside. Mostly they had fired shotguns at clay pigeons, but occasionally he had brought military weapons—machine pistols, rifles, and Luger pistols to practice with.

"I will not let you seize the cargo," Gretel stated in a matter-of-fact voice. "I will kill you first. And you know too much for me to let you go. Your government put considerable effort into positioning you to steal what is mine. They will provide you another ship to follow us. So you are going with us.

"I don't know who you are," she continued, looking at Jerry. "But I can't let you go either."

Paula interrupted. "He's with the oil company that's doing a geophysical survey up the river. Name's Jerry. He's a good guy. Tried to get me to Caracas to make a flight. But I agree—he has to come with us. He'll tell the Americans where we are headed."

Gretel picked up the submachine guns that Tom Barber and Matt had surrendered and told Paula to go onto the wing deck and throw them over the side of the vessel.

Gretel turned to Gordon. "I can't get this ship to Buenos Aires. Tell me what you want to do. Either get us to Buenos Aires or join these men and I'll promote someone else to captain."

"You've contracted the *Estrella Blanca* to transport your cargo to Buenos Aires. I keep my word to those who hire my ship. When we arrive there, I'll turn these men over to the authorities as pirates. They can then make their explanations that they represent the American government, or whatever. I like Jerry, but he deceived me."

"Then put all three of them in the hold and chain them down. We'll figure out something longer term after we get out of here. And get underway. Tow that boat they came in out to sea, and then we'll sink it."

Gordon paused for a second. "There's a stairway outside that goes down to the main deck. We need to go down, then forward to that first hatch. From there there's a ladder down to the cargo deck. We can chain them to some pipe down there."

He looked at Liam. "Get the anchor up. Then steer down to the river mouth and head due east. The boat they came in is still tied up. Make sure it's secure and tow it behind us."

"You go first," Gretel told Gordon when he had finished speaking. She looked at the three Americans. "Follow him. There's no place to run. If you try, I'll kill you."

Convinced, they followed Gordon out the open doorway.

Watching as Gordon and Liam pried open the gratings covering the hatchway, Gretel turned to Paula. "Go on down. I'll send them down one at a time. When they get to the bottom, tell them to lie flat on their stomachs with their hands stretched out. If they move, shoot them. When they're all down there, I'll come down with Gordon to chain them."

Paula nodded, and descended the ladder, her nightgown catching her shoe on the ladder and almost tripping her. Once she stood on the deck that stretched the length of the ship in the cargo hold, she looked up and nodded to Gretel.

"You first," Gretel said to Jerry. He looked like the least dangerous, and she wanted to see what happened when she sent the first one down.

Jerry turned to face the ladder; a set of steel rungs thirty feet high. He descended carefully, turning to face Paula at the base of the ladder. "You heard what she said," Paula told him.

He lay flat as directed.

"Now you," Gretel instructed Tom. He was obviously the leader of the raid, and probably the most dangerous. She wanted him separated from the others and prostate on the deck below.

Tom climbed down the ladder and lay flat beside Jerry. He looked sideways at Jerry and started to roll toward Paula, who was obviously a novice with firearms and might not be willing to actually shoot another human being.

Paula pointed the pistol at his head. "One more inch and you're dead," she said in a convincing tone. Tom lay still as Matt preceded Gordon and Gretel down the ladder.

Releasing a lever that secured a chain around a cluster of steel drums, Gordon pulled the chain across the steel floor with a clattering sound. He stretched it between two pad eyes that were welded onto the deck. Then he opened a chest to remove a roll of heavy steel cable and a crimping tool.

Cutting a section of cable, he made a loop between the last link of the chain and the pad eye and threaded the ends through a steel tube. Placing the tube between the jaws of the crimping tool and pushing down hard formed a connection that could not be removed. Repeating the process at the other end resulted in a twenty-foot-long section of chain that was secured to the deck.

"Sit down at that end," Gordon said to Jerry, motioning him to move near the pad eye. He wrapped a loop of cable around Jerry's wrist, securing it with a crimp. Leaving three feet of slack, he attached the other end of the harness to the chain. Jerry could sit or lie down, but not stand. After Tom and Matt had been latched to the improvised shackles, Paula stepped back and lowered the Luger pistol.

"That should hold them," Gretel said. "Let's go back to the bridge."

CHAPTER EIGHTEEN

JAN HAD SET up an awning by the tent that he used as an office, shading a set of old wicker chairs painted white with canvas cushions. The improvised gazebo provided Maria with a place to sit while she watched the river. Jerry had boarded the *Osprey* before dawn after a heated argument the night before, when she told him that whatever happened to the uranium was none of his business.

"You almost got killed in Everglades City," she said. "Wasn't that enough of the war for you? What are you trying to prove?"

"I didn't like getting shot at then, and I certainly don't want to experience it again," Jerry had replied. "But I think I can talk everyone down and convince Gordon that he has no choice. If I don't go, it will look like pure piracy—which it's actually pretty close to—and Gordon may resist handing over the uranium. Tom's going to take it regardless. I don't want anyone to get hurt."

"The best way to not get hurt is to stay away from people who might hurt each other." Maria had learned that while working in her uncle's bar in Queens. Once two or more of the customers were headed toward a violent encounter, her only recourse had been to get out of the way. There was a point where the men who frequented the bar could not be talked down, and fists or worse would determine the outcome.

"I'm responsible for the situation," Jerry argued. "I let George convince me to let Tom and Matt join the survey crew, and I knew what they were going to do. I can't just let things go without trying to keep someone from getting killed."

Maria had not replied, and Jerry had left her staring at the canvas ceiling of the tent. Now she watched the river flow slowly toward the Atlantic as the midmorning sun produced tendrils of vapor rising from the marsh. Large patches of porous peaty soil bound together by a network of roots eroded from the grassy banks drifted eastward in the central channel. Eddies of countercurrents circled closer to the shore, carrying in flotsam that washed up onto the sandy bank.

Debbie walked down from the office tent and sat down next to Maria, sipping coffee.

"You've been here all morning," Debbie looked downstream, seeing nothing out of the ordinary.

"I've been up all night. Jerry's taken off on the *Osprey* with Tom Barber and Matt. I can't sleep or hold anything down in my stomach until he gets back."

"I'm sure they'll be okay. Where'd they go? We've finished this part of the survey and I thought we were going back to Trinidad as soon as we finished packing up."

Maria liked and trusted Debbie, but she remembered the warning Jerry had given her about top secret information. She didn't care about what the government might do to her, but she didn't want to get Debbie involved in what was turning into a spiderweb of espionage and intrigue. "They're going to get something from the *Estrella Blanca*, whether the people who have it want to give it up or not. That's all I can tell you."

Debbie looked startled but didn't say anything. She reached up and brushed a strand of curly hair away from her eyes. "That's okay. I'm here as a guest, finishing my research. I don't expect to be told everything about Pride Oil's business."

"It's not Pride Oil," said Maria. "It's the damn government. They've gotten Jerry tangled up in something way over his head."

"Well, I haven't seen Jerry over his head yet. I'm sure he can handle whatever he's doing."

"I hope so," Maria said despondently. "I know he's done a lot for you. But he's not a cop or a soldier."

"I know you can't answer this, but I'm sure it's something to do with the uranium. The government sent a guy named Sam out to the *Estrella Blanca* with a gamma ray spectrometer. That's how we found out the radioactivity was from uranium. Someone in Washington is obviously very interested in it."

Maria stayed quiet, looking for the *Osprey* and finally sighted it moving rapidly up the center of the channel. As it drew opposite the camp, it turned and coasted into the shoreline, the bow bumping onto the sandbar at the edge of the river.

Jan emerged from the office tent and joined the two women as they ran to the bank, shouting to the helmsman through the open windows of the pilot house. Maria recognized one of the *Osprey* deckhands as the man steering the boat.

"Why are you driving? I thought all of the crew had come ashore before they left. And where is Jerry?" Maria shouted, frightened by the appearance of the *Osprey* without her husband.

"I was asleep below when they started the engine and headed downstream." the seaman replied. "By the time I got up to the helm, we were ten miles downriver and Jerry said they couldn't bring me back. They pulled up next to the *Estrella Blanca* and threw a ladder up, then boarded. Told me to stay on board. Then the ship pulled anchor and left while we were still tied on. Tom, Matt, and Jerry are still on it. I had to cut the line so I wouldn't get towed out to sea, and there was no way for them to get back on board the *Osprey*. They headed out the channel to the Atlantic. Don't know where they're going after that."

"Gordon told Jerry that their original destination was Buenos Aires," Maria said, looking at Jan. "They must have overpowered Jerry and the others and are taking them with them. Can we follow them?"

"Not in this boat. We've only got enough fuel to get back to Trinidad, not chase them out to sea. And even if we catch them, they are armed, and we are not. There is no way to stop them."

"Can you radio the Navy to send a ship after them?" Maria asked.

"Yes. We can reach our base in Trinidad and ask them to relay the message. In the meantime, we're going to finish packing up and return to Trinidad tomorrow morning."

Wanting to go after the *Estrella Blanca* in hot pursuit, but not seeing any other option, Maria acquiesced, then sobbed. Her face covered with tears, she returned to the wicker chair, staring quietly at the river, and listening to Jan talking on the radio. His conversation lasted for a few minutes, becoming heated at times. She heard him sign off and slam a clipboard to the ground.

"Well, that was not a good conversation," he said, sitting in the chair next to her. "I had to explain to the Pride office that we let a couple of commandos use our survey and our boat for a privateering expedition. They were not happy about it. Jerry is going to have some explaining to do."

"I don't care about Pride," said Maria. "What about the Navy?"

"The Navy isn't going to send a destroyer just because three people have been kidnapped. We still have a war going on. But I told them that George Morales in Maracaibo was the one who was responsible for this disaster. They're going to contact him. Maybe he can get something moving."

Disappointed, Maria nodded. If the U.S. government had enough reason to send Tom and his companion to seize the uranium, that was probably sufficient cause to send a warship after it. She would have to return to Trinidad on the boat, find her way back to Maracaibo, and get George to tell her what was going to happen. She regretted ever meeting him in Maracaibo.

"I couldn't help hearing that conversation. I'll pack up your things along with mine," Debbie said, wrapping her arm around Maria's shoulder.

The *Osprey* departed for Trinidad the next morning. It ran through the night and arrived in Port of Spain the following day. Maria listened as Jan spoke on the radio, then turned to her. "There is a flight to Maracaibo to-morrow morning. I procured you a seat. You will need to spend the night in a hotel."

* * *

In ordinary circumstances, Maria would have been fascinated by the flight along the Venezuelan coast, looking down at the ribbon of sand between the blue water and the jungle. But she was oblivious to the scenery, looking at her watch and willing the aircraft to go faster until it descended at the Maracaibo airport. Rushing to a taxi as soon as the door was lowered on the DC-3, Maria fretted as the driver navigated the crowded streets between the airport and the U.S. Consulate. She paid the taxi with a handful of Bolivars—evidently enough to make him more than happy—and entered the lobby of the build-ing, sprinting up two flights of stairs. Brushing past the secretary outside of George's office, she entered and closed the door.

"Do you know what's happened?" she asked abruptly.

"Yes, the Pride office called me and told me the situation. Jerry wasn't supposed to be involved. I can't understand how the crew of a derelict freight-er could have gotten control over Tom and Matt. They're supposed to be pro-fessionals. Tom was a Texas Ranger."

"It doesn't matter how it happened," said Maria. "It did. What's the Navy doing about it?"

"They've detached a destroyer escort from Trinidad to go after them. They left this morning. It will take them about two days to get to the *Estrella Blanca's* last location. Then they'll take the most direct course to Buenos Ai-res, hoping that they spot them or that another ship does."

"I blame you for this," Maria snapped. "You put Jerry in a bad place. He was worried about losing his job when Pride Oil found out but was willing to take the risk for his country. Now he's been kidnapped with no chance to help himself."

"I don't feel bad about asking him to take the risk as I understood it. I didn't think there was any chance that the ship's crew could prevent Tom and Matt from seizing the cargo, much less overpower them. But I do feel responsible that Jerry's ended up in danger," George replied.

"Keep me posted," Maria said, and walked out without another word. She hailed a taxi, giving the address of the house she had rented with Jerry in what seemed like another life. Unlocking the door, she threw her suitcase on the bed and picked up the telephone, responding when the operator asked, *"Que numero, por favor?"*

Maria gave the number she remembered from childhood, the bar in Queens owned by her Uncle Ignatius. She recalled his words when she had married Jerry. *"You're going to live in a different world, now, sweetheart. I'm happy for you. But if you ever need help, I'll be there."*

"Gracias," replied the operator, putting through the call. Maria heard the phone ringing in New York City, followed by a gruff voice.

"Yeah?"

"Uncle Ignatius?" she said. "This is Maria."

The tone of the voice in New York City changed from challenging to delight. "Yes," Ignatius replied. "How are you? Are you home? Can you come by for dinner?"

"No. Still in Maracaibo," Maria said. "Jerry and I were going to come back next month. But I have a problem. Jerry's missing."

She relayed the story of seeing Jerry leave with the armed men to board the tanker and learning from the returning *Osprey* seaman that he had been abducted with the rest of the party. "The Navy is supposed to be looking for them," she said. "But it's probably not high on their list, and they don't have a lot of ships in the south Atlantic. I thought you might know someone who can help find him."

"Where did they leave from and where are they going?" Ignatius asked.

"They left the Orinoco River and are almost certainly headed to Buenos Aires. But I don't know what route they'll take to get there."

"I know some people. Let me talk to them. Call me back about midnight tonight," Ignatius replied and hung up.

Maria sobbed. The strain of the last few days caught up to her, and an offer of help from a familiar source overwhelmed her. Jerry had tolerated her cousins, ignoring their background and how they made their living, and they had grudgingly accepted him. Maria had never proposed asking them for help with anything, wanting to put that part of her life behind her and sure that Jerry would refuse to get involved with them in any way. But she would not turn down any help in trying to rescue her husband.

She called back at midnight, and heard the phone pick up after one ring. "Uncle Ignatius?" she asked.

"Yes, sweetheart. I talked to some people who have contacts with the seaman's union. They will put the word out to pass on any sighting of the *Estrella Blanca*, and two of your cousins have put up enough money to make sure that it happens. I don't know much about the shipping business, but these people do, and they said it would be impossible to sail from the Orinoco to Buenos Aires without being sighted. So we wait. I'll call you with any information."

Maria had regained her composure after the first call. She felt like she was back in the bar in Queens with Ignatius and her cousins taking care of any threats. She had never doubted then that they would keep her safe. And she felt confident that they could find Jerry.

"I can't thank you enough, Uncle Ignatius," she said. "Please tell everyone who's helping that I'm grateful."

"Come see us soon," Ignatius replied. "Sophia will make tiramisu."

CHAPTER NINETEEN

Off the Coast of South America, July 1944

MANGROVE TREES PASSED by on the north bank of the river, then the ship turned with the twisting channel and the green forest was replaced by a sandbar extending into Atlantic Ocean. Waves broke against the bar, flooding over its seaward side, and white birds marched back and forth perpendicular to the direction of the waves, picking up small crustaceans washed ashore by each succeeding breaker. The *Estrella Blanca* cleared the pass into the Atlantic. As the ship steamed toward the horizon, the muddy river water abruptly ended in a tidal rip, replaced by the green water of the nearshore ocean. A collection of weeds, branches, and man-made flotsam had collected along the rip.

Gretel stood on the wing deck of the bridge looking down at a line of coconuts, broken pieces of lumber, fishing net buoys, and a small wooden doll. She wondered how the doll had washed into the ocean and how far it had drifted. Had it floated downstream from a Venezuelan village, or come south with the longshore currents from Trinidad? She put the thought aside as the bridge door opened and Gordon stepped out on the wing deck.

"That was not a good beginning," he said. "We're going to have to deal with prisoners now for several weeks. And their boat is gone. They must have left someone on it who cut the line when we started to move."

"They shouldn't have tried to steal the cargo. Pirates get what they deserve. Actually, these won't. They should be hanged. But I'm not expecting you to do that."

Gordon ignored the remark. "We can't just leave them chained to the deck like slaves in the middle passage. We have a compartment where we store spare engine parts and tools, a steel room with no window. I'm going to put them in there. We can lock them in and give them food and take out waste."

"I want to look at it first," Gretel told him. "These are dangerous men. The U.S. government wouldn't have sent amateurs to seize the cargo. Except for that one man—Jerry—who seems to have ended up in the wrong place at the wrong time."

"Okay. Let's go take a look." Gordon ducked back through the door. Gretel followed him down to the main deck of the freighter and to a steel box welded to the deck. A square structure about twenty feet on each side, it had been repainted a dull white during their hiatus on the Orinoco riverbank. The interior was accessible by a single door, the latch secured by a metal pin. Gordon removed the pin and pulled on the handle, swinging the door open.

Gretel stepped inside, peering around in the dim light. With no other openings to admit light or air, the room would be pitch black when the door was closed. "This will do," she said. I don't see how anyone can get out of here if the door is locked shut. Put a padlock on it in place of that pin and keep the key yourself. And make sure that you or Liam are here when the crew delivers food. It would be easy to bribe one of the crew."

"I'll have to cut some window slots in the sides," Gordon said. "They can't breathe in there if we don't. But a narrow slot won't help them escape."

"All right. Cut the slots and then we'll move them up." Gretel stumbled slightly as the freighter encountered the first of the rollers coming in from the open Atlantic. The freighter had a different motion than the smaller *Oso Negro*, more of a sliding than a rocking movement. She grabbed Gordon's arm to regain her balance. "I'm going to return to the bridge," she said, walking unsteadily across the deck.

Two hours later, two steel slots had been cut into the rusted sides of the intended prison. Meant to be rectangular, the rusted metal falling away from the cutting torch had resulted in an irregular oblong shape. Inspecting it, Gretel nodded approval to Gordon. "Let's go get the prisoners," she said.

* * *

A dim light penetrated the cargo hold through grated hatches on the main deck, enough for the three men to see each other. No one was hurt, but they were helpless. Jerry reached for the shackle around his wrist and tried to wiggle the steel wire, hoping he could pull it through the tube that Gordon had crimped around it. After a few minutes, he gave up and looked around. "There's nothing down here but bales of something that looks like wool," he commented.

"I see some wooden crates underneath it toward the bow," Tom said. "That must be the uranium. It looks like they tried to hide it by piling these bales on top. At least we've found what we came for. It will be a lot easier to handle in boxes than loose metal rods or ingots."

Jerry said nothing, convinced that they weren't going anywhere until someone came and released them. He wondered if he would see Maria again. She would do something to set the Navy in pursuit but finding them on the open ocean wasn't going to be easy. Sitting below the waterline of the old freighter, Jerry could hear the sound of water moving on the other side of the hull grow louder as the ship gathered speed.

A crewman brought some blankets and a bucket to the imprisoned Americans.

"Pirates, eh?" he said. "You will be hanged when we get to Buenos Aires. In the meantime, here is something to sit on and a bucket to piss in. Don't spill the bucket."

Through the open door, Jerry saw Gordon and Liam descend the ladder, hoping something relatively good was going to happen and not the beginning of physical brutality. It was obvious that Gordon now regarded him as a part of a pirate crew and had no use for him, regardless of their former semi-friendship. Imprisonment for several weeks would be bad enough. Beatings to extract more information or simply to amuse the crew would not be totally unexpected.

Gordon stopped before the line of chained men sitting on the floor, looking first at Jerry. "We're going to move you to a room on deck. You can stay there without the chains if you don't try to escape. If you do, we won't bring you back here. We will tie a weight to your feet and toss you over the side, executed as pirates."

"Remember we are representatives of the U.S. government," Jerry said. "The geophysical crew knows where we are. Sooner or later, the Navy will find you, and if we are harmed, the *Estrella Blanca* will be seized, and you will be shot as spies."

"We'll see," Gordon said.

"The U.S. Navy knows that the Americans have been taken on the *Estrella Blanca* and will be looking for us," Jerry continued. He wanted to convince the captain that he should stay on Jerry's good side. The war was going to end soon, and the losers would be punished, as they always were. "You'll need someone to put in a word for you someday."

"We're taking you up one at a time," Gordon said, not responding to Jerry's statement. "You're first." Liam cut the wire that secured Jerry to the chain, motioning him to the ladder.

"If you try anything, the other two are going over the side," Gordon added. "You can't overpower the entire crew by yourself. And Gretel is at the top of the ladder with the machine pistol."

Jerry hesitated, thinking about his days in the boxing club at the University of Oklahoma. He could easily subdue Gordon, probably quickly enough to turn to the tougher looking man, Liam. But he wouldn't be able to knock them both to the ground and free Tom and Matt before Gretel came down with the firearm. Convinced, he climbed the ladder to the deck, followed by Gordon. Gretel stood by the open door to the now empty toolroom holding the machine pistol. Gordon pushed Jerry through the opening, slamming the door shut and securing the latch.

"That was the easy one," Gretel said. "Take down a couple of the crew and cut the one called Tom loose next. I don't think he'll try and take on four men. If he does, get out of the way because I'm going to come down and shoot him."

Gretel's plan left the FBI agents no options for escape, and shortly afterward they heard the click of a padlock outside the door to the metal room.

"Well, this is a lot better than the hold." Jerry sat on the deck and leaned against the wall of their improvised jail cell.

"Certainly is," Tom agreed. "We can get out of this place sooner or later. And it's a lot more comfortable. Feel that breeze."

* * *

The slots in the side of the compartment admitted a cooling airflow as the ship moved steadily at ten knots. Fresh white paint had been applied to the top as well as the sides of the boxlike structure, reflecting at least some of the radiant heat from the sun. Tom idly picked at the wall of their prison. Unlike the exterior of the compartment, it had not been repainted and areas of rust covered about half of the surface. He pulled at a piece of metal that had been partially separated from the wall by a layer of rust. Putting the tips of his fingers between the thin fragment of metal and the wall, he pulled hard, bending and separating the smaller piece. He motioned to Matt. "You have smaller fingers. See if you can pry this loose."

Matt grasped the upper edge of the metal fragment, forcing his fingers into the gap, then pulled back hard. He fell backward onto the deck as the metal shard pulled free from the wall, a piece several inches long with a pointed tip.

"Excellent," Tom said. "Give it here." Taking the newly available tool, Tom scraped softly in the middle of the largest rust spot, grunting in satisfaction as brown powder fell to the deck, coating his hands.

"This spot is about to go. We'll etch a groove around a spot big enough to crawl though, then we can kick it in. Should take about a day to scrape enough away to weaken the edges, then we're out of here." Sitting on the floor next to the wall, he started to pull the sharp point repeatedly through the rusted metal.

CHAPTER TWENTY

THE *ESTRELLA BLANCA* steamed east by southeast on a cloudless day, the mid-day sun baking the decks and bulkheads until they were hot to the touch. As the freighter paralleled the coastline of South America, the shoreline of British Guiana was visible in the distance, a thin line of green above the horizon.

Gordon had set a course to keep the freighter in deep water but stay within sight of land. They were south of the trade winds now, and the surface of the ocean was a glassy calm, greenish blue in color with occasional lines of Sargasso weed. The ship was running smoothly. Originally built to burn coal but converted to oil after the Great War, the engine was noisy but reliable. A constant effort by the engine room crew was required to lubricate, adjust, and tighten the moving machinery, but years of experience made the work routine. Unless something unexpectedly shattered or twisted off, the propulsion system would move them to Buenos Aires without incident.

Gordon did not trust the makeshift steering cable repair, however, and was grateful for the calm seas. If it had parted once, another break was possible—if not likely—and they had no means to repair it at sea. If the cable separated again, they were better off in the calm waters near the equator. There, the jury-rigged fix that had steered them into the Orinoco could be called upon to navigate the ship into one of the small rivers emptying into the Atlantic from the forested mainland of British Guiana. Once they passed the equator and rounded the easternmost shoreline of Brazil, they would be back in more temperate climes and rougher waters. But the repair was holding well, and his confidence increased with each passing mile.

They passed fishing boats and coastal traders, moving between the rivers where the small villages were situated. But nothing larger, neither warships nor freighters, had been sighted by the lookouts that Gordon had posted on both wings of the bridge.

There were two pairs of binoculars on board. One belonged to Gordon, and one had been traded for a case of beer long ago in Lagos. They were held by the lookouts, who were changed at two-hour intervals, each charged with repeatedly scanning a designated sector of the horizon. Gordon wasn't worried about a threat from land but hoped to avoid being sighted by an Allied or American warship. The Germans had largely disappeared from this sector of the Atlantic. The U-Boats concentrated on the shipping lanes between the northeastern U.S. and Britain, but the German submarine threat was still present.

A warship from either side would likely board the *Estrella Blanca*. If it was an American vessel, Gordon, Gretel, and Paula would likely end up changing places with the prisoners. A U-Boat would probably just sink them once they realized there was nothing on board worth taking, unaware of the uranium's value.

The home port of Buenos Aires lettered on the stern designated them as a vessel from the still neutral country of Argentina and should provide them some protection. But a U-Boat might suspect that they were headed to pick up a cargo of bauxite, the source of the aluminum that the Allies turned into airplanes and landing craft.

* * *

Gretel slouched in one of the chairs behind the helmsman on the bridge with Paula, watching the passing shoreline. Last night, she had heard Paula's and Hans' door opening stealthily, followed by light footsteps in the hallway. She surmised Paula was visiting the captain, either to pay for her passage or for romantic reasons—or both. Hans had spent the night in an alcohol-induced stupor, waking late in the morning after his travelling companions had finished lunch. Gretel heard rusted hinges squeal behind her as the German businessman opened the door to the bridge deck.

"No one could bother to wait for me in the wardroom?" Hans asked in an irritated voice. "I had to eat lunch alone." He peered through the salt encrusted windows. "Where are we? This coastline all looks alike. No towns, cities, mountains, or beaches—just jungle. I hope Argentina doesn't look like this."

"Ask Gordon," Paula replied, clearly irritated. "I have no idea. But we're going south. I can tell that from the sun, and you should be able to. And Argentina is south, so we're headed the right way."

"I guess so," Hans said. He stood up and walked to the helmsman. "Where are we?" he asked. The man did not reply, under orders not to take his attention from the wheel and the compass when steering. Hans turned to Paula and Gretel and asked, "Where's Gordon? I hope he can tell me where we are."

Neither woman answered and Hans turned away, saying, "I'm going to take a few turns on the deck. Sitting for hours isn't too good for anyone." Still not getting a response, he descended the steel spiral staircase and opened the door to the main deck, then started to walk in a clockwise direction near the rail. Gretel watched through the bridge windows as Hans completed his first turn around the deck, three hundred feet long and fifty feet wide.

"I'm going back to my cabin" she told Paula. "I brought a travel guide to Buenos Aires with me, and I want to read some more about what to expect."

A few minutes later she heard a tap on the door. "What is it?" she asked as she opened it. Her tone wasn't friendly or dismissive, but a simple interrogatory.

"I just stopped by to say hello," Hans said. "If there's anything I can do for you, let me know. You might need a man's protection on this expedition."

"Really?" Gretel wondered what type of assistance he might ever provide.

Certainly not in any type of confrontation, armed or verbal. But he might be of some use, and she didn't want to offend him. Yet. "I'll let you know if I need help."

Hans smiled and stood outside the door, obviously hoping to be invited in. Gretel looked at him appraisingly. About five and a half feet tall, with thinning brown hair and a greying mustache, he was leaning toward fat. He obviously spent a lot of time on his appearance, she thought, although it appeared that he was having to clip his own fingernails and his hair needed cutting. Apparently, the only clothes he owned were business suits and shirts. He wore a white shirt with cuffs slotted for cufflinks, the sleeves rolled up above his wrists, and a pair of gray silk pants that were obviously the bottom half of a suit. Two weeks exposure to the sun had tanned his face and arms. His expression reflected an expectation that he would always get what he wanted but did not show the underlying self-confidence to make things happen when necessary.

A nice-looking man, but soft, Gretel thought. Her Gestapo lover and Dussell both possessed a hard, merciless core that Hans did not. They would step on him like a bug if needed.

She smiled at Hans and closed the door.

After seizing control of the ship and the uranium cargo, the voyage seemed to be on track to reach Buenos Aires in two weeks. Gretel was concerned about running into the U.S. Navy, but Gordon was hugging the coastline and had told her that the naval vessels would probably be offshore in deeper water, hunting for the few U-Boats left in the equatorial Atlantic. The weather was expected to worsen as they reached the higher latitudes below the equator, but as long as the freighter's mechanical systems kept functioning, Gordon seemed confident that the ship could handle the seas.

Gretel expected to be in Buenos Aires by August.

* * *

After locking Tom, Jerry and Matt into their steel cell, Gretel had coded a message to Dussell:

```
July 8, 1944. Have control of Estrella Blanca and the
cargo. An incident with pirates met with satisfactory
outcome. Will give you more details in Buenos Aires.
Expect to arrive early August.
```

She handed the coded cable to the operator and listened to him tap the Morse code, then hand the paper back to her.

"I expect a reply, but not right away," she had told him. "Send someone to my cabin immediately when you receive it."

* * *

That had been two days ago, however, no reply had been received. Unaware that he had left Germany and was making his own way to Buenos Aires, she wondered if the theft of the uranium had been discovered, and he was a broken man in a Gestapo prison. Gretel had no idea who to contact when she reached Buenos Aires. Dussell had told her that Juan Peron would want the metal cubes, but she was sure it would be in conjunction with the expertise in the physics of nuclear fission that Dussell could bring. She guessed that Juan Peron would want to somehow have a bomb made from the two thousand pounds of metal. *If Dussell doesn't show up, I need to be able to take advantage of the uranium.*

She had established a routine of visiting the bridge after breakfast when the morning air was cooler and settling into one of the metal chairs facing the open forward windows. As long as the ship was not moving directly downwind, a cooling breeze provided a few hours of tolerable conditions, if not comfort.

The next morning, she smiled at Hans as he settled into the chair next to her. "*Guten Morgen,*" she said cordially. "Sleep well?"

Pleasantly surprised, Hans took a second to reply. "Very well, thank you.

And yourself?"

"Pretty well. But I keep wondering about what to do with this cargo we're carrying to Buenos Aires. Do you know anything about physics?"

"Actually, it was my major at Heidelberg. "It is the most basic of sciences," he said in an authoritative voice. "All other sciences, chemistry, biology, geology, are built on it. Without an understanding of physics, one cannot pretend to understand the natural world."

Gretel was skeptical but somewhat interested. Perhaps he really did understand something that might be useful. She had no way of interrogating him to find out. She decided to assume that he might have some useful knowledge, although certainly not the expertise he was advertising.

"What do you think of nuclear fission?" she asked. "Is it real?"

"I believe that it can happen under the right conditions. But the mathematical description is very complicated."

"Well, I'd like your opinion on uranium," Gretel said. "Apparently there is a possibility it could be used to make some sort of super bomb."

"It's a process with enormous potential. But the details require a thorough understanding of quantum mechanics to appreciate," Hans said confidently.

"You'll need to explain it to me some time," she said.

Hans started to reply, but Paula had appeared on the bridge and was showing an interest in the conversation. He simply said, "At your convenience," and turned toward his wife.

* * *

In their cramped cabin after lunch, Paula looked at Hans and laughed. "Physics! You don't know Newton from Einstein. What the hell was that all about?"

"I took a physics course at Heidelberg," he whined defensively. In reality, he had nearly failed the one physics course he had been forced to take in order to graduate with a degree in business. He vaguely remembered the equations, expressed in symbols from a calculus course that had also been another waste of time for someone who was going to be a businessman.

The conversation with Gretel about fission, uranium, and bombs had made no sense to him, and he tried to think of anything that might help him understand whatever she had been talking about. He picked up one of the few books they had packed for what they thought was going to be a long flight to Argentina, an English dictionary. He flipped to the word *nuclear*. It evidently referred to the nucleus of an atom. Then he looked up *fission*. It meant to split apart. The uranium must have something to do with splitting the nucleus of an atom. An absurd concept, but who was he to make judgments? He remembered reading a copy of *Life* magazine on the ship that had brought them from Germany to Venezuela. The cover story had been on a new field of physics called quantum mechanics. A German physicist named Becker evidently knew more about it than anyone else.

He thought about what he might say to Gretel and left the cabin.

* * *

Gretel was not surprised to hear a knock on the door in the mid-afternoon. She knew that Paula took a nap during the heat of the day, leaving Hans to his own devices. She turned the handle that sealed the door against the watertight gaskets and pulled it open. Hans stood in the hallway outside, his hands clasped behind his back. Still not certain if he could be of any use, Gretel greeted him cordially.

"*Guten Nachmittag.* What brings you here in this heat?" she inquired.

"This morning you mentioned that you would appreciate an explanation of nuclear fission, and how it might relate to uranium and a bomb. Do you want to talk about it now?"

"Surely," she said. "Please come in."

Hans ducked through the oval opening, looking around the small cabin. Gretel motioned him toward the single chair and sat on the bed forcing him to look into the light from the porthole. It put him at a disadvantage, with her face in shadow.

"The term nuclear fission refers to splitting the nucleus of an atom," Hans said portentously. "Every atom has a nucleus. It can be split by a process that is difficult to explain to an amateur. But if it can be split, it could release a lot of energy."

"Enough for a bomb?" Gretel asked, looking at him skeptically. She was beginning to think that Hans was an impostor who knew nothing about theoretical physics.

"Yes, possibly." Hans asked if she had a sheet of pencil and a paper.

Gretel reached into the briefcase that had accompanied her from Maracaibo and handed him a spiral notebook opened to a blank page and a pen.

Hans sat next to her on the bed, pressing his leg against hers, and started to write mathematical symbols on the paper. He filled in the paper with meaningless scribbles—Greek letters, integrals and derivatives, arrows indicating a greater or less amount separated by plenty of dots and parentheses and brackets—until it looked like the blackboard for a lecture on higher mathematics.

As he wrote, he talked rapidly to Gretel. "If you describe the initial state of the nucleus thus, and the fissioning power is sufficient to overcome the initial state, then the resultant power can be quantified by this expression, to the sixteenth power. I have written it in calories, which is the standard unit for energy in physics. Thus, we can determine the energy and compare it to what would be needed for a bomb, calculated by this equation. As you can see, it would be very close."

Gretel looked at the paper with interest. It resembled some of the writing she had seen in Dussell's notebook. Incomprehensible to her, but similar, like two pages of Latin might have a resemblance. Perhaps Hans *did* know what he was talking about after all. She felt his hand on her thigh and allowed it to remain there while she asked, "Well, does that mean if we had some uranium, we could turn it into a bomb?"

"I could, if I had the right laboratory and equipment," Hans said. "It would take a lot of money to get set up. Perhaps we can find that in Buenos Aires."

"Perhaps," Gretel said. "Let's think about the next steps. Now it's time to go to the bridge and see where we are." She stood up quickly, motioning him out of the cabin. She followed, closing the door behind her. She put her foot on the stairs leading upward to the bridge without waiting to see if he shadowed her. Entering the bridge, Gretel was not surprised to see Paula seated behind the helm next to Gordon, listening as he described their current position and projected course.

"We are about twenty miles off the coast of British Guiana," Gordon said. "We're going to pass offshore of the border with Brazil tonight, but it won't look any different—"

"A ship approaching, bearing one hundred degrees," the helmsman shouted from the port wing of the bridge. "It will pass us about five miles to port if we keep our current heading. It looks like a small tanker."

"That will be close enough for them to see the name of the *Estrella Blanca* on the stern with a pair of good binoculars," Gordon said.

"Do you want to change course?" asked the helmsman. "Put more distance between us when we pass?"

"No. That might look suspicious, and there might be Brazilian navy personnel on board who would react by closing the distance and challenging us. Stay on course." Gordon commanded. The tap-tap of the wireless started at the rear of the bridge deck. "They see us and they're making contact."

Francis tore off a flimsy paper and handed it to Gordon. "Uncoded," he said.

July 12, 1944. This is the tanker Tucuma. Headed northwest, approaching vessel at 6.54 North, 52.34 west. What vessel are you?

"What are you going to tell them?" asked Gretel.

"We could not reply or reply with a false name. But either one might result in raising suspicions even more than a change in course." He dictated a reply to the wireless operator of the *Estrella Blanca*:

July 12, 1944. Freighter Estrella Blanca. Carrying
cargo from Venezuela to Buenos Aires. How is the
weather ahead?

Apparently satisfied, the *Tucuma* radioed back:

July 12, 1944. Wind SE at 10 knots, few showers for
next 100 miles.

Gordon watched the tanker approach, passing less than three miles on
the port side. He handed his binoculars to Gretel, who focused them on the
bridge of the other vessel. As she steadied the binoculars, she saw a lookout on
the *Tucuma* staring back at her.

CHAPTER TWENTY-ONE

Maracaibo, July 1944

MARIA AWOKE FROM a nightmare in a sweat. She had been searching for Jerry in the swamps of southwest Florida; she could see him through the mangrove trees, but the dense thicket of roots prevented her from reaching him. The phone was ringing, and she realized that the insistent noise had awakened her. She sat up, glad that the dream was over—but then the awareness that Jerry was indeed missing made her heart skip.

Picking up the receiver, she heard the gruff voice of her Uncle Ignatius on the other end of the line, the familiar late-night noises of the Queens bar audible in the background.

"Hello, sweetheart," she heard through the scratchy background of the overseas line. "This is Uncle Ignatius. We heard something."

Maria swallowed, anticipating bad news. Perhaps the *Estrella Blanca* had been sunk.

But the message that Ignatius relayed was somewhat reassuring. "The *Estrella Blanca* was sighted eight hours ago off the coast of British Guiana by a Brazilian tanker. The wireless operator on the tanker owes somebody in Rio a favor and sent a message that was relayed to us. We have the position and the course. Do you have a pencil?"

"Wait a second," she said. "Okay."

"They are at 6.54 North, 52.34 West. Whatever that means. And they are steering a course of one hundred degrees."

As Maria wrote down the information, Ignatius asked, "What do you intend to do? If they go into port, we can probably find an excuse to send someone on board and see what's happening. I don't think we have a way to do that while they are at sea."

"Let me contact the Navy," Maria said. "If they know where to look, they can find them and take the ship and get Jerry back. I don't know how to thank you."

"Come see me when you get back to Queens," Ignatius said. "And good luck."

Maria dressed quickly in a simple skirt and brown, low-heeled shoes. She didn't want to attract attention at 2:00 a.m. and be mistaken for a streetwalker. She picked up the phone again, dialing the home number of George Morales. It rang several times before she heard the voice of someone obviously aroused from a deep sleep.

"Hello. Who is this?"

"Maria. I have some information. Can you come over here? I don't want to give it over the phone, and it's not safe for a woman on the streets of Maracaibo at 2:00 a.m."

"Can't it wait until morning?" George asked plaintively.

"No. If you won't come here, I will be there in a taxi shortly and make sure that the State Department knows you are too much of a coward to do your job."

"Okay," he agreed sullenly. Relieved, Maria started making coffee. She had been prepared to bang on his door if necessary, but it would be simpler to wait for him to arrive. Thirty minutes later, he knocked on her door.

"Come in," she said.

"I'm sorry for putting you off. I'm not at my best when I first wake up. What do you have?"

Maria handed him the paper with the coordinates and course of the *Estrella Blanca* written in pencil. "This is where Jerry was earlier today. I want you to tell the Navy so they can find the freighter and Jerry."

"How did you get his?" asked George. Information came from strange sources in wartime Maracaibo. "I didn't think that you had any connections beyond Pride Oil."

Maria had been anticipating the question. The Navy wasn't going to send a ship chasing off to some unknown location based on her word, without an explanation of how she had received the information.

"I grew up in Queens," she explained. "My uncle is Ignatius Magianni. He owns a bar where some people you wouldn't want to know hang out. Some of them have connections, and they located the ship."

"Can I use your phone?" George asked.

"Smithfield 60535 in Washington," he said when the operator picked up. "Collect."

George waited a moment before speaking into the telephone mouthpiece. "I have a location for the *Estrella Blanca*. It came through organized crime in Queens. I believe it's reliable. The ship was sighted today, and I have the coordinates and course heading."

He listened for a moment and then said, "Ignatius Magianni. Doesn't get much in the paper, on purpose. Ask the FBI to check him out."

Lowering the phone, he told Maria, "They're going to make some calls to verify your information. If they believe it, they'll send a destroyer escort to intercept the *Estrella Blanca*. Since they don't have any other information and want the uranium back, I suspect that they're going to assume that the information is credible. They're going to call me back in about an hour."

Relieved, Maria offered coffee as they waited for the phone to ring. They sat silently, drinking out of the china cups that had come with the furnished house. Too anxious for small talk, Maria answered George's attempts at conversation with monosyllables. All she wanted to hear was that the Navy was pursuing the *Estrella Blanca* to the right place in the Atlantic Ocean.

The phone rang forty minutes later, and George picked up the receiver after a nodded assent from Maria.

"You are. Good. Keep me posted." He hung up. "They are sending the *Livingston* to the location you gave us. It's a destroyer escort normally used for anti-submarine operations. They should arrive in about two days."

"What happens then?" Maria asked. Although she was grateful that the Navy was searching for Jerry in the right place, apprehension about the outcome of an armed encounter replaced her fear that he had simply disappeared.

"They are going to board the ship and take the uranium," George said. "They will also rescue Jerry, Tom, and Matt. They can easily overpower the crew of a freighter."

Unless they can't, Maria thought. *Tom Barber and Matt Richards, two well trained FBI agents, had somehow been overpowered.* She didn't know what else to hope for.

"How much do you know about the uranium?" George asked her.

"Not much," Maria replied. "A graduate student with the survey party found it with her Geiger counter. Jerry said it had a use that was top secret and that no one knew about, but some people in Washington were interested enough to involve you and send a young man with a special instrument to the freighter to make some readings."

"I shouldn't be telling you anything," George said. "But you are the reason that we might be able to find the *Estrella Blanca* and seize the uranium. A special project going on right now in New Mexico is attempting to make a new type of bomb out of it. No one knows if it will work or not. But if it does, one bomb could level a whole city—something that takes days of air raids with conventional bombing."

"I see. I thought it might be worth more than gold, like platinum. But that wouldn't result in sending armed men to seize it. The government doesn't have enough people like Tom Barber just to take something valuable in dollars. But what you're telling me makes sense. I wish Jerry had known more. He might have stayed behind when they took off for the freighter."

"I'm sure he guessed something close to the truth," George said. "He's too smart to think that the government would do all of this just for money. He took a risk by involving Pride Oil and probably felt he needed to see things through."

"Well, he got in over his head. I hope they find the *Estrella Blanca* soon and send him back. I'm going to tell him he needs to stay in the office for a while. He got promoted to be a manager, not be out in the field, anyway," she said with conviction.

But Maria knew how much Jerry wanted to see the frontier areas of the world. That was why he studied geology. She knew that he merely tolerated the time spent in the office and looked for opportunities to visit a new wilderness. Maria had enjoyed traveling with him and seeing a new world outside of Queens. But at some point, soon, she wanted to live on Long Island and raise a family while Jerry worked at the Pride office in Manhattan, commuting on the Long Island Railroad to Penn Station. Maybe Amityville.

"There are a lot of people in over their heads right now," George reminded her. "No one grew up learning how to man the guns on a battleship or pile out of a landing craft to assault a beachhead. Jerry did what he thought he had to do."

Maria stood up, ending the discussion. "Please let me know as soon as you hear anything." George took the dismissal politely, leaving her to brood for the remainder of the night.

＊　＊　＊

The largest window of the house that Jerry and Maria had rented look out at a small garden, an area enclosed by a stone wall topped with broken glass. Built in the 1920s for a Standard Oil executive, the house was not a mansion but still far more than two people needed. The front of the house, facing the street in the upscale neighborhood, had narrow vertical windows covered with steel bars flanking a heavy wooden door. But upon entering the foyer, a visitor could see through a room with tall ceilings, electric fans, and large windows to a courtyard containing a fountain surrounded by flowering plants growing in clay pots. A dining area was to the right as one entered, adjoined by a large kitchen attended to by the cook Maria had hired on Paula's recommendation. A wing with three spacious bedrooms was on the far side of the courtyard, connected to the main part of the house by a hallway with whitewashed walls, a tile floor, and a collection of brown clay pots.

The low mountains of Colombia, rounded by erosion from the tropical rainfall, were visible in the distance above the garden wall as the sun rose above the horizon, turning the green hills from shadow to light green. Maracaibo is situated at the western edge of Venezuela on a narrow plain between the lake shore and the foothills of the mountains. Some ancient Spanish politics had determined the border which had never been a factor for the indigenous people who lived and fished on the lakeshore.

Maria was not a morning person and only saw the sunrise when awakened early to leave on a journey. But this morning, the glow on the distant mountaintops made her resolve to get up before dawn more often and experience the beginning of a new day. Her mood quickly shifted to despair, however, as she realized the night had passed with no word from George Morales. She hadn't expected anything—even with if information Uncle Ignatius had provided was accurate, any pursuing ship was still hours away.

Pacing the floor, she tried to think of something else to do. Looking across the courtyard, she saw the lights go on in the kitchen as Ana, who served as maid, cook, and Spanish instructor, started making coffee. Still dressed from the night before, Maria washed her face and followed the hallway to the kitchen.

"*Buenos dias, Ana,*" she said. She practiced her Spanish at every opportunity. Reading it was getting easier, and she could make out the menus in the restaurants that she and Jerry frequented with no problem, ordering the delicious fish and beef dishes that exemplified the Maracaibo cuisine. But speaking it was another matter. Her Italian accent overrode the Spanish vowels, and sometimes she thought that being understood by a taxi driver or waiter would never be possible, much less one of the diplomats at the embassy parties she sometimes tried to converse with. After listening to her attempt a few words, they usually switched to excellent English.

"*Buenos dias, Señora*," the cook replied. "How did you sleep?"

"I didn't," Maria said, shifting to English. "Jerry is in trouble, and I don't know how to help him. He's on a ship somewhere, and the U.S. Navy is looking for it, but haven't found it yet."

Ana poured coffee. "Why is he on a ship?" Maria had told her about Jerry's trips to the Orinoco delta shared her excitement about finally getting to accompany him. "I thought they were in a camp."

"It's a long story. I can't tell you more now, but someday I will."

"Are you hungry?" Ana asked. Jerry always wanted breakfast before he left for the Pride office. Maria was often still asleep when he came downstairs and many mornings wanted only coffee.

Maria thought for a moment. Her stomach was in a knot, and her mouth tasted like dry soap from the sleepless night. She just wanted to drink coffee and worry and had no desire for food. But she realized that the day ahead could be long and uncertain, and she might not have a chance to eat again. "Yes. Can you cook me some eggs?"

"*Perico*." Ana said. "That will be enough to last you all day." She broke three eggs into a skillet, then added tomatoes and onion. It wasn't an omelet, just scrambled eggs and vegetables. But accompanied by the cornbread Ana called *arepa*, it was a delicious and filling breakfast. Maria sat down at a wooden table that had come with the house, scarred on the top by years of food preparation. Ana had tried to convince her and Jerry to eat breakfast in the formal dining room, but they preferred to sit at the battered table in the kitchen, reminded of the Queens apartment that had been their first home. Ana brought the iron skillet to the table and spooned in the *perico*, placing a dish of butter next to it. Maria started to eat, realizing that she was indeed hungry.

Finished with breakfast, she returned to her room to bathe and dress. She put on a white dress that she had worn to fly to Maracaibo from New York. It was more formal than she usually wore, but she wanted to look polished and feel at ease with her appearance if she needed to make an appearance at the U.S. Consulate or somewhere else. She looked at herself in the mirror. Slim, dark haired, and beautiful, she decided. Maria wasn't given to self-deception, either positive or negative. She knew she was good looking, and glad that God had given her the gift of beauty. Looking forward to having children, she hoped that one was a girl who would resemble her, imagining how her extended Italian family in Queens would adopt the child.

The telephone rang again, a jarring noise. It was not George Morales, but a clerk at the U.S. Consulate.

"The Consul would like to meet with you this morning, if you are free," the woman said.

"I'll be there in thirty minutes," replied Maria. She knew the Consul, Richard Longstaff, and didn't ask what the meeting was about. She might learn something about Jerry, and if not, it would be a welcome distraction. Anything to get out of the house. Returning to the kitchen, she asked Ana to call her a taxi and watched through the barred front window for its arrival. An old Ford with *Taxi* painted on the doors pulled up opposite the front door. After shouting goodbye to Ana, Maria left the house.

The driver opened the back door, bowing his head. "*Buenos dias,*" he said.

"The American Consulate office," she told him in halting Spanish.

"*Si,*" he replied.

The ride took ten minutes through the narrow streets, at times requiring the taxi to halt and back up to allow oncoming traffic to proceed. Maria had never learned to drive. There was no reason to own a car in New York City, and she had been unable to afford one in any case. Jerry had done all the driving in Florida, and they had not purchased an automobile after their transfer to Maracaibo. She planned to obtain a driver's license when they returned to the U.S. and thought she would have no trouble navigating the small towns and rural highways of Long Island. But driving in New York City was unimaginable, dodging the men pulling racks of clothing on 34th Street and coping with the constant honking of other drivers.

Maracaibo was much worse. The city had been built before the advent of the automobile, and the twisting, narrow streets were lined with buildings at the very edge. Some appeared to be one way. Some were open to traffic in both directions but too narrow for vehicles to pass. People pressed against the buildings to let cars go by, and dogs were a constant presence. Maria wasn't sure who owned the dogs. They didn't appear dangerous but were generally ill fed and mangy. The taxi driver knew the unwritten rules, backing up at times and taking the right of way at other times, constantly honking to communicate irritation, agreement, or bluffing.

The car eventually arrived in front of the American Consulate, a two-story stone building in the center of the area where the other diplomatic offices were housed. Maria paid the driver, adding a small tip. She had ridden with him before, and he seemed as safe as any of the taxi drivers. She wanted him to keep coming to pick her up when she wanted to go somewhere.

Entering the Consulate, she walked to the reception desk occupied by a young man whose duties included being the public face of the U.S. Government to the community of American expatriates in Maracaibo.

"Good morning," Maria said. She knew the clerk and did not introduce herself. "I understand Richard Longstaff wants to see me."

"He's waiting for you," the man replied. "Go on in. They're in the conference room at the end of the hall." He waved toward a hallway leading toward the back of the building, an open door visible at the end.

Maria entered the conference room to see Richard Longstaff, George Morales, and a third man whom she did not know. The Consul stood, saying, "Good morning, Maria. Thank you for coming so promptly. You know George, of course. And this is Alan Courtney from Pride Oil."

"Pleased to meet you," Alan said. "Mike Woods sent me down. I understand that Jerry has gotten himself in a bit of trouble. Someone I know from the State Department called and told me what happened. I gave Mike Woods a briefing before I flew down."

CHAPTER TWENTY-TWO

Off the Coast of South America, July 1944

A SMALL SHIP with a narrow beam that made it prone to roll unbearably, the destroyer escort *Livingston* cruised east by southeast off the coast of British Guinea. Designed for convoy escort duty in the North Atlantic, the ship was smaller and slower than a conventional destroyer, lacking the speed and range to serve as part of a task force led by battleships and aircraft carriers. Armed with cannons and depth charges, it was more than a match for the German U-Boats, sinking two since being commissioned. The U-Boat threat had greatly diminished in the Gulf of Mexico and the Caribbean since 1943, as the German U-Boat command concentrated on interrupting the increasing flow of war materiel between the U.S. and Britain. But occasional sightings and torpedoed ships had kept the *Livingston* based in Trinidad, patrolling the Leeward Islands and the eastern coast of South America.

Two days ago, an urgent message from CinCLANT—the Commander-In-Chief, US Atlantic Fleet—had resulted in the crew being recalled at midnight from the wharf-side bars and brothels.

Lt. Commander Allen Cunningham, an Annapolis graduate commissioned in the aftermath of the Great War, was the son of a wealthy farmer in the Iowa corn belt. An only child, his father had urged him to return and take over the planting and harvesting on the family estate. But four years at Annapolis, with two summers at sea, had left him determined never to leave the ocean. He had worked his way up the ranks of the peacetime Navy, until the rapid expansion of the fleet in 1942 resulted in being given command of a minesweeper. Then he was promoted and assigned as the *Livingston's* commanding officer.

The orders that had been handed to him by the admiral's attaché in Trinidad instructed him to intercept a freighter named the *Estrella Blanca*, free three U.S. prisoners, and seize the ship and its cargo. He would be given further orders once that had been accomplished. The location of the *Estrella Blanca* and its presumed course and speed were stated in the orders. It was up to him to find it.

*　*　*

Two days later, the was crew relaxing in the calm seas south of the trade winds.

The radar operator called out, "Contact. Thirty miles ahead. Course 120 degrees."

Cunningham called out to one of the lookouts perched in a crow's nest at the top of the mast. The pitching and rolling of the small ship often made it impossible to scan the horizon with binoculars from the precarious perch, but today the flat seas provided an opportunity for another fifty feet of elevation above the bridge deck. "Anything in sight?"

"No, sir. Empty horizon."

"Steer toward the contact," Cunningham ordered the helmsman. The *Livingston* closed the gap at twenty-five knots. Twenty minutes later, a hail came from the masthead.

"Ship in sight. Looks like a freighter. Stack of cabins aft. The hull is still below the horizon."

"That should be the *Estrella Blanca*," Cunningham commented. At this rate, they should close on their quarry in less than an hour. "Radio Trinidad that we have visual contact with a freighter we assume to be the *Estrella Blanca*."

The radio operator spoke into the microphone. The radio on the *Livingston* was capable of reaching Trinidad with voice communication, eliminating the need to tap out the message in slow and complicated Morse code. The operator listened through headphones for a response. "They are telling us to abandon the chase and pursue a U-Boat sighting," he said. "They gave us a position, about one hundred miles from here."

The operator handed a sheet of paper from a scratch pad to Cunningham, who looked at it briefly, then passed it to the helmsman. "Change course to these coordinates. All ahead full."

Although curious about the cargo and the American prisoners on the *Estrella Blanca*, Cunningham was happy to be once again engaged in pursuing the destroyer escort's arch enemy, a German submarine.

The ship's engines pushed it at flank speed toward the presumed location of the U-Boat, the knife sharp bow pushing aside the four-foot rollers. The *Livingston* was two hours from the reported location of the submarine when the radio operator called out to Cunningham. "They're telling us to abandon the U-Boat pursuit and resume our pursuit of the *Estrella Blanca*, sir."

Cunningham swore. "Those assholes don't know what they want us to do. Assume the *Estrella Blanca* is proceeding at ten knots and plot a course to intercept. If there was a U-Boat, this is their lucky day."

The *Livingston* turned to the southeast, once again steering a course to intercept the *Estrella Blanca*. As night fell, Cunningham went to his cabin after ordering the executive officer to call him with any contact. *We should intercept the freighter after daybreak. I have time to catch a few hours of sleep,* he thought.

*   *   *

At 2:00 a.m. a violent thunderstorm to the west concealed the *Estrella Blanca* from radar and the lookouts' binoculars. It proceeded slowly at two knots, reducing the stress on the mended steering cable in the rough seas brought on by the storm.

Unaware of the *Estrella Blanca's* slow progress, the *Livingston* bypassed its quarry in the dark night and plunged ahead through an empty ocean. By dawn, it was fifty miles past the *Estrella Blanca*. The rising sun revealed an empty horizon, and Cunningham decided that the *Estrella* Blanca, making better speed than he anticipated, was still ahead of the destroyer escort. Unaware that the *Estrella Blanca* was now behind them, he ordered the helmsman to maintain course and the warship continued to increase its distance from the freighter.

✳   ✳   ✳

Bauxite, the aluminum ore essential for factories manufacturing aircraft and other machinery needed for the war, is transported by sea from the mines of British Guiana to the smelters in the United States. For the German U-Boat campaign in the waters off of Venezuela, interrupting the supply of bauxite was second only to torpedoing the oil tankers that carried crude from the Lake Maracaibo fields. In the summer of 1944, most of the U-Boats had been ordered to the North Atlantic to intercept the convoys carrying reinforcements and equipment to support the landing in Normandy, but the U-770 had been instructed to finish its cruise off the coast of British Guinea.

Idling slowly on the surface, the U-770 was recharging its massive batteries and flushing the stale air below decks. Unaware of the pursuit by the *Livingston*, the submarine was taking advantage of the darkness, prepared to submerge as dawn broke off the coastline. It had been a successful cruise, with eight freighters sent to the bottom. One torpedo was left onboard, and the Kapitan was reluctant to return to Lorient without using it. But no ship had been sighted for five days. Diesel fuel was running low, and they would have to begin their return voyage to France the next day.

The submarine's routine was interrupted by a shout from the lookout atop the conning tower: "Ship at 280 degrees!"

Climbing to the bridge above, the Kapitan looked to the west where the upper silhouette of a freighter was outlined against the horizon. Then he shouted down to the helmsman on the deck below, "Steer 280 degrees. Prepare to submerge but remain on the surface for now." He did not expect the freighter to be armed, and there was no airbase to respond to a radioed SOS from the freighter if it was attacked. The U-Boat approached the freighter at twenty knots, slowing when it was within five hundred yards of the slower ship and paralleling its course.

"Call them on the radio," ordered the Kapitan. "Tell them they have ten minutes to get in the lifeboats before I sink them."

The wireless operator picked up the ship-to-ship radio microphone and transmitted the message in Spanish. The Kapitan could see a sudden commotion erupt on the freighter's bridge. Two men and a woman appeared on the wing deck of the bridge, scanning the U-Boat with binoculars. Evidently the ship's crew had been unaware of the approaching submarine until the radio message interrupted their somnolent passage. Frantic words came over the static on the radio.

"This is the vessel, *Estrella Blanca*. We are neutral. From Spain, going to Argentina. Do not sink us."

The wireless operator repeated the message up the open hatchway, waiting for instructions from the Kapitan.

"Tell them this is not the route between Spain and Argentina, and they are going in the opposite direction to get there. They have eight minutes left to abandon ship and take to the lifeboats."

The operator complied and listened as another transmission came through his headphones. "They're broadcasting their position and stating that they will be sunk by a U-Boat," he told the Kapitan.

"That's okay," the Kapitan replied. "We'll be a long way from here before any help reaches them. Tell them six minutes left."

This last transmission resulted in the desired effect—the two lifeboats stored immediately forward of the superstructure on the *Estrella Blanca* were lowered over the side, and people started descending into them by rope ladders. Men picked up the oars and pushed away from the vessel.

Suddenly, a tall man emerged from a ragged hole in the side of a metal shed on the deck. He looked around in puzzlement until his gaze fell on the nearby U-Boat and the freighter's lifeboats pulling away. He ran to the side of the freighter and jumped, obviously confident in his swimming ability and aware of the impending end of the *Estrella Blanca*. Two more individuals escaped from the metal box and followed him over the side. One of the lifeboats stopped rowing, allowing the swimmers to be pulled aboard.

With all crew members apparently clear of the vessel, the U-Boat pulled up to the two lifeboats.

"You know your position," the Kapitan said. "You are only thirty miles from the coast of British Guiana. About eight hours of rowing. Good luck." Satisfied that he had done what he could to prevent the slaughter of fellow seamen, he turned to his men. "Fire the torpedo to sink it. Then we are going home."

Anticipating the order, an officer below pushed the button actuating the release of the torpedo from the bow tube, sending it on its way to the now abandoned ship. An explosion rocked the ocean, sending spray over the lifeboats still frantically rowing away.

The *Estrella Blanca* shuddered as the blast broke the keel, then the bow tilted skyward, and the stern was pulled under by the weight of heavy steam engine. The ship became a vertical spear that accelerated toward the seafloor one hundred feet down. As the stern struck the ocean bottom, the shock shattered the rusted hull, breaking the *Estrella Blanca* into two sections where the torpedo had shattered the keel welding the vessel together. The bow section rested upright on the seafloor with a cavernous opening where it had been blown apart from the stern section. The stern section rolled over, resting on the port side, the bridge wing deck submerged in the muddy sediment.

The U-Boat turned to the northeast, beginning the long voyage to return to Lorient, a trip that would end in the North Atlantic, sunk by a depth charge from a British destroyer.

CHAPTER TWENTY-THREE

British Guinea, July 1944

JERRY SAT ON the bottom of the lifeboat, happy to be alive. Ready to kick out the weakened section of the rusted toolroom wall as soon as darkness fell, the three prisoners had been slumped on the floor when the noise of the ship's engine suddenly ceased. Shortly after that, he heard something heavy bump and scrape down the rough metal side of the ship.

"Something's happening!" Tom yelled. "We've got to get out of here now." He kicked hard at the section of wall that had been scribed by the scraping wedge, creating an open crack at the top where sunlight streamed in. He kicked again, and the opening enlarged, the flap of steel still attached at the bottom and bending outward. "Put your foot on it and help me push down."

Jerry rose and stepped onto the metal panel along with Tom. Their combined weight folded the rusted section downward, enlarging the opening enough for the prisoners to crawl through.

Jerry was the first to escape. He stood up as soon as his feet cleared the jagged steel to see a German U-Boat at a distance of several hundred yards The ship's two lifeboats were slowly pulling away from the *Estrella Blanca*. The noise that he, Tom, and Matt had heard must have been the sound of the lifeboats being lowered into the water. He couldn't see any life jackets nearby, and in any case, they would slow down his race to catch up with the closest lifeboat. After stepping on the rail and jumping, he struck out with an over-hand stroke that slowly closed the distance between him and the skiff. He was confident that once on board the closest lifeboat, he could force the crew to turn and pick up Tom and Matt.

The man steering the lifeboat looked Jerry's way and then yelled some-thing to the two men rowing. They stopped and the boat drifted in the water, allowing the three swimming men to catch up and clamber over the gunwale.

Jerry collapsed on the deck near the bow, watching as Tom and Matt shoved aside Gretel and Paula and pushed their way toward the stern where Gordon held the tiller. Tom grasped Gordon by the collar and slapped his head to one side, then the other. Then he picked him up by the feet, lowering his head into the water.

"Leave us locked up to drown like rats!" Tom yelled.

Matt picked up Gretel and suspended her the same way, her skirt drop-ping down over her head. He and Tom were obviously intending to drown them, enraged by their callous decision to leave the Americans locked in their steel prison while the *Estrella Blanca* sank to the floor of the ocean.

"Wait," Jerry said. "They might be useful to us. We don't know where we are or how to get ashore in this lifeboat."

Tom hesitated and then pulled Gordon's head out of the water, nodding Matt to do the same with Gretel.

Gordon and Gretel coughed and spat, close to drowning but still alive. Tom picked up Gordon by the belt and threw him roughly to the floor of the lifeboat. Gretel landed on top of him a second later.

The FBI agent searched them both and quickly announced, "No weap-ons."

Gordon coughed and pushed Gretel off. "I sent a man to unlock the toolroom." He pointed to the other lifeboat, gasping for air. "He's in the oth-er boat. I guess he panicked and got in the boat without letting you out. I thought you were free but weren't going to get in the lifeboats with us—maybe take to the raft instead."

Tom breathed deeply. "All right. I'm going to talk to that guy and bounce him around some. If he backs you up, I might drown him for cowardice, but I won't hold you responsible."

He pointed at Gretel, who was leaning on the side of the boat and trying to sit up. "And you. You're the one who locked us in there. I won't kill you yet. But watch yourself. I've no reason not to."

Jerry watched the exchange, satisfied that the FBI agents had taken control of the situation. The three Americans might be outnumbered, but the crew and the German passengers were too frightened to challenge them.

"Get us ashore, Gordon. Then we can decide what to do next," Jerry said.

Seated in the stern of the lead boat and grasping the tiller in one hand, Gordon resumed steering southwest as the two seamen pulled on the oars.

The lifeboats were open skiffs constructed of wooden planks equipped with two sets of oars and a rudder. The oars were provided to pull the boats away from a sinking ship and avoid being sucked under. They weren't intended for long sea voyages, but the light easterly wind was sufficient to steadily move them through the water.

There's no reason why we won't reach land, Jerry thought. The weather was good, the boats weren't leaking more water than could be handled by occasionally bailing, and they had enough drinking water. The boats pulled slowly through the water toward a shoreline that was becoming visible as a dark smudge above the horizon. Jerry watched the rowers bending to pull the oars through the water, then sitting up straight as they lifted the blades and lowered them for the next stroke.

*   *   *

Eight hours later, as the shoreline drew nearer, Jerry saw a beach bordered on its landward side by a solid green wall of vegetation. The boats neared the beach and grounded a few yards from the water's edge. The crewmen, passengers, and former prisoners climbed out and waded ashore, grateful to have reached dry land after seeing the *Estrella Blanca* explode and sink below the ocean surface.

A seaman walked up to the line of green at the landward edge of the sand and disappeared into the dense foliage. He came running out a second later, swatting his face and head, yelling a warning about the dense clouds of mosquitos inhabiting the tropical jungle. They didn't appear to live on the beach, at least not in the daytime hours, but they made even a brief walk into the trees impossible. The survivors of the torpedoed ship would have to stay on the narrow strip of sand between the water and the jungle.

The crew of the *Estrella Blanca* stood by nervously, waiting for direction but uncertain about who would give it after they had watched their captain unceremoniously dunked in the ocean.

Jerry and Tom stood to the side as Gordon approached.

"We need him to oversee the crew. He knows things that we don't. And we will still need the boats," Jerry said in a low voice.

"I agree." Tom replied. He stared at Gordon. "You're still in charge of the crew and the boats for now. I'll let you know if that changes."

Turning to his former shipmates, Gordon gave quick orders. "We need to get everything out of the lifeboats and then pull them onto the beach above the high tide mark. We have some biscuits, enough water in the emergency beakers to last us for a few days, and some signals if we see a ship offshore. We'll turn the boats over to create shade and keep the rain out."

A crew member began opening a beaker of water.

Gordon spoke sharply. "No. Put the water on the beach. We have to ration it until we find more." The seaman hesitated but placed it in the growing stockpile and continued to unload the lifeboat.

Six crewmen grabbed the sides of an empty lifeboat, sliding it above a patch of dry sargassum weed that marked the high tide line. They flipped it over and tilted it on its side, resting the gunwale on a mound of sand and creating a two-foot gap to crawl under the boat. Repeating the exercise on the other lifeboat created enough shade for the two women and sixteen men to escape the sun. Satisfied, Gordon turned to the provisions that had been placed in a pile on the beach.

"Thirty gallons of water in five beakers. Chlorine tablets. Four tins of biscuit. Some fishing lines and hooks. Two sets of flares. Two signaling mirrors. Some rope, life jackets, and two knives." Gordon inventoried their supplies, already knowing what had been stored in the lifeboats. At least none of it had been stolen from the covered boats and sold in one of the ports they had visited over the last year. The crew knew the *Estrella Blanca* was an elderly lady, and a broken hose or a boiler explosion could send her to the bottom any time. They also knew they might need the lifeboats someday, so mutual suspicion and surveillance had left the minimal stores intact—nothing like what might have been found on a more modern ship, but at least a start.

Jerry turned to Tom and Gordon. "Let's ration the water to last five days. Tom and I will walk north along the beach and see what's there. Gordon, pick two of the men and send them south. If we can find a river, then at least we won't have a water problem, and maybe there will be a village. But be back before dark."

"Let's go." Tom looked at Matt and added, "Make sure they don't drink all of the water the first day."

"They won't," Matt stated harshly. Jerry and Tom had put the experience of being locked up in the toolroom while the ship was torpedoed behind them. Matt still looked like he would require little provocation to soundly beat someone.

Without another word, Jerry started walking north, stepping close to the water where the sand had been more tightly packed by higher waves. Adjusting his stride to the angled beach, he took faster steps with his uphill leg. A rogue wave had soaked his shoes, so he walked barefoot along the narrow strip with his footgear tied together by the laces and slung over his shoulder. Tom followed him.

"Do you know where we are?" Tom asked.

"Not exactly. But a few rivers flow down to the coast of British Guiana. I remember that from looking at maps of the Orinoco delta before I came to Maracaibo. And there are villages near the mouths of the rivers. But the closest one might be twenty miles north or south, so I'm not optimistic we'll find anything with our little afternoon walk."

"We'll have to take a longer walk tomorrow," Tom mused aloud. "Plan to stay overnight. Gordon said Francis sent our position before we were torpedoed, so we might get rescued sooner rather than later. A freighter isn't going to come in and get us off the beach, but the Navy might send in a boat if we send up a flare. If we're strolling north and they come in for the rest of the group, we'll miss being picked up. But we can't just sit on the beach and hope somebody comes for us."

Jerry thought about it. *Well, if the rest of the group gets picked up and I'm not there, at least they'll get word to Maria that I'm alive and on the way home somehow. And I want to see British Guiana while I have the chance.*

"We'll both go tomorrow," he told Tom. "You might need a geologist."

Tom laughed and continued his irregular gait.

The water near the beach was muddy, the waves stirring up clay and sand. Evidently the water was shallow for some distance from shore because it stayed brownish green for a long way out. The jungle on their left rose vertically, the border between sand and vegetation marking the point where regular incursions of salt water prevented the rainforest from expanding seaward. Exotic plants that one might grow in a flowerpot in New York City grew to fifty feet in height, and every inch of space between them was filled with vines and creepers, green leaves competing for the sunlight.

Jerry walked up and peered between two vines. The jungle floor opened up away from the dense growth near the beach. The leaf canopy starved the forest floor of sunlight, so packed leaves sprouting mushrooms and other fungi filled the space between towering trunks. After a few seconds, the mosquitoes found him and he quickly returned to the open beach, striding faster to catch Tom.

A small inlet intersected the sand path connecting a small lagoon to the ocean. Jerry stopped and tasted the water, hopeful that the lagoon was created by a freshwater stream flowing toward the sea. He spat out the brackish solution. "Just a tidal lake behind the berm. But the inlet looks pretty deep.

I think we should turn around, and we'll wade across when we come back tomorrow."

The lagoon was about twenty yards across and paralleled the beach for several hundred yards. A marsh of tall grass grew on the inland bank, reminding Jerry of the Florida Everglades. Fish swirled in the center of the salt pond, feeding on minnows, and birds dived to pick up broken pieces of bait. The tide was falling, and a swift current flowed from the lagoon to the ocean. The inlet looked to be at least six feet deep in the center, and crossing it would require a man to swim.

"Best to cross this at slack tide tomorrow," Jerry said. "It's falling now, and dead low tide should be in about three hours. So it will be low again at about eight tomorrow morning."

"That'll work. We can get back here by then if we leave at six. But once we cross, it might be difficult to get back if the tide's coming in."

Jerry tossed a stick into the inlet, watching as the current carried it seaward. "If we're going to see what's farther north, we have no choice. We can swim it on the way back if we have to. Let's plan to cross at eight tomorrow and hope we find a river and a village not too much further north."

"The best plan we've got." Tom turned to retrace their path, Jerry following in his footsteps.

*　　*　　*

The tired group of men and women were sitting under the improvised shelters when Jerry and Tom returned to the lifeboats at dusk. Gretel, Paula, and Hans sat under a boat with Gordon, next to Liam, who had scouted the beach to the south with another seaman. The remainder of the crew huddled under the other boat, dozing in the heat. A slight breeze kept the mosquitoes at bay, and the survivors of the *Estrella Blanca* looked reasonably secure, if not comfortable, for the oncoming night.

"Did you find anything?" Jerry asked Liam.

"No, just empty beach and jungle. We did see the wreck of a fishing boat on the beach a few miles south. Might be something useful on it if we're stuck here for a while."

"We didn't find anything either," Jerry said. "There's an inlet north of here we'll have to swim in the morning to go further than we did today. Tom and I will head north again tomorrow, and the rest of you can stay here. We're about a hundred miles from the mouth of the Orinoco. If we end up going that far, we should be able to flag a fishing boat or a native canoe. If we split into three groups and go north and south again, we'll leave two groups behind instead of one if a ship comes.

"I'll go with Jerry and Tom," Liam said.

"Walking takes more water than sitting," Tom protested. "There's no reason for three of us to go."

"We'll find some water somewhere," Jerry interjected. "Let him come. A larger group might be a good idea if something happens, like meeting unfriendly natives. The three of us need to leave at sunrise. We'll carry some of the tinned biscuits and enough water for two days."

"What do you want us to do?" Gordon asked.

"The rest of you will wait here in case a ship comes. If you get picked up, you can guess how far we might have walked and send someone to find us," Jerry told him.

*　*　*

The continent of South America resembles an ice cream cone, rounded at the top and tapering to a sharp point at the base. Near the easternmost point at Cabo Branco, the coastline forms an almost exact match to that of Africa, a result of the two continents splitting apart 140 million years ago. North of Cabo Branco, the edge of South America faces northeast, the shorelines of French Guiana, Dutch Guiana, British Guiana, and Venezuela looking toward Europe.

*　*　*

Trudging along behind Tom and Liam, Jerry picked up a handful of sand. It was dark in color, incorporating grains of rocks from the Guiana Shield, the igneous core of the South American continent. There was little potential for oil exploration inland where the sedimentary rocks that formed oil reservoirs were not to be found at depth. The mineral wealth of British Guiana was bauxite, formed as intense tropical rainfall weathered the Guiana Shield. But the endless supply of sand created by tropical moisture as it eroded the hard rocks might form oilfields offshore. He wondered if it would ever be possible to drill under the deep water of the Atlantic.

He saw the inlet ahead marked by a break in the height of the jungle growing near the beach. Seeing slack water in the strait that interrupted the sand highway, the group stopped at the water's edge. All three men were barefoot now. Each carried only a beaker of water tied to a piece of rope around their waists and a tin of biscuit in their pockets.

There was no reason to hesitate. Tom started wading across, stepping through waist deep water until he was about one hundred feet from the northern side of the inlet. He suddenly stepped into water over his head and swam strongly to the bank. The tidal currents had evidently scoured out the northern edge of the inlet with deep water immediately adjacent to the shoreline. Tom clambered up the steep shore, and then sat facing the water to watch the progress of the others.

Jerry traversed the inlet without difficulty, pulling himself up with a hand from Tom. He watched Liam wade gingerly into the deeper water as if he were nervous. When the water reached his chest, he started dog paddling to keep his head up, and he focused on the dry land ahead.

At least he can swim, unlike most mariners, Jerry thought.

About fifty feet short of his goal, Liam started thrashing about. Tom slid down the bank into the water and swam out to him, shouting, "Grab my shirt and I'll pull you in."

Liam grabbed Tom's shirttail as Tom stroked back to the bank. Treading water, he pushed Liam up the bank to grasp Jerry's outstretched hand.

Liam collapsed on the sand. "Thanks. You could have let me drown."

"That's true," Tom said. "But I don't hold any grudges against you for locking us up. You were just doing your job."

Jerry stood up and started walking, the sun now almost at his back. The dense green jungle wall reached down to the water's edge in places, forcing the three men to wade through the shallows as they continued plodding toward the Orinoco River. Jerry saw a flight of birds that resembled ducks circling about a mile inland, descending to some unseen body of water. They reminded him of mallards flaring over a pothole in the Oklahoma prairie before landing.

He pointed at the birds. "Those ducks must be going down to some fresh water."

They walked up to the edge of the jungle, peering at the thicket of bushes and vines.

"Should we try and go inland to find the water?" Liam asked.

"Let's keep going along the beach," Jerry replied. "It will take a lot of energy and all of our water to go a mile through this mess. If there is water back there, maybe it's a river that drains to the ocean up ahead."

Taking a sip of water, they resumed their trek along the beach. New flocks of birds circled and landed a short distance inland, an encouraging sign that fresh water was close by and might indeed be a river draining into the ocean ahead. They waded around a stand of palm trees to see that the beach became a headland, curving back to create a point of land. Following the shore around the headland, Jerry looked back in the direction from which they had come. A river flowed toward them, its course a straight line that paralleled the beach. They had been walking within a mile of the stream for the last two hours, separated from it by a band of jungle.

Sloshing through the shallow water, the three explorers waded upstream. The water changed from a muddy brown mix of seawater and fresh river water to a darker and clearer appearance as tannic acid from the decaying rain forest colored the stream.

Jerry scooped up a cup of water with his hand, tasting it and nodding. "Fresh," he said. "We can drink this."

Jerry and Liam filled the empty beakers and dropped a chlorine tablet into each one. The water tasted of rotten eggs but was drinkable. They had been rationing the water for two days as they walked in the tropic heat, and the torment of thirst had been constantly present. Unlimited fresh water had never seemed a luxury, but it was now. They sat on the edge of the estuary and ate a biscuit, washing it down with more river water.

"We can't swim this inlet," Tom said. "It's too wide, and the current in the middle looks too strong to get across. But we can bring the lifeboats up from where we are now and cross with them."

Jerry agreed. "The only reason to stay where we are is the wireless transmission. If anyone received it with the position where the *Estrella Blanca* sank, they'll be looking further southeast for us on the beach. But we can't stay there for more than another couple of days without water. So let's move up here."

* * *

The *Estrella Blanca* survivors listened as Jerry described what they had found on their expedition to the north and his decision about what they would do next. They departed their campsite at dawn the next day, loading the provisions back into the two lifeboats. Gordon had decided that the boats would make better progress with only the men rowing onboard, and the remainder of the party trekked north along the narrow beach. Their ability to walk along the soft, sloping sand was limited to that of the slowest person in the group, who happened to be Hans. The German businessman had kept his shoes and socks on, afraid of cutting his foot on a shell or piece of flotsam, which forced him to walk in the loosely packed sand above the high tide mark. His shoes had sunk down inches with every step, requiring twice the effort his companions were expending as they walked on the packed sand at the edge of the waves.

Aided by the wind and a longshore current, the boats progressed with less effort by the oarsmen than expected, and Gordon ordered everyone to board the two small vessels. Happy with the decision, the crew and passengers relaxed as they coasted along a short distance from the beach.

Paula looked at Hans with disgust. "You really have to get in better shape after we get to Buenos Aires. You're holding up the entire group."

Still breathing hard, Hans didn't reply.

"You can buy new shoes in Buenos Aires," Paula continued. "If you insist on keeping them on, just get them wet. Otherwise, you'll never make it out of here."

Hans sat up straighter and struck her face with an open hand, a smack that shook the dozing passengers out of their sun-induced stupor. "Quiet!" he shouted. "When we get to Buenos Aires, you will have to relearn the attitude and manners of a proper German wife. Until then, keep your mouth shut."

"Throw him overboard," Gordon said to the two seamen sitting closest to Hans. Happily complying, one put an arm under his legs and lifted them over his head while the other pushed down on his shoulders, flipping him into the water head down.

Panicking, Hans flailed at the water, struggling to keep his head above the waves. "Don't leave me," he yelled. "I can't swim with all these clothes on. Pull me back into the boat. I'm drowning."

"Just stand up," Gordon laughed. "The water's only about four feet deep here."

Hans stood up in the shoulder-deep water and his face flushed.

"Fighting is punishable by imprisonment on any ship," Gordon told him. "I won't tolerate it. Never have. We don't have a prison. So we're going to leave you standing here. You can walk ashore. If you make it, you'll find us a few miles up the beach."

"Keep rowing," he ordered the two men at the oars. Lowering the blades into the water, the boat gained way as they leaned backwards, leaving Hans to start wading toward the beach. Hans looked back at the occupants of the boats, who stared back at him with expressions of satisfaction. His mouth twisted in a grimace as a look of intense hatred covered his face.

Jerry had watched the incident without intervening. He had told Gordon he was in charge of the crew and the boats, and felt no sympathy for Hans, especially after his outburst to Maria on the *Estrella Blanca*. But he did wonder if Paula's husband was being sentenced to death for slapping her. "Can he make it? He knows nothing at all about the outdoors."

Gordon shrugged. "We may be stuck here for a while, and I can't have fighting. All he has to do it wade two hundred yards and walk five miles along the beach. This will scare him, but it won't kill him."

CHAPTER TWENTY-FOUR

Maracaibo, July 1944

THE HANDSET ON the old telephone rang shrilly and Maria answered it nervously, praying it was George Morales calling to tell her that Jerry had been rescued.

George's voice came over the line—but not with the message she had hoped for. "Maria. Bad news. The *Estrella Blanca* was sunk by a U-Boat."

Maria stared at the wall in disbelief, hearing the words but unwilling to let her mind acknowledge what they meant. A few seconds passed, and shock was replaced by anger. She hated the war, Pride Oil, and especially the U-Boats, who had all conspired to kill her husband. She said nothing, her chest moving with sharp, shallow breaths. Then sadness overcame her, and her eyes filled with tears.

"There is some better news, not good, but some hope," George continued after a brief pause. "The *Estrella Blanca* radioed their position before being sunk. Maybe the U-Boat let them get into the lifeboats before they sank it."

Maria was quiet. She gathered herself and then said, "Tell me the position." She wrote down the coordinates, hung up the telephone, and picked up Jerry's briefcase. Rummaging through the pockets, she found a business card printed with the image of a floatplane and placed another call.

"*Hola.*" A man's voice answered.

"I need to talk to Rulof, the pilot," Maria answered in Spanish. "Right away."

"He's down at the end of the dock working on his plane. I'll go fetch him."

"*Gracias,*" Maria responded and waited.

*　*　*

Rulof stood on a ladder propped against the engine compartment of the old floatplane, trying to fit a wrench around a sparkplug located beneath a rat's nest of wiring and hoses. The plane was back in service after flying back from the Orinoco delta with a new propeller brought from Trinidad. The engine ran smoothly, and there was no evidence of damage to the crankshaft from the sudden impact with the floating log. An air taxi service in the United States would have had to pay a mechanic to dismantle the engine, inspect, and reassemble it. In Venezuela, no one cared as long as the plane could fly, and Rulof had resumed his one aircraft flying service. He had a charter tomorrow and was catching up on the routine maintenance. The Venezuelan authorities might not require rigorous inspections for airworthiness, but that didn't mean losing the single engine at ten thousand feet was an acceptable risk.

A young man wearing ragged pants and a white t-shirt headed down the seaplane dock toward him carrying a piece of paper. He shouted to Rulof when he was still a hundred feet away. "You have a telephone call from someone named Maria. Need to call her back at this number."

Thanking the messenger, Rulof carefully climbed down the ladder, laying it on the dock so that it didn't slip into the water. The dock ran perpendicular to the shoreline, giving the seaplanes a place to tie up without running up onto the shore and scraping the bottoms of the floats. A gas pump stood at the end next to a small office with a telephone. Rulof gave the number to the operator, waited for a ring, and then heard Maria's voice on the other end of the line.

"Rulof? This is Maria, Jerry's wife with Pride Oil. Thanks for calling so quickly. I need you to fly me to the Orinoco delta right away." She sounded flustered.

"Can I ask why?" Rulof asked. "It will take me an hour to finish putting the plane back together and get gas. We can't fly there and back before dark. And I have a charter tomorrow. A Standard Oil executive wants me to fly him to Caracas and it's the first time they've hired me. Can't it wait?"

"No. I think you've heard that Jerry's missing. If not, I'll tell you the story while we're flying. But he's on a ship that's been torpedoed, and I have the position. I want to go get him."

"If you know the position, doesn't the Navy know too? Won't they send a ship?"

"They haven't done much of anything that I can see. Anyway, we can see a lot more from the air than they can from the sea. I don't want to wait on the Navy when we can be there in five hours."

Rulof didn't reply for a few seconds. Pride Oil had kept his flying service occupied for months, and now that the plane was repaired, they could be the foundation for a future of lucrative charters.

"If you don't help me find Jerry, that will be the end of your work for Pride. I can guarantee that," Maria added after a few more seconds.

Rulof acquiesced. "Okay. Be on the dock at dawn tomorrow. We'll stop for fuel where we did before. Then we'll have enough to search for an hour and get back here before dark. I can only do this tomorrow. The Standard Oil people know Jerry. They should understand—I hope."

* * *

Maria leaned forward in the harness, looking ahead through the windscreen of the floatplane. She felt the aircraft losing altitude as Rulof slowed and dropped the nose to give her a better view. The beach to her right stretched away for miles, a strip of brown sand sloping toward muddy brown water, interrupted in places where vegetation grew down to the water's edge.

"We'll be over the water in a few seconds," Rulof yelled above the engine noise. "Then over your position in about twenty minutes."

She suddenly grabbed Rulof's shoulder and pointed, "Look! There's someone walking along the beach. Go in closer."

Banking to the right, Rulof circled and turned the nose of the plane. Below them, a man walked slowly, head down, oblivious to the approaching aircraft. When they approached within half a mile, the noise of the engine caused the plodding figure to suddenly look up and turn toward them, waving frantically and pointing toward the water near the beach.

"Can you land here?" asked Maria.

"Yes. It's not too rough. And I don't see any logs. But I can't get all the way in—it looks like there's a shallow bar right off the beach. We don't want to get stuck again."

"Land and let him come out to us," Maria said. "He can wade."

Rulof flew inland over the jungle and landed into the wind a hundred yards from the water's edge. The propeller turned slowly, providing enough forward motion to keep the plane turned into the wind and maintain position just seaward of the shallow bar. Maria opened the door. She waved to the unknown party on the shore and motioned for him to walk out to the floating plane.

"Wade on out," she yelled. "It's not deep."

Hans stepped into the water, still wearing his shoes and socks, and stepped forward cautiously. By the time he reached the seaplane, he was in waist deep water.

"Hello, Maria. It's good of you to rescue me."

Ignoring his salutation, Maria responded, "I haven't rescued you yet. Where are the others? Where's Jerry? What happened?"

"We were torpedoed. I'm the only survivor."

"How did you get ashore?" Rulof leaned over Maria to get a closer view of the shipwrecked German.

"I had on a life jacket and grabbed onto a floating pallet," Hans said. "I drifted into the beach and started walking. I don't know where I am. I really want some water. Do you have any?"

Maria could see that Hans was an indoor person, unaccustomed to walking in a wooded park in Germany, much less a wilderness like the coast of British Guiana. Forced by the high tide to stay close to the jungle, he must have been apprehensive that an animal was going to burst from the thick brush and kill him. Perhaps a jaguar. The experience had worn him out. She passed him a bottle, heartbroken but skeptical. Waiting until he had drained half of it in a few swallows, she asked, "Why were you the only one? Didn't anyone else have a lifejacket on?"

"I don't know what happened to them," Hans answered. "It was all I could do to save myself. But I haven't seen anyone alive since I came ashore."

"Get in," Rulof said. "We're going to fly out to where the *Estrella Blanca* sank, then back in, and look for anyone still alive."

Hans climbed onto the wing of the seaplane, clumsily squeezing past Maria to the back row of seats. His face had a worried expression that puzzled Maria.

If it was me, the only thing I would be feeling is overwhelming relief at being rescued. I wonder what he's worrying about. Jerry was right not to trust him, and I don't, she thought.

The plane spun around and taxied into the wind as Maria closed the cabin door and Hans struggled to fasten his seat harness. The small aircraft skipped along the wave tops. Then it broke free of the water and climbed into the sky, heading southeast toward the position that Maria had handed Rulof on a slip of paper.

"I'm accustomed to navigating by comparing landmarks below with notations on a map clipped to the dashboard of the plane," Rulof said. "The waterway below must be the Waini. It flows parallel to the coast, meeting the sea a few miles to the north of us."

Maria watched him use a set of parallel rulers to determine a new heading and distance to the presumed location of the sunken *Estrella Blanca*. "Thirty miles on a heading of one hundred degrees. We'll be there about ten minutes after takeoff," he said. As the plane gained speed and altitude, he noted the time and turned the nose, heading almost due east.

An empty ocean greeted them as they circled above the location where the *Estrella Blanca* rested on the seafloor, the highest part of the vessel only about thirty feet below the surface. The outline of the wreckage would have been clearly visible in clear water, but the turbid sea obscured anything below the surface.

Rulof flew in ever-increasing circles for thirty minutes, searching for any trace of floating wreckage that might support a swimmer. They saw nothing but empty ocean.

"Let's fly back in and then go southeast along the beach." Hans suggested a course directly away from his former companions. "If anyone made it to shore, they would be walking in that direction. Otherwise, I would have run into them."

"That makes sense." Rulof flew back to the spot where they had picked up Hans on the beach, and then banked to the left, following the narrow strip of brown sand toward Georgetown. Flying only a few hundred feet above the sand, Maria saw a nesting sea turtle plodding back to the water after laying her eggs the night before. Shorebirds worked the sand at the water's edge, running down with the receding waves and retreating with the next surge up the sloping sand. At one point she saw an animal that looked like a rat digging in the soft soil, searching for turtle eggs. But there was no sign of human presence.

"They couldn't have walked any further southeast than this if they reached shore when Hans did," Rulof said. "That's all we can do. We have to go back to Maracaibo while I still have fuel and daylight."

I can't believe he's dead, thought Maria. *Somehow, I would feel it, and I don't. I don't believe Hans is telling the truth. But I don't know where else to look.*

"Are you sure no one came ashore northwest of you?" she asked Hans.

"Impossible. I was making good time. I would have caught up with them."

"Well, let's return," Maria said. "I think Jerry's alive somehow. And he will find me. But he'll have to look after himself for a few more days until he reaches some help."

CHAPTER TWENTY-FIVE

Buenos Aires, July 1944

THE VOYAGE FROM Spain had been uneventful, uninterrupted by weather or war. Intrigued by Dussell, his mysterious passenger, the captain had invited him to visit the bridge at any time. Dussell had spent most of the voyage watching the ocean through the windows forward of the helm. As a tugboat escorted the passenger freighter into the harbor, he looked down at the shipping along the wharf in Buenos Aires, searching for the *Estrella Blanca*. The port was busy, ships departing with beef and hides from the South American country and unloading manufactured goods.

Strock had described the *Estrella Blanca* as old and rusty with the profile of a tramp steamer—a long flat deck with a tower aft that housed the accommodations and the bridge. Dussel saw twenty ships matching that description tied bow to stern along the wharf as longshoremen maneuvered cranes over open hatches to unload the cargo. He couldn't tell if the *Estrella Blanca* was tied alongside the wharf or had not yet arrived.

"I have a friend who booked passage on the *Estrella Blanca*," he said to the first mate in broken Spanish. "Are you familiar with the ship?"

"*Si*," the officer replied impatiently. He kept his gaze on a section of vacant dock at the end of the port where the harbor pilot was directing the tugboat to take them. The pilings were tilted at different angles and the planking was collapsing into the water.

"We can't dock there," the first mate told the pilot. "That section of the wharf is too rotten to unload our cargo."

"This is all that is available, *señor*," the pilot replied. "The harbor is full. If you want to tie up, this is where it will have to be."

Frowning, the first mate acquiesced, and the tugboat moved amidships to the freighter and started pushing it sideways to the dock.

"Do you see the ship here?" Dussell asked.

"No, but I haven't had time to do any sightseeing," the first mate replied irritably. "Let us get docked, and I'll look around." The ship bumped into the pilings where men stood on the dock to catch the messenger lines and haul in the heavy cables.

When the ship was secured, the officer turned to Dussell. "Can't see anything from down here. They've stuck us at the end of nowhere."

"Can you call on the radio and see if they answer?" Dussell asked.

The first mate nodded to the wireless operator, who picked up the microphone of the ship to shore radio. "*Estrella Blanca, Estrella Blanca,*" he said. "This is the vessel, *Carmenita*. Can you read us?" There was no answer. "Either they're not listening or they're not within range," the operator said.

"I'll go look around," Dussell replied. He put on a coat to ward off the southern winter chill and walked to the port captain's office, dodging the cranes lifting pallets of merchandise from the holds of moored ships. Carts loaded with baled hides, destined to be made into shoes in New Jersey, were wheeled down the dock to a waiting ship with a U.S. flag. The scene was bedlam, but everyone appeared to know what they were doing.

The port captain had offices in an old wooden house across the street that bordered the wharf. Dussell opened the door to see a room full of desks, some with women typing manifests and other shipping documents, some with men talking on the telephone to arrange dockage for incoming ships. No one looked up when he walked in or seemed to care that he was there.

A middle-aged woman finally looked up from her typing, staring at the newcomer. "Are you here for an exit permit?" she asked. "If so, you'll have to wait."

"No, I just arrived. I wondered if a ship named the *Estrella Blanca* was here."

"You'll have to ask the harbor master to be sure," she replied. "He's not here now. But I don't recall a ship of that name berthing here, and I type all of the contracts for dockage."

"That's probably good enough for me. Is there a telephone office nearby?"

"There's one next door," the woman said. "They'll want cash. But they can place a call anywhere."

There was a line at the telephone office, ship captains calling to schedule loading and unloading or to make arrangements for new cargo. Telephones were placed three feet apart on a long table furnished with chairs and ash-trays. Everyone smoked, and the air was a bluish haze. Dussell finally got a seat after a two-hour wait. He gave the attendant a U.S. dollar bill and received a handful of coins in return. Picking up the phone, he gave the operator the number of a contact in the Argentinian government that Peron had given him at their last meeting. Struggling to understand the rapid Spanish as the opera-tor gave him instructions on payment, he finally just deposited all of his coins into the slot. He heard a clicking noise as the operator made the connection. A phone rang on the opposite side of the city.

"*Hola.*" A man's voice, sounding brusque and uninterested.

"I am calling for Antonio Gonzalez," Dussell said. "Is this you?"

"Yes," the speaker replied. "Who am I speaking to?"

"I am Ernst Dussell. I have arrived from Germany and am in the tele-phone office by the Port captain. I was told to contact you when I reached Buenos Aires."

"I will meet you at the port captain's office in an hour." The telephone went silent.

* * *

"We have been expecting you. But we thought that the cargo would precede you. We have had no word of it." Antonio had an expensive suit, a military bearing, and an impatient manner. He had taken them to a small café near the waterfront and ordered coffee for them both. Dussell could tell that he was suspicious of the German's arrival without the promised uranium.

"They must be late," Dussell said. "The ship's name is the *Estrella Blanca*."

"Oh," Antonio said. "It was sunk by a U-Boat off the coast of British Guiana two weeks ago. Don't know why. They were a neutral vessel and not obviously carrying anything of value. But the Germans must have thought they were Brazilian and torpedoed them."

"Are you sure?" asked Dussell.

"Yes. They radioed their position before the U-Boat torpedoed them. The Germans gave them time to get in the lifeboats. Haven't heard of any survivors, though."

"Well, I still have the knowledge that Señor Peron wants," Dussell said. "We can get more uranium."

"Uranium. Hmm. Well, let me talk to some people about what to do with you now. I'll be in touch. Where are you going to stay?" Antonio put down his cup and signaled the waiter for the check.

Dussell had expected to be welcomed and put up in a luxurious house. Now it appeared he was on his own to find lodging until Antonio learned that he was a crucial asset to Argentina, even without the uranium. "I don't know. Any ideas?"

"They have rooms upstairs. I would get one and stay here. I'll be back in a couple of days."

*　*　*

Three days later, Dussell sat across from Antonio in the café, listening to a summary of his new status and predicament.

"The government has no interest in you without the uranium," Antonio told him. "We don't need a physicist without the means to do anything. But we do know where the uranium is. You need to go get it and bring it here like you promised."

"How? It's at the bottom of the ocean."

"We have the position. And the water is only a hundred feet deep there. We are willing to pay for you to charter a vessel with a diver to bring it up."

"And how do I go about this? "

"We know a man named Sergio in Maracaibo," Antonio said. "He knows lots of people. Here is a ticket to Maracaibo and Sergio's address. He is going to arrange for a boat and a diver. Look him up, and he will tell you what to do."

"Why do I need to go if you know where it is and how to get it?" asked Dussell.

"Because we need someone to tell the divers what to look for. They have no idea what uranium looks like. Neither do I."

✳　✳　✳

Dussell climbed the steps to the shaded porch of the Novella Cantina, pausing as the barista approached him. The flight from Buenos Aires had taken two days with an overnight stop in Arequipa. He was tired but impatient to make the contact that Antonio had set up for him.

"Do you want a table and a menu, *señor*?"

"Maybe. I am looking for a man named Sergio. Do you know him?" Dussel asked.

"He's at the table in the corner. The one with two people. Sergio is the dark haired, good looking one." The barista laughed softly. Sergio was obviously a familiar customer, perhaps more.

Another man, a European, was seated at the table next to Sergio smoking a cigarette. Dussell walked over to the table and looked down, addressing Sergio directly and ignoring the other patron. "I'm Ernst Dussell. I believe that you have been told to expect me."

"Señor Dussell, meet Señor Hans Diess." Sergio made the introductions and continued. "You both seem to be here for the same reason. The unfortunate sinking of the *Estrella Blanca*. Before I make any arrangements, I thought it might be useful for you to meet and see if some common purpose might exist."

"Who are you?" Dussell asked Hans rudely.

"I am a businessman who was making a living here in Maracaibo. My wife and I took passage on the *Estrella Blanca* for Buenos Aires. The ship was sunk with no survivors except myself, but I got to shore and was picked up by a seaplane looking for the wreckage. I just want to get to Argentina."

"You might be useful," Dussell said. "You know what the ship looked like. Come with me, and I'll take you to Buenos Aires after we retrieve what we're looking for." Not waiting for a reply, Dussell turned to Sergio. "I understand that you can arrange for a boat with a diver."

"Yes, I have found a boat. It is named the *Oso Negro*—a sailboat. It left here with a woman named Gretel to meet the *Estrella Blanca* in the Orinoco River, then go to Buenos Aires. She decided to continue to Argentina on the *Estrella Blanca* and paid off the charter. The *Oso Negro* had some repairs to do after an encounter with a whale. It is still in Trinidad and available. They can hire a diver in Trinidad to dive on the wreckage. What they will find, I don't know."

Dussell said nothing for a minute, his face expressionless as he considered what he had just been told. *The same boat. If I had told Gretel to continue on it instead of boarding the Estrella Blanca, she would still be alive.* "How do we meet this boat?"

"You can fly from here to Trinidad on Pan Am," Sergio replied. "You can board the *Oso Negro* there, and they will take you to the wreck of the *Estrella Blanca*."

"Can you book me on a Pan Am flight to Trinidad?"

"Yes, for a hundred dollars U.S. I'll have to get you onto the priority list. The oil people here seem to want to fly to Port of Spain constantly and fill up the flights. But I can do it. Come by tomorrow and I'll have the ticket."

"I'll be here," Dussell said. Looking at Hans, he added, "You need to come up with a hundred dollars if you're coming with me." Descending the steps to the sidewalk, he strode away.

*　*　*

Hans remained on the porch of the Novella Cantina after Dussell departed. Since returning to Maracaibo with Maria and the pilot, he had retrieved new clothes from his apartment, dressing in an expensive suit that drew the attention of passersby. Paula had given Sergio her jewelry to purchase their tickets, but she had left behind a set of gold flatware, hoping to somehow retrieve it after they reached Argentina. Hans had taken it to a small shop that purchased valuable goods without questions. The exchange had provided him sufficient funds for one last chance to fly to Buenos Aires.

"Is this my only chance to get to Argentina?" he asked Sergio.

"I can get you a flight from Maracaibo this time. Leaves in two days. Will cost you five hundred instead of one hundred dollars."

"I'll take that one," Hans said. I've had enough of boat rides. I don't want to go to Buenos Aires on a sailboat."

"Come back tomorrow with the cash, and I'll have the ticket." Sergio waved to the waiter. "For now, have another glass of wine. I'm happy to have sold two tickets in one afternoon."

CHAPTER TWENTY-SIX

British Guinea, July 1944

EXHAUSTED FROM A day in the humid heat, the *Estrella Blanca* survivors camped on the beach bordering the eastern edge of the river mouth. Gordon had suggested stopping early to rest for the night before rowing across the estuary, and Jerry had concurred. Three seamen carried the almost-empty beakers upstream to collect fresh water. The rest of the marooned party settled under the boats, shaded from the midafternoon sun.

The sudden drone of an airplane engine roused them enough to crawl out from underneath their improvised shelter, waving frantically as the aircraft appeared in the western sky and passed over the route they had taken that day. It flew away from them toward the open ocean, then suddenly turned back toward land, losing altitude, and appeared to touch down close to the beach a few miles away. Hoping it would pass closer to their position when it took off again, Gordon told Liam to unwrap the package of flares and ordered the youngest seaman to run down the beach and see if he could reach the plane before it took off again. The pilot might have touched down due to a mechanical problem but could not be expected to remain drifting in the choppy surf for an extended time.

Jerry shaded his eyes as he gazed intently down the beach. The seaplane lifted into the haze rising from the water and headed away from land again. A few minutes later, the young runner trudged back into camp and reported he saw the plane disappear along with any reason to keep running toward it.

"Well, that's that," Jerry said. "We're here for now. Gordon, can you send a man back the way we came and see if he can find Hans? He should have been able to walk this far with no problem."

Gordon motioned to the seaman who had chased the plane, ordering him to retrace their steps to the east and look for any trace of the German they thought they had only temporarily abandoned. He trudged back into camp four hours later, his feet soaked and his face red with sunburn.

"I don't know what happened to Hans," he reported. "The tide came in and put most of the beach underwater, so I didn't see any footprints."

"How far did you walk?" Jerry asked.

"For two hours, further than the point where the captain ordered him ashore," the man replied.

Jerry looked at the beach where they were camped, the water lapping at the base of the jungle along much of the shoreline. It would have forced Hans to wade in knee-deep water much of the time. He wondered if Hans had stepped into a deep pothole and drowned. Or had been killed by a jaguar and dragged into the jungle to be eaten.

"Well, we can't stay here and wait for him," Jerry said. "He might still be alive somehow. But we can't just sit here and hope that he might show up. We're about forty miles from the mouth of the Orinoco and another hundred miles from Trinidad. We can probably find help in the delta or continue in the boats to Trinidad."

"Let's go straight to Trinidad," Tom said. "If we get there, I can radio for instructions on what we're supposed to do. We know where that uranium is, and it's only under one hundred feet of water. Should be able to get it up if it's not buried in the ship."

"What does Paula want to do?" Jerry asked.

"She doesn't care," Liam interjected. "She's sick of him. That slap was the end of a marriage."

Jerry turned to the rest of the group. "We'll leave at first light for Trinidad. Get some rest and drink plenty of water because we're going to be spending a few days in the boats."

*　*　*

The sun had not yet appeared above the horizon the next morning when four crew members of the *Estrella Blanca* pushed the lifeboats out into the shallow water, clambered over the sides, and dropped the oars into the oarlocks. They held the boats bow on into the waves while the remainder of the party waded out and boarded the boats, some headfirst, the more competent sitting on the gunwales and swinging their legs inboard.

Gordon steered the first boat toward the northwest across the mouth of the estuary. A slow current of muddy water flowed from the mainland causing them to drift out to sea as they passed the river mouth bar. The sun was well above the eastern horizon by then, and the tropical day had begun, forcing the occupants of the lifeboats to cover their heads with any spare article of clothing they had available.

With full water beakers and expecting that they would encounter fresh water at the mouth of the Orinoco the next day, Gordon did not enforce water rationing. The seamen traded places on the oars every two hours, and the boats moved steadily north at two knots. The shoreline became a line of jungle behind a narrow beach again, interrupted periodically by small streams that had split off from the main channel of the Orinoco. In some areas, marshy vegetation covered a flat plain shoreward of the beach creating a sanctuary for birds that rose from the small lakes in huge flocks. Tidal rips began to appear, marking boundaries between fresh river water and the salty brine, signaling that they were approaching the area where the second largest river in South America drained into the sea.

"How wide is the delta?" Jerry asked Gordon.

"It's about thirty miles across. There are about twenty passes where the river reaches the Atlantic, and only one that is navigable—the one we came up. We're going to stay far enough out so that we don't get caught on a sandbar in breaking waves. We should be able to drink the water, and it will take us about a day to row across."

* * *

Five days later, the lifeboats surfed onto the beach that formed the island of Trinidad's southern shoreline. They had come farther north into the latitude of the trade winds, and the skiffs had rolled heavily in the swells, shipping water that required constant bailing. Their biscuits had all been eaten, along with some eggs they had scooped from bird nests along the beach, but they had caught enough fish to sustain them.

The settled part of the large island was mostly on the western shoreline, sheltered from the heavy seas that battered the eastern side. The south shore where the lifeboats landed was largely deserted.

The first lifeboat struck on the shoaling bottom and threatened to broach and turn sideways.

"Ship oars and get out to hold us," Gordon yelled.

Six men jumped over the sides, holding the boat with the bow toward the beach and struggling to keep it from turning. A large wave crested but did not break before lifting the stern of the boat and pushing it in to ground on the beach.

The second boat was not so fortunate. Liam steered it toward the beach, attempting to keep the stern toward the waves—but he turned slightly so that the waves came on the port quarter, pushing the stern of the boat toward the shoreline. The next wave broke onto the side of the boat, capsizing it and spilling the passengers into the surf. Finding their feet in the shallow water, they managed to wade ashore, leaving the lifeboat behind to surge back and forth in the breakers.

Jerry looked past the beach to see a wall of jungle resembling what they had encountered when they were swept ashore in British Guiana, but instead of the chattering of birds he heard the passing engine of a motorcar. "There must be a road close by," he announced to no one in particular. "I'm going to go have a look."

Working his way inland while watching for snakes and ducking below vines and low branches, he encountered a narrow dirt road created by horses and wagons and now partially utilized by automobiles and trucks. A dust cloud visible beyond a curve to the east announced an oncoming vehicle. Standing in the center of the road, he waved both arms over his head as a large tank truck came toward him, slowing to a stop as the driver drew even with Jerry. A yellow pecten on the side of the door announced that the tanker was part of the Shell operation in the Trinidad oil fields.

"What's happening, mate?" asked the driver, a tall, light brown man. "Are you lost?"

"No, shipwrecked," Jerry replied. "I'm with Pride Oil in Maracaibo. It's a long story, but I was on a ship that got torpedoed off British Guiana. Eighteen of us took to lifeboats and came north, and here we are."

"Get in and I'll take you to the field office. You can telephone from there."

"Let me tell the others I'm going. They're back on the beach. Be right back. And thanks."

* * *

Jerry sat on the edge of the bed in the Port of Spain hotel room, talking to Maria on the telephone. Or rather listening to Maria. She had cried upon hearing his voice when she picked up the phone in Maracaibo, and then the days of uncertainty and despair launched her into a fusillade of grievances.

"We picked up Hans who said he was the only survivor of the *Estrella Blanca*. I thought you were dead," she said tearfully. Then her tone changed from grief to anger. "What the hell did you think you were doing? You're not in the Navy. You survived the U-Boat raid on the Sunniland well. Are you just trying to get killed one way or another before this war is over?"

"No," he said reassuringly. *Hans is alive,* he thought. *But didn't tell them we were still alive.*

"I met an Alan Courtney from Pride Oil in Maracaibo—do you know him? He said that Mike Woods knew nothing of all of this and was going to be pissed."

"I'm sure he will be," Jerry said with a sigh. "I'll probably be looking for another job."

"When do you get back to Maracaibo?" she asked. "I hope that Pride will still pay for a plane ticket before they fire you."

"I haven't called Mike Woods yet," Jerry replied. "I have to do that next. Let me do that and I'll know more about what's going to happen."

"Okay. Don't do anything else stupid. I'm mad, but I want you back in one piece so I can keep telling you what I think of your half-assed schemes."

"I love you. See you soon one way or the other." Jerry hung up. He rang the operator and asked for the New York number of the president of Pride Oil. It took a few minutes for the call to go through the poorly connected network of telephone lines to the mainland of North America.

Finally, a woman's voice answered. "Mr. Wood's office."

"Hi, Ellen. This is Jerry MacDonald. Is he available?"

"Jerry! We thought you were dead. Where are you?" Ellen had moved up to the president's suite when Mike Woods had been promoted. Jerry had met her during her days in the secretarial pool when she typed his reports, occasionally sharing lunch at the automat and going to the theatre. That had stopped when he met Maria, but Ellen seemed to accept the end of their relationship gracefully and got along well the outgoing Italian girl. She had attended their good-bye party at the seedy bar owned by Maria's uncle when they left for Maracaibo.

"I'm alive and in Trinidad. It's a long story I'll tell you at another time, but I'm fine. But I need to talk to Mike," Jerry explained.

"I'm glad you're alive. How's Maria?" Ellen asked.

"She's fine but mad at the fix I got into."

"So is Mr. Woods. I'll put you through."

The phone went silent, then Jerry heard the familiar voice of Mike

Woods. "Jerry! Where the hell are you? We thought you were dead."

"I'm in Trinidad. I've spent the last three weeks as a prisoner on a ship with two American FBI agents, then as a shipwrecked beachcomber. But now I'm in a hotel in Port of Spain."

"Alan Courtney told me about your conniving with the State Department and these FBI agents. What the hell did you think you were doing with a Pride operation? And why didn't you ask me before you agreed to put us in the middle of some sort of raid?"

"I thought it was the right thing to do in wartime. I was told that it was top secret, and I couldn't tell anyone. I thought that Tom Barber and his companion would just carry off the uranium, and that would be that. But it didn't work out that way."

"No, it didn't. We'll talk more about it when you get back to New York."

Well, at least I won't be fired until I get back to New York, Jerry thought. "I'll be there as soon as I can book a flight," he said. "I think Standard Oil has enough people going back and forth to New York to keep a daily flight going. I'll call them next."

"No, there's something else I need you to do first," Mike said. "You got us into this, and we might as well get some credit for it. The State Department appreciates what we tried to do. They want to go after the uranium with a diver—they say it's in shallow enough water. And they need a boat. Asked for the *Osprey*, and I told them they could use it. I want you to do whatever it takes to transport these FBI agents, a diver, and whatever else is needed to the wreck site. They may need to blow up the wreckage to get at the uranium. And you need to go."

"What about the U-Boats?" Jerry asked. "We got sunk by one. They're still around."

"They tell me they can get a destroyer escort, the *Livingston*, to patrol around the wreck site while you're on location. That should be enough."

"Do you know if this is still top secret?" Jerry desperately wanted to tell Maria everything if he was going on another paramilitary expedition. He would in any case, but it would be nice if he wasn't risking trial and imprisonment for doing so.

"Yes, so I've been told. Everything about uranium is top secret. But I've been briefed, so keep me up to date. No more clandestine Pride operations."

"Yes, sir." There were times when Jerry fell into a formal, subordinate-superior mode with Mike Woods. It seemed to be the best approach after a contentious discussion.

CHAPTER TWENTY-SEVEN

Trinidad, August 1944

WITH ITS SINGLE window covered in tarpaper, the interior of the Quonset hut was dark except for the overhead lights. A metal table was bolted to the floor in the middle of the room with four chairs from the dining hall scattered around it. The metal door was reinforced and had a sliding window with a screen. It reminded Tom of the speakeasies that had flourished before the repeal of Prohibition, checking out potential customers before opening the door. But this peephole was for looking in, not out. Tom stooped slightly to see through it, watching and listening to the conversation taking place inside.

Two men in khakis were seated facing the door and across the table from Gretel, who had been brought from a cell in the Army stockade. The older man introduced himself as Captain Russell and seemed to be in charge. The handcuffs on Gretel's wrists had been removed and she flexed her fingers, rubbing the skin where the circles of steel had enclosed her wrists. Looking tired but defiant, she did not respond to the pleasantries offered by the two interrogators.

Changing to a more antagonistic tone, Captain Russell started reading from a notebook. The second man shook his head and left the room, his manner suggesting that an unpleasant episode was about to commence and that he did not want to be present.

"We know your real name is Gretel Mannheim, the former mistress of Captain Blanchard of the Gestapo in France," Captain Russell began. "The French are looking for you, and you were identified from a poster they've plastered around Orleans. You apparently went to Germany and disappeared. And now you've reappeared trying to transport uranium to Buenos Aires. Imagine that."

He paused and looked up at Gretel, who had no reaction. "We want to know everything about the uranium—who sent you on this journey, how much there is, and where it is intended to end up. Tell us what you know, and we'll let you go free here. Maybe you can find a way to Argentina."

Gretel said nothing.

"Or we can send you back to France. There are a lot of people who were imprisoned and tortured by the Gestapo who would like to see you. Your choice." Russell stopped talking, leaned back in his chair, and lit a cigarette.

Gretel remained silent.

"Take her back to her cell." The interrogator looked at Gretel. "You have until midnight to decide to tell us everything. Otherwise, you're on a ship to Marseille and then a train to Orleans to reunite with some old acquaintances." He motioned to the door, and Tom Barber entered the room with two guards. Gretel was handcuffed and escorted from the cell, and Tom took her place at the table.

"I think she will break," Tom commented. "She's a tough lady. But she really doesn't have a choice, and she knows it."

"I think she will too." Russell had been briefed by Tom on the story of discovering the metal cubes on the *Estrella Blanca*, seizing the ship, and then being overcome and imprisoned by Gretel. The uranium appeared lost to whoever it was destined for in Argentina, but its appearance in the western hemisphere had alarmed someone in Washington.

Two hours later, Gretel was back in the interrogation room after banging on her cell door to call the guard. This time, Tom entered the room and sat at the table with her and Russell.

"A man in Berlin—a scientist—shipped the uranium to Buenos Aires on the *Estrella Blanca*," she said. "He sent me to Curacao, and I was to then meet him in Buenos Aires. But before I could leave Curacao, he sent me to Maracaibo to charter a boat. I was supposed to get the uranium from the freighter and take it to Buenos Aires. You know about the ship losing steering and having to stop in the Orinoco River."

"What was his name?"

"Becker," she replied.

"Who is that?" asked Russell.

"A German scientist, a world-famous physicist. You should know that if you're asking questions about uranium."

Tom seemed to accept her answer as at least plausible. "Tell me about this boat you came on."

"The *Oso Negro*. The captain is called Carlos. We sailed to the Orinoco delta, but when we got there, they had fixed the steering on the freighter and Becker told me to continue to Buenos Aires on the ship."

She looked at Tom. "Then you and your compatriots tried to steal the cargo."

"The *Oso Negro*," Tom said thoughtfully. "I saw it in the harbor."

"Put her back in her cell." The khaki clad interrogator pushed back from the table, putting his notes in a briefcase.

"I thought you were going to let me go," Gretel protested. "I told you all I know."

"Maybe later. At least you're not going back to France tomorrow."

* * *

The *Oso Negro* was hauled out of run-down boatyard on the Port of Spain waterfront, the keel kept upright by huge timber and wooden supports. A man wearing rust-stained overalls watched a carpenter tapping caulk into the seams between newly fastened planking, easily distinguished from the weathered appearance of the lumber comprising the original hull. The man doing the tapping stood on a ladder using a screwdriver and a hammer to drive the caulk in.

Dussell approached the decrepit looking boat with suspicion. Sergio had assured him that it was capable of making the voyage, but it looked like the planking was about to fall off the frame. "I understand that you were struck by a whale," he said to the man in coveralls.

"That is so. You must be Dussell," the man replied. "Have you heard what kind of whale it was?"

"A sperm whale, that's the story that's being told. Are you Carlos?"

"*Si*. I was told you want to charter the *Oso Negro* for a diving expedition. A treasure hunter, eh? We used to see a lot of that before the war. You must know where there is a Spanish galleon for sure."

"I'll tell you more when we get there," Dussell replied. "I have some co-ordinates. The first thing is to get this boat back in the water. Does it have a motor?"

"No, I don't need one," Carlos said. "We can sail as fast as a motorboat when the bottom is clean. And it will be clean for your voyage—we just scraped and painted it."

"Where did you come from?" Dussell asked.

"Maracaibo. A pretty lady who referred to herself as Gretel chartered me. We were supposed to pick up a cargo in the Orinoco delta, then sail to Buenos Aires. But when we got to the ship with the cargo, she decided to go with them and cancelled the contract we had. I needed some bottom work done on the *Oso Negro* anyhow. She gave me a bank draft. It was good, so I can't complain."

Dussell looked at the boat that had carried Gretel from Maracaibo to the Orinoco delta. *Even more primitive than I thought.* "We were told that you could provide a diver. With equipment. Is that correct?"

"Yes, I think so." Carlos watched the man caulking as he answered. "I know two, but they both just got a contract on a Pride Oil boat. Must be doing some pipeline repair or something. But I'll ask around—I'm sure we can have one on board when we leave."

"I want to go tomorrow. Get this back in the water and be ready to leave at dawn."

CHAPTER TWENTY-EIGHT

THE ARMY CORPS of Engineers had constructed a huge new airfield in Trinidad's interior, bulldozing away the jungle, flattening the rolling hills and laying down a gravel runway. Hastily constructed Quonset huts lined the field, serving as housing and office space for the air traffic controllers, mechanics, armorers, and radar operators that were required to support a continuous air operation. The roar of airplane engines at full throttle, accelerating as they took off into a sky marked by approaching thunderstorms, made conversations difficult.

Jerry stood with Tom Barber and Matt Richards outside the door of a hut that was evidently the Trinidad FBI headquarters. They watched as a B-24 coasted to a stop on the nearby taxiway. He could see Maria through the window, waving as she recognized him.

George Morales was the first one down the stairway after the door opened, shaking hands with Jerry and yelling over the noise of another Navy plane taking off to patrol for U-Boats. "Found out the Army had this plane stationed in Maracaibo and managed to persuade the Colonel to fly us over here. He's on board, along with Maria. You need to thank him."

Jerry wasn't surprised that the vanished uranium was important enough for the Army to fly George to Trinidad, but they didn't have to bring Maria. He had tried to call her back after his conversation with Mike Woods, and

Ana had told him she had gone to the airport. George must have decided that he owed Jerry something for almost getting him killed.

A tall man in summer khakis with silver eagles on his collar stepped aside to allow Maria to descend the ladder first. As she rushed to hug Jerry, she dropped the small suitcase that she had been carrying on the tarmac and smothered his face with kisses, crying.

"I thought you were dead and would never be found. Uncle Ignatius helped to find the *Estrella Blanca,* but you got torpedoed before the Navy could get there. Somehow you managed to stay alive again. But this is it. You're not in the Navy."

"This is Colonel MacKenzie," Jerry heard George saying in the background.

Jerry turned to acknowledge the introduction. "Thank you for bringing Maria."

"Glad to. I'm looking forward to hearing your story."

"We'll need to talk to you," George said. "The Colonel has the clearance to hear what happened. Why don't you get Maria settled in the hotel and meet us in the lobby at 17:00 hours? Tom, you and Matt can come with us now."

Colonels rated jeeps with drivers, and Colonel MacKenzie settled into the front seat of one that had driven up when the plane landed, letting his three passengers crowd into the back. The small vehicle sped down the road to the edge of the airfield and disappeared into the dense jungle.

Jerry turned to Maria. "I have a car and a driver from the Pride office," Jerry told Maria. "They'll take us to the hotel."

* * *

Two hours later, Maria leaned against the headboard of the hotel bed, tasting a martini brought up by room service. "Not too bad," she murmured. "But I could make a better one. Too much vermouth."

She listened intently as Jerry described his experiences since he had told her good-bye and boarded the *Osprey* with Tom Barber and Matt to seize the uranium. "You have nine lives," she told him. "First in Florida, and now here. But that's enough. If you're going back to New York to see Mike Woods, I'm going with you. I need to see Uncle Ignatius and thank him. And I hope Pride doesn't fire you and gives you an assignment in the U.S. for a change."

"Well, actually, there is one more thing I need to do here," Jerry offered diffidently. He described his conversation with Mike Woods and the instructions to organize a diving expedition to recover the uranium. He watched as Maria listened, glad to see that she was disappointed, but not angry.

"I understand," she said. "You have to do it. I don't mind as much when I know where you're going and that you're not going to be involved in any more gunfights. A salvage operation shouldn't be too risky. I want to go too. If I could stay on the *Osprey* in the Orinoco, I can manage on this trip."

Jerry hesitated. They had been sunk by a U-Boat in that location days before. But George Morales had assured him that the *Livingston* would remain in the area, and a U-Boat probably wouldn't bother with a salvage operation.

He kissed Maria. "That'll be fine. We leave in the morning. I need to tell Jan we're taking the *Osprey* for a few days. He's expecting to return to the Orinoco and shoot another seismic survey farther upstream than the last one. And Debbie's still here. She's been trying to get priority on a flight back to New York since you arrived on the *Osprey* but hasn't so far. I'm going to ask her if she wants to come with us."

"What about the top-secret warnings you've been given?"

"She's the one who found the uranium in the first place and knows that it's on the *Estrella Blanca*. I'll just tell her that we're going to get it. She doesn't need to know anything more than that. Although she'll probably figure out what's going on."

* * *

Debbie followed Maria up the steep gangway the next morning, a duffel bag slung over one shoulder, the case for her Geiger Counter in the other hand.

Wonder what she thinks she's going to do with that? Jerry thought. Through the open doorway of the pilothouse, he could see Tom Barber and Matt Richards talking to the two divers and their assistants who filled out the passenger list. With space for a crew of thirty while conducting seismic operations, the accommodations were luxurious. Only the captain, first mate, a cook, and four deckhands were needed to operate the vessel for the salvage operation. The rest of the seismic crew was happy to be relaxing in a Port of Spain hotel paid for by Pride Oil.

The voyage was expected to last a little more than a week; an overnight voyage to the location of the *Estrella Blanca*, several days of diving and hoisting the cargo to the *Osprey*, and two days returning to Trinidad.

"Is that all of you?" the captain called through the wheelhouse aft window.

"That's everyone," Jerry replied. "We're ready to go when you are."

The *Osprey* navigated through the harbor slowly, weaving between the anchored fishing boats, and then accelerated when they cleared the breakwater. As the boat gained cruising speed, Jerry watched as they passed a sailing vessel on the same heading, the slower boat rocking in their wake.

He translated the name from Spanish: Black Bear. *Oso Negro.* An unusual name for a boat. It seemed familiar somehow.

"Seen that boat before?" he asked Tom.

"No. But Gretel told us that it's the one that brought her to the *Estrella Blanca*," Tom replied. "Must have gotten another charter."

*   *   *

Moving through the water at the speed of a slow walk, the geophysical boat executed a rectangular search pattern, working outward from coordinates marking the presumed location of the *Estrella Blanca*. Repeated measurements with a sextant of the altitude of the sun, consultation with the expensive chronometers that had been installed in Miami, and a three star fix the night before had given the captain confidence that he was within several hundred meters of the sunken freighter. But no evidence of the wreckage was visible below the milky green water. The crew had deployed a magnetometer on a cable behind the boat—a tool used to map the magnetic field of the earth for geophysical surveys—and they watched for an anomaly that would indicate a mass of iron influencing the magnetic field.

The *Osprey* was halfway through one side of the rectangle when the first mate shouted, "Here's something. Watch the sonar."

The sonar ping changed from a soft reflection on the seafloor to a hard echo from something metal. One of the seamen threw a buoy over the side to mark the spot as the *Osprey* continued, finishing the leg of the survey and then returning to the buoy.

"This might be it," Jerry said. "Let's send a diver down to see what's there. Anchor so that we can hold position at the buoy."

"I'll go down first," volunteered the older of the two divers, who had introduced himself as Nicholas. A heavyset man with thick black hair that reflected his Greek heritage, he donned his suit of heavy rubberized canvas and equipped with boots and a metal ring around the neck that sealed to the helmet.

The surface crew for the diving operation had already assembled a network of air hoses and telephone wires, and the air compressor was humming. Two men lifted Nicholas's helmet and settled it onto the metal ring, tightening bolts to form a watertight seal, then snapped a cable to a ring on the back of the suit. Nicholas stepped through an opening on the transom of the *Osprey*, lowering himself into the water, his weight partially supported by the cable running over a sheave on a crane.

As the cable paid out, he descended below the surface, his voice crackling through the telephone speaker. "Visibility improved below that layer of dirty water. About twenty feet."

The Waini and smaller rivers had pushed a layer of fresh, muddy water along the shoreline, overriding the clear seawater. When a diver descended below the interface, it was possible to see about fifty feet—more than sufficient to make out a sunken ship.

Approaching the bottom, Nicholas continued to relay his observations. "I can see something directly below. Looks like wreckage. Lower ten more feet and stop.

"It's the bow of a ship, resting on the bottom, right side up. The back end is open. It looks like the stern was blown off. Some bales of something spilling out."

One of the surface crew held a microphone that was connected to the speaker in the diving helmet, conveying instructions to the man eighty feet below.

"Tell him we need to know how far from the bow to where it's been blown apart." Jerry said.

The assistant relayed the information to the diver.

"I'd guess about two hundred feet," Nicholas replied. "Is that close enough? Otherwise, I'll need you to move the *Osprey* to the bow, let me attach a line, then back up."

"That's close enough," Jerry said. "What we're looking for is going to be about fifty feet forward from where the back end of the ship was blow off. The hold is packed with bales of wool that are going to have to be pulled out somehow to get in from the stern, or we'll have to blow the deck off."

"Anything else?" Nicholas crackled over the telephone speaker.

"Not now." Jerry turned to the diving assistant. "Bring him up and let's decide what to do."

∗   ∗   ∗

The *Osprey* captain and his passengers were seated at the dining table in the wardroom where Jerry had laid out a sketch of what they believed to be on the seafloor below them. The front half of a ship, resting upright, had an *X* marking the approximate position of the uranium. Jerry had described the cargo to the captain and the divers, deciding that it was unreasonable to expect success if they didn't know what they were looking for.

"We need to blow the deck," Matt said.

"I agree," the captain said. "We can lift up the crates with a crane if they're still intact. And we can lift the wool bales that are in the way. But we can't pull anything out of the open back end. No leverage. All we could do is tie on a cable and pull with the *Osprey*, but that would move us off the location."

"We can do it." Nicholas spoke confidently. "Used explosives a lot of times to clear obstacles in the oil field. But we'll need to drill some holes to get the charges underneath the deck. Otherwise, they'll just dent the deck downward without blowing it off."

"How many holes will it take?" asked Giorgios, the second diver and Nicholas's longtime partner. They were both from the Greek colony in Tarpon Springs, diving for sponges when they were young, then leaving to pursue more lucrative work in the oilfields of the Caribbean.

"About ten. One for each charge. Through the deck and into the hold." Matt spoke with authority, the only one in the cabin with a knowledge of ship construction.

"That's about a day's work," Nicholas said. "We've got a compressed air drill in the kit we brought with us."

"Let's start tomorrow at dawn," Jerry said. "Get everything ready. If we have time to set the charges after the drilling, we can blow the deck tomorrow evening, then start hauling up the uranium the day after."

CHAPTER TWENTY-NINE

Off the Coast of South America, August 1944

DUSSELL WATCHED AS Carlos stood on the rail, steadying himself by clutching a shroud with one hand while he held a pair of binoculars with the other. Five miles ahead, the outline of the *Osprey* was visible at their destination, still too distant to discern what it was doing there. The *Oso Negro* closed the distance without having to tack, and in thirty minutes Dussell could see a suited diver pulled to the surface and helped up a boarding ladder.

"What's going on?" Dussell asked.

"Somebody has the same idea," Carlos replied. "That's the *Osprey*. It belongs to Pride Oil, and they use it for geophysical surveying. Right now, they're sending divers down to the *Estrella Blanca*."

Verdammt. That's a complication I hadn't expected. That Hans fellow told me there were no survivors except himself, Dussell thought. *Someone else got ashore alive and had the connections to get that boat here ahead of us. Pride Oil isn't interested in bales of wool. They know what they are looking for.*

"Call them on the radio," he instructed Carlos. "Speak English."

"This is the *Oso Negro* calling the *Osprey*," Carlos spoke into the microphone of the ship to shore radio.

"This is the *Osprey*," Dussell heard on the radio speaker. "What's up with you?"

"We're going to Georgetown," Carlos said. "Have a load of lubricating oil from Trinidad. What are you diving on?"

"A wreck, the *Estrella Blanca*. Sunk by a U-Boat two weeks ago."

"Doesn't seem like a normal operation for a geophysical boat. What are you looking for?"

"Can't say," was the reply. "You'll have to ask someone with Pride Oil."

"Any one from Pride on board?" asked Carlos.

"Yes. A Jerry MacDonald. He was on the ship when it was torpedoed. About twenty of them made it to Trinidad in the lifeboats."

Dussell picked up the microphone. "Can I talk to Mr. MacDonald?"

"I'll get him," replied the speaker on the *Osprey*. A few minutes later, Jerry's voice came through the loudspeaker on the *Oso Negro*.

"This is Jerry MacDonald."

"Hello, Mr. MacDonald. My name is Ernst. My nephew was a seaman on the *Estrella Blanca*, and I understand that you are a survivor of the shipwreck. Can you tell me what happened?" Dussell's English was excellent, but his German accent unmistakable.

"We got torpedoed, but the U-Boat captain gave us time to get in the lifeboats. We rowed ashore, then up the coast to Trinidad."

"Did you bring everyone to safety?" Dussell asked.

"We did lose one man, Hans Diess. He started a fight, and the captain made him walk ashore for a few miles as punishment. But he never caught up to us. We don't know what happened to him. Was that your nephew?"

"No. So I guess he survived. Good luck with whatever you are doing," Dussell said. *So, Hans lied, and Gretel is still alive. I hope that she can convince the Americans that she doesn't know anything.*

Dussell waited for Jerry to say more but was met with silence. He chuckled to break the tension.

Jerry still didn't respond, and Dussell hung up the microphone. Telling Jerry that he knew someone on the torpedoed freighter had probably been a mistake, but he had hoped that Jerry would volunteer more about the survivors. Jerry's abrupt responses made him uneasy. He had wanted to establish a rapport with the Americans, but the opposite had occurred for some reason.

He turned to Carlos. "How long would it take to get to Georgetown and back here?"

"Two days. It's about a hundred miles. Eight knots. That's thirty hours of sailing, and ten hours of unloading."

"Let's sail there and back. Show up here day after tomorrow. Offer to help with an extra diver. At least we can see what's going on, and maybe something will happen to give us a shot at the cargo."

*　*　*

The *Oso Negro* sailed east southeast along the coast, approaching the capital city of British Guiana at dusk. Carlos made no attempt to enter the harbor, turning the boat due east to make the second leg of a triangle that he had agreed on with Dussell.

Dawn broke over the Atlantic, deep blue this far offshore, and the *Oso Negro* turned again, setting course to return to the wreck of the *Estrella Blanca*. Sailing under only a reefed mainsail, they would arrive at the *Osprey* the next morning. Carlos instructed the diver to be ready to go down as soon as they arrived.

"I'll need another man to work the pump," the man stated. The only diver Carlos had been able to recruit on short notice, he made his living picking up dropped objects on the bottom of the harbor at Port of Spain, not a lucrative trade. Possessing a worn and patched diving suit and a scratched and dented helmet, he was reliant on a manual air pump that required a man to constantly pump, compressing air that flowed to the diving helmet. It was an antiquated system, used for years by Greek sponge divers in the earlier part of the century, but now replaced by engine driven compressors.

"Miguel can do that," Carlos answered. "Not sure what you're going to be able to do. But we'll make sure you get enough air while you're doing it."

The *Oso Negro* sailed uneventfully through the equatorial sea, the crew watching the sun disappear over the jungle to the west. Shortly before the orange globe disappeared, they heard a booming noise from the direction of the *Osprey.*

"Dynamite," the diver said, "Set off underwater. They must be blowing a hole in the wreck to get inside."

"Good," Dussell said. "If they opened it up, maybe they can use some help."

Dussell turned to the diver. "We're going to offer to send you down to help. They are picking up cubes of metal, about two inches in size. If they agree, see if you can hide some of the cubes where we can come back and find them later. I'll pay a dollar for each cube." That was all he could think of at the moment. Showing up in Buenos Aires with some uranium would at least give him some credibility with Juan Peron's government, even if it wasn't enough to start building a reactor. And maybe something would happen that would give him a shot at seizing all four hundred blocks of the gray metal.

* * *

The next morning, Jerry stood on the deck with Maria, drinking coffee and watching Giorgios climb into the heavy canvas suit, weighted down by the heavy boots that allowed him to walk on the seafloor rather than float. They stood aside as the support crew helped him clump to the boarding ladder by the rail opening and descend to the water where he disappeared from view, accompanied by a stream of bubbles from the engine driven air pump. Sounding like a bad telephone connection, his voice came over the speaker on the deck.

"Descending. No problems. I'm getting below the surface water and can see some pieces of debris on the seafloor."

"We used too much dynamite. The deck has been blown off, and the wool bales are scattered over the seafloor," the raspy voice continued after a pause.

Jerry picked up the microphone. "What about the wooden crates below the bales?"

"Lower me another ten feet . . . I can see where they were. The crates have been broken apart. I see some blocks of metal in the hold, scattered around on the lower deck. Cubes about two inches square."

"Great," Jerry said. "We'll have to pick them up one by one and bring them to the surface."

"How many are there?" asked the captain.

"We don't know," Tom told him. "Send a basket down and tell him to start picking them up. We'll get all that we can."

The diving crew brought a metal basket used to collect sponges off the west coast of Florida and lowered it over the side. A rope attached to the basket was passed over a pulley attached to the crane, and two crew members watched the line spiral from a coil on the deck, careful to not let the basket descend too fast and tangle the rope. When the line slackened, they pulled on it until it was taut, lifting the basket a foot above the sea floor. Jerry and Tom watched the surface of the water where the lines, hoses and cables descended to the diver.

The speaker crackled. "Slack off. I'm pulling it over to the hold. I can walk into it from the open end where the ship broke in half." A few minutes passed before they heard from the diver again. "Filling it," the diver announced. "These are heavy, even under water. Feel like lead weights." More silence, and then the speaker crackled again. "Half full. Probably a hundred pounds. Pull it up and send it down again."

The two crew members pulled on the rope, and the basket broke the surface of the water, swinging level with the deck of the *Osprey*. One of them grabbed the side of the container and pulled it inboard while the other slackened the rope until basket settled onto the deck. Twenty metal cubes, about two inches per side, covered the bottom of the basket. Dark gray in color, they resembled lead blocks.

Jerry picked one up, looking at it closely. "So, this is it. A lot of effort to bring them here."

Debbie looked at the gray metal blocks with curiosity. "I had imagined something totally different, something that looked like a lava flow from an erupting volcano. A uniform cube shaped by ordinary tools in a machine shop isn't what I expected. "

She picked up one of the cubes, her fingers almost slipping off at the unexpected weight, and she held it next to the Geiger Counter detector. The buzzing increased sharply, to the highest level she had heard the instrument make, several times more intense than when she had made the original measurements on the *Estrella Blanca*.

"I need a scale so I can measure and weigh one of these to determine the density," she said. "That way I can tell if it's pure uranium or some kind of alloy. Not that it matters—I sure won't be able to publish any of this—but I want to know."

Tom picked up another cube and motioned to Matt, who focused a camera on a block of the recovered uranium, snapping a photograph.

"Well, let's stay here and keep picking them up until we have all we can find," Jerry said. "Or until the weather changes."

"We can keep one diver on the bottom for two hours a day," he continued. "That's four hours a day of work. We don't know how many there are, so we don't know how long it will take. But let's work as fast as we can before we get a storm that makes it impossible to dive."

Four more baskets were pulled up before Giorgios ascended to the surface, climbing up the ladder and sitting down heavily on a bench.

"That's all of the ones that I could see easily in the hold," he said. "But some have scattered around the cargo space, and some were blown out of the ship. I could see a few on the sea floor. We'll need to mark off a grid and do a search for a hundred yards around the ship."

Already suited up, Nicholas walked to the ladder and began to descend. He would stay below for an hour while Georgios decompressed and then they would trade places. That would allow them to maximize their bottom time while avoiding the potentially fatal effect of dissolved nitrogen in their bloodstream expanding, giving them the bends. Without a decompression chamber on board, there would be no way to treat the painful symptoms.

"Any weather updates?" Jerry asked the *Osprey's* captain.

"I'll call on the radio. Might be able to get a report from some shipping. But no one will want to give away their location with the U-Boats out."

"This could take days," Jerry said. "How long would it take to train one of us to dive?"

"You would have to start off in shallower water," Giorgios told him. "Starting out with a one-hundred-foot dive would probably kill you. And we'd have to use the other suit to send someone down to train you, so it couldn't be used by one of us to pick up cubes."

Jerry grunted in agreement and started to pick up the metal cubes. "We'll need something to put these in," he told the captain. "See if you have any boxes that will hold something heavy."

The work continued through the afternoon with eighty-seven cubes recovered. Maria had volunteered to tally the results on a notepad, counting the blocks of recovered uranium as they were emptied from the basket. Their bottom time expended, the two divers relaxed on the bench, their gear piled on the deck. The smell of frying steak came from the galley window as the cook prepared dinner. Nothing could be done until the next morning when each of the divers could descend for an hour, alternating until both had worked two hours each.

* * *

"That's about all I can see in the hold." Nicholas' detached-sounding voice emanated from the deck speaker the following morning. "We'll have to get a line and move some of these bales out of the way. They've shifted and may be sitting on top of some cubes. Or we can start working the grid on the seafloor."

"What do you think?" Tom asked Jerry.

"Let's get the ones on the seafloor first. If the weather changes and we have to leave and come back, anything in the ship will probably stay put. But mud might shift over anything sitting on the bottom."

Hours passed, and an additional fifty-three cubes were recovered. The work slowed as the divers pulled the basket around the sunken ship, picking up widely scattered blocks. Nicholas was halfway through his second shift with only two more hours of salvage time remaining in the day.

Jerry turned his attention from the rising bubble train to look around at the green sea, startled to see the *Oso Negro* approaching to within less than a mile. When the old sailboat had passed them two days earlier, the coincidence of encountering the vessel that had brought Gretel to the Orinoco delta and the *Estrella Blanca* had raised his suspicions. But the worn and battered-looking boat, struggling to make a living by plying the coastal waters of South America, did not appear to be a threat. He accepted that the end of Gretel's charter marked the end of any connection of the vessel with the uranium, and that they were engaged in a separate enterprise. But he was irritated to see their distance decrease to a hundred yards, risking entanglement with the bundle of cables that connected the *Osprey* with the diver below.

"Stay off. We have a diver in the water," Jerry shouted.

Jerry saw Carlos tell the helmsman to turn into the wind, and the smaller vessel coasted to a halt, the sails flapping. Carlos reached above his head to remove the radio microphone from its holder, and his voice came over the radio on the *Osprey*.

"We have a diver on board. Do you have any work for him? Usual oilfield rates."

Tom turned from watching the approaching sailboat to look at Jerry. "Ask them why they have a diver. Seems unusual."

"Why do you have a diver, and what are his qualifications?"

"We're bringing him back from Georgetown. He was down there on a repair job welding on a freighter that hit a log and had a sprung plate. He's from Trinidad. Done some oilfield work as well as ship repairs. But we only have a manual air pump."

"We could let him use our pump, and that would give us another two hours a day," Tom said. "But if he can work at the same time as our divers, that would be better. It may take two men to move some of those bales out of the way."

Jerry picked up the microphone, calling the *Oso Negro*. "We'll hire your boat and your diver. Anchor to the west of us and come over in your dinghy. We'll show you what to look for."

A few minutes later, Dussell stood on the deck of the *Osprey* with Carlos and the diver, introducing himself as part owner of the *Oso Negro* without offering any further details or a last name.

Dussell looked at the cube of uranium that he had last seen in the Berlin laboratory. "Not very remarkable," he said to Jerry. "Why is it worth the effort to bring it up?"

"Don't know," Jerry said. "But we're doing it. The cargo was packed in crates in the *Estrella Blanca*, which broke in half when it sank and hit the seafloor. We blew the deck off and shattered the crates. Now we need to move some bales of wool out of the way to get at the cubes underneath them."

The diver from the *Oso Negro* picked up the cube, surprised at its weight. "Okay," he said. "I can be on bottom in thirty minutes."

* * *

Jerry stood at the rail next to Giorgios, both of them watching the crewman on the *Oso Negro* pumping steadily, turning a flywheel to provide air to the man walking the seafloor below. It was a simple setup that lacked the sophistication of the *Osprey* gear, including a telephone connection.

Giorgios shook his head in disbelief. "I wouldn't go down ten feet with that equipment. You only stay alive when your gear works like it's supposed to. That outfit looks like it's about to fall apart. All it would take is for that man pumping to get a stomach cramp."

* * *

With the help of the third diver, thirty more cubes of uranium were hoisted to the surface when the need to decompress forced Nicholas to start his ascent to the surface. He told Giorgios to bring him up, motioning to the *Oso Negro* diver to also ascend. The other diver started walking to a position directly below the sailboat as if preparing to be picked up—until Nicholas disappeared into the brightness of the sunlit shallow water.

Alone on the seafloor, he started to pick up cubes, loading his basket with all he could carry. He deposited six cubes near the bow of the broken ship, directly below the opening for the anchor chain where they could easily be located. Satisfied, he pulled on the cable to signal that he was ready to ascend to the *Oso Negro*.

* * *

"Six, eh," Dussel said when told of the results. *If we stay here three days, that might be twenty cubes*, he thought. He considered various ways to seize the cubes being boxed up on the *Osprey* for the hundredth time, but none of them seemed feasible. Especially considering that while Carlos was agreeable to pilfering a few cubes, he wasn't going to get involved in an altercation with Jerry and the crew of the *Osprey*. He was a boat captain, not a pirate.

* * *

The diving operation continued until the afternoon of the following day. Dussell estimated that about half of the four hundred cubes had been recovered, when the voice of the *Osprey* captain came over the radio speaker.

"*Oso Negro*, this is *Osprey*."

Carlos picked up the microphone. "*Osprey*, this is Carlos. Go ahead."

"A ship to the east of us, the *Livingston*, reports a tropical storm headed this way. We will have to seek shelter in the Orinoco delta, then return when the weather improves. Thank you for your help. Pride Oil will pay you for your services when you return to Trinidad."

"Understood." Carlos turned off the radio and turned to Dussell.

"They're leaving. We need to leave too. This will be too much storm to ride out in the open ocean."

"Let's act like we're pulling the anchor and getting ready to leave, until the Osprey is over the horizon. Then stay another day," Dussell replied. "We can pick up another fifty cubes on the seafloor. I'll pay you twice what we agreed on. And let's go into Georgetown when we do leave. We might be able to get back here before they do—they won't be in a hurry."

When Carlos hesitated, he added impatiently, "You've been stranded in Trinidad since the voyage to the Orinoco delta, and this is the first money you've earned in a month. And the *Oso Negro* needs a new mainsail."

"We can make another dive today," Carlos decided. "And two tomorrow. Maybe the storm will veer to the north, as most of them do. But we'll probably have to leave for Georgetown tomorrow afternoon."

"Excellent." Dussell turned to the diver. "Remember, I'll pay you a dollar for every cube you bring up. And we'll return after the storm, so if you can't put them all in the basket, hide them so we can find them."

✳ ✳ ✳

The *Osprey* was over the horizon when the diver lowered himself over the side of the *Oso Negro* again. Back on the bottom, walking in heavy boots and tethered by a hose and a line to the surface, he trudged around the *Estrella Blanca* picking up the cubes that littered the bottom. They were hard to see in the dim light, their color providing little contrast to the gray mud. The ones closest to the bow of the ship were hidden, the ones further away were carried to a basket that was raised when he pulled on the attached line. After an hour, he signaled that he was ready to ascend, relaxing while he was hoisted to the surface and helped up onto the deck of the *Oso Negro*.

With nothing to do until the next day while the nitrogen in his bloodstream diffused out of his body, he opened a beer and drank it thirstily. Alcohol was not recommended while decompressing, but Carlos didn't bother enforcing safety regulations. It was the diver's decision. He could do what he wanted and accept the consequences.

CHAPTER THIRTY

The Orinoco Delta, August 1944

ANCHORED IN THE lower delta of the Orinoco River, the *Osprey* was sheltered by Isla Tercera from the increasing wind and waves of the approaching storm. Brown water flowed slowly eastward into the Atlantic Ocean. The current's strength diminished as the channel split into multiple passes. Bands of gray clouds passed by rapidly to the south, interrupted by intervals of clear sky as the eye of the tropical storm passed offshore.

A safe place to ride out the storm, and close enough to return to the wreck in a day, Jerry thought. There wasn't much to do while they waited out the weather. Maria and Debbie were playing gin in the pilothouse, using the chart table to lay down the cards. The graduate student was no match for the bartender from Queens, who had a pile of matchsticks in front of her taking the place of chips.

Jerry looked out of the windshield impatiently, watching the Pride Oil flag snap straight out when another band of rain passed over. The diving operation and the dynamiting of the wreck had been a new experience for him. Caught up in the excitement of bringing up something of value from the seafloor, he wanted to get back to it. He picked up the report on the geological mapping he was halfway through writing, stared at it for a few minutes, then put it down.

"What do you think of me learning how to dive?" he asked Maria as the band of rain passed.

She put down a king of hearts, then turned to look at him. "Just like that? I didn't know you liked to swim."

"I'm an excellent swimmer. Anyhow, I understand that you walk on the seafloor. No swimming involved. And here's a chance to learn while we're doing nothing."

"Not for me," Debbie chimed in. "Seems too much like the time I rode down the mine elevator with my brother. I wanted to see what it was like. Felt like being buried alive."

"Think they'll teach you?" Maria wasn't surprised that Jerry would want to learn to dive. Anything to see another part of the planet.

"All I can do is ask," Jerry said. There was nothing in their contract that said they had to instruct him. But he had made friends with Nicholas and Giorgios while they worked the salvage operation, and they might be willing to use the downtime to teach a novice.

He left the crowded pilothouse, occupied by almost everyone on board who had nothing to do. The crew was relaxing, and the captain was sleeping soundly in his cabin below deck, satisfied that the anchor was holding firmly in the river bottom and there was nothing that might require his immediate attention. Jerry walked out on deck, happy to see Nicholas on the aft deck where the diving equipment was stored.

The diver was inspecting the fabric of one of the suits, carefully going over it inch by inch, looking for tears or worn places that might leak and allow water to enter. Jerry hesitated. It had been necessary to stay out of the way while the divers worked at the site of the *Estrella Blanca*. But now that they were forced to remain in the river for at least two days, there was no reason not to ask Nicholas for some instruction.

"Nicholas, is it hard to teach someone to dive?"

"No, not if you are a good swimmer, comfortable in the water, and don't get claustrophobic. The thing one can't do is panic. The equipment will keep you alive if you keep your head."

"We have a couple of days. Can you show me?"

"Gladly. You can learn to suit up and go down here. But the water is very muddy. You won't see much."

"That's better than nothing," Jerry said. "If I learn, maybe I can help with the salvage when we go back out, and the visibility is better. Or at least if I know how, maybe I can arrange something in clear water next time I'm in Curacao."

"Okay. Let's get started," Nicholas agreed. "We'll go through the equipment, and I'll show you how it works."

He walked over to the diving helmet resting on a bench, the glass ports on the front, sides, and top. Each port was open and drying after being rinsed with fresh water. It was made of copper, the bottom a ring pierced by holes where it bolted onto the suit.

"You've seen how this is worn. It is attached to the suit with a shoulder harness to support these weights which keep it from floating upward, since it's filled with air. This valve attaches to an air hose connected to a pump at the surface. The pump forces air down at a pressure a little higher than the water at the diver's depth. That lets him breathe. Otherwise, he couldn't expand his lungs against the water pressure. The air flows continuously and comes out of the helmet through this valve. That makes the stream of bubbles that you see coming up to the surface. The bubbles let us know where the diver is," Nicholas explained.

Jerry picked up the helmet, anticipating its weight. He could see why Nicholas had mentioned claustrophobia. A man's head would be constrained to a small space in the helmet, and he would be unable to remove the copper headpiece without outside help.

Nicholas walked back to the suit he had been inspecting. It was made of heavy rubberized canvas, with tight cuffs at the wrists and a metal ring where the helmet bolted on.

"Air from the helmet fills the suit, too," he said. "The pressure has to be the same everywhere. If the air pump stopped working and the pressure in the helmet dropped, the seawater pressure could force the diver's body up into the helmet. Happened in the old days. But now we have a one-way valve in the hose so that can't happen. Theoretically, at least.

"When the suit and the helmet are filled with air, you would float. So, you need these weighted boots, and a weight belt to keep you down. You can control your buoyancy by the relief valve that lets air out of the helmet. More air and you float. Less air and you sink and can walk on the bottom."

"That's a lot of weight," Jerry said. "I see why you need help getting over the side."

"About a hundred and fifty pounds," Nicholas agreed. "Diving is for young men. Want to try on the suit?"

"I sure do."

Nicholas waved to the other diver. "Giorgios, our employer wants to learn how to dive. Come help me suit him up."

Maria and Debbie had come on deck, watching with interest and amusement as the two divers encased Jerry in the canvas and metal armor that would allow him to breathe and walk on the river bottom. It seemed to be safe enough in the river, only thirty feet deep, with two professionals teaching him. There wasn't much else to do while they waited out the storm.

Maria went below to get her Kodak and snapped a picture of Jerry's head sticking out of the metal ring. "Uncle Ignatius will enjoy seeing you look like a cautious turtle peering out of his shell," she said.

With the helmet lowered over his head and bolted down, Jerry clumped to the opening in the rail, aided by Nicholas and Giorgios. They each held an arm. He backed up and slowly descended the ladder into the water. The weight that made walking slow and difficult on the deck suddenly disappeared as the air-filled suit became buoyant and he started to float.

"Open up the valve," Nicholas said into the telephone. "You've got too much air. When you start to slowly sink, it will be about right. Remember, don't hold your breath. If you start coming up while you are not breathing, an air bubble in your brain can expand and kill you"

Jerry felt the suit partially deflate as the stream of bubbles increased, and he descended to the bottom of the river, lowered by the line secured to the front of the suit along with the air hose and telephone cord. The air pumping through his helmet made a rushing noise, like the air brakes on a train, but continuous. He spoke into the microphone to make sure it was working.

"Going down. Can you hear me?"

"Yeah. Go down. That's the idea," Nicholas replied.

Jerry looked up through the clear glass at the top of the helmet, then down. He could barely see his feet encased in the weighted boots. Then he felt the temperature drop. The water cleared slightly so that he could see the approaching riverbed. His boots dropped into the soft mud as he landed, kicking up a cloud of suspended sediment, and he felt the weight on his legs as the lifting line slackened. It was much less than he had experienced at the surface, the weight of the diving gear counterbalanced by the buoyancy of the suit and helmet.

He saw a few large fish that resembled the catfish he used to catch in Oklahoma, and a school of smaller fish that swam rapidly, twisting and turning in unison. They resembled the piranha he had seen in the river at the encampment, and the thought unnerved him. He knew they were not reluctant to attack large animals. A school could quickly devour a cow or a person. The adventure had suddenly become potentially deadly. He hoped that a diving suit didn't look or smell like something good to eat.

Putting the thought out of his mind, he walked along the riverbed, holding the assemblage of lines and hoses out of his way. He found it easier to hop than walk, jumping about three feet at a time, and moving about thirty feet from where he had been lowered.

This must be what it would be like to walk on the surface of the moon in a spacesuit, held down by gravity one sixth that of the earth. He looked down at the sandy bottom forming ripple marks as the current pushed the sediment downstream. Jerry had seen similar marks on ancient rocks created by rivers that flowed millions of years ago. He reached down and picked up a handful of mud, putting it into a pocket of the dive suit. He wanted to keep it as a souvenir of his first dive.

"Don't go any further," Nicholas's voice echoed in the helmet speaker. You're only down about thirty feet, and we don't want the line to go too far out horizontally. How do you feel?"

"Fine. This is fantastic. Thanks for letting me do it."

"Okay. Time to come up. You don't need to decompress with the depth and time you've been down, so we'll bring you straight up. Remember, don't hold your breath."

Climbing the ladder, even assisted by the hoisting line, required all of Jerry's strength as he rose from the water and the weight of the suit rested on his legs. Standing unsteadily on the deck, he moved cautiously to the bench where Nicholas and Giorgios unbolted the helmet and lifted it off his head.

I've seen another part of the world, he exulted. *I can't wait to see a reef.*

CHAPTER THIRTY-ONE

Off the Coast of South America, August 1944

THE FOLLOWING DAY broke with clear skies and a moderate wind, but huge waves still crashed onto the beaches of Isla Tercera, forcing the *Osprey* to remain at anchor in the Orinoco River. Jerry made another dive, becoming more familiar with the equipment and proficient in moving about, both on the deck of the *Osprey* and on the river bottom. He saw another school of the small fish that he was now certain were piranha, but they seemed uninterested in an object of metal and rubberized canvas. The wreck of a small boat emerged from the cloudy water when he walked in the opposite direction from his first dive, the single mast broken off and a large hole evident in the bottom planking. It must have hit something and sunk. He picked up a bronze bolt as a souvenir, seeing nothing of value in the open boat, and told Nicholas he was ready to return to the surface.

* * *

The waves subsided overnight, and morning found the *Osprey* shouldering aside the diminishing seas as it returned to the site of the *Estrella Blanca*. Debbie stood at the rail, looking down into the green water and watching a dolphin ride the bow wave. As they drew closer to the buoy that marked the location of the sunken freighter, they could see a boat anchored over the wreck site. Its distinctive silhouette identified it as the *Oso Negro*. With a single crewman working the manual air pump, it was obvious that they had a diver below.

"They've got a diver down," Debbie called to Jerry.

He waved an acknowledgment as he picked up the radio microphone in the pilothouse.

"*Oso Negro*, this is the *Osprey*. What are you doing here?" Jerry spoke into the microphone with an irritated voice. He didn't want any more complications. He wanted to get the uranium and get back to Port of Spain.

"We went into Georgetown, and thought we'd come back and continue working for you," Carlos replied. "We expected you back today. Thought we'd go ahead and get a man in the water and keep bringing up the cubes."

"Okay," Jerry said. "But it would have been better if you had waited for us before you started diving. We're going to send someone down shortly."

He turned to Tom. "I want to go down with Nicholas. We'll use both suits. Let's see the condition of the wreck, and then we can put together a plan. We can write on a slate with crayon to tell their diver what to do. While I'm doing that, why don't you go over to the *Oso Negro* and get the cubes they've brought up so far. I'm not happy about having them on another boat."

Nicholas listened to the exchange. "Your decision. But one hundred feet in the open ocean is a step beyond thirty feet in the river. Your ears are going to hurt as you go down. Swallowing should help. And after you spend an hour on the bottom, you'll need to decompress for thirty minutes at twenty feet."

Nicholas started to pull on the heavy rubber suit, and Jerry sat next to him, trying to remember the sequence. He saw the stream of bubbles rising from the *Oso Negro* diver and wondered what he was doing. They had something lowered over the side which was being pulled up by two crewmen. A wire basket broke the surface of the water and was hoisted onto the deck of the *Oso Negro*. It looked empty from a hundred feet away where Jerry watched from the deck of the *Osprey*, but one of the men dropped the hoisting line and picked up some small objects from the basket, presumably cubes of uranium.

Jerry sat upright as the copper helmet was lowered around his head, feeling the wrench tug as the diving assistant tightened down the bolts that secured the helmet to his diving suit. Looking through the helmet's glass, he saw the assistant give a thumbs up, indicating that he was ready to be lowered into the water. Nicholas was already descending the ladder as Jerry stood by the gap in the rail, waiting for him to reach bottom and move out of the way. This was the first time that two divers had been deployed from the *Osprey*, and Nicholas had been adamant they ensure the lines did not tangle.

The bundle of hoses and lines tethering Nicholas to the *Osprey* started to move away from the vessel.

Nicholas's voice came over the telephone speaker. "On bottom. The wreck hasn't moved. But a lot of mud was stirred around by the storm."

"Tell him I'm starting to come down," Jerry said. He backed cautiously down the boarding ladder, the diving assistant holding the line secured to the front of his suit. He started to float and opened the valve on his helmet to release air faster, partially deflating the suit. The loss of buoyancy resulted in him starting to sink rapidly, halting when the lifting line came taut.

"Close the valve a quarter turn," directed the diving assistant from the telephone speaker.

Complying, Jerry noticed that it gave him only a slight negative buoyancy, enough so that he sank slowly as the lifting line was slackened. A few minutes later he passed through the thermocline that separated the muddy surface water from the colder, denser, and clearer seawater below. He could suddenly see the wreck of the *Estrella Blanca* and two suited divers on the seafloor. One was obviously Nicholas, suited up with gear identical to Jerry's. The other was dressed in the patched outfit that Jerry recognized as the diving suit utilized by the diver from the *Oso Negro*. The man was standing on the seafloor near the bow of the ship, oblivious to the arrival of two more divers, and picking up cubes from a pile to deposit in the basket that had been lowered again from the *Oso Negro*.

* * *

Dussell watched as the small boat was lowered over the side of the *Osprey*, two men rowing it across to the *Oso Negro*. It pulled alongside and Tom stepped from the rowboat onto the deck. "Where are the cubes that you've picked up so far?" he asked abruptly.

"We only have a few. About six. Just got started." Dussell pointed to the small pile that he had placed on deck when he saw the rowboat leaving the *Osprey*, leaving about one hundred cubes hidden below deck on the *Oso Negro*. Since they had arrived that morning, the diver had filled the basket several times from the pile of cubes hidden under the bow of the wreck. After surfacing to decompress, he had just returned to the seafloor when the *Osprey* arrived.

Tom looked at him suspiciously but placed the six cubes into a bag offered by Carlos. "I'm going to send someone over to take the cubes as you bring them up," he said.

"That will be fine," Carlos said. "We're very happy that we can continue to help you."

As soon as Tom stepped into the rowboat, Dussell turned to two crewmen waiting to raise the basket. "Bring it up quickly before he sends someone over." The two men pulled on the line, raising the basket in a matter of minutes. This one was filled with thirty-six cubes, the remainder of what the *Oso Negro* diver had hidden near the bow of the *Estrella Blanca*.

That's about a hundred and fifty since we got back here, thought Dussell. *About two hundred on the Osprey, so there's about fifty more down there. We won't be able to get the ones on the Osprey, but if we can get what's still on the bottom, it should be enough to convince the Argentines that I can start building a reactor. But I suspect that the Americans are going to search the* Oso Negro.

Dussell turned to Carlos." Do you have a place where we can hide the cubes below while they search the boat?"

"*Si.* There is a place in the bilge where we sometimes store cargo we don't want the authorities to find. It's big enough."

"Good. Put all the remaining cubes in it, and make sure they can't be found."

With the problem of hiding the one hundred and fifty cubes he had already salvaged temporarily solved, Dussell turned his attention to the uranium remaining on the seafloor. The divers from the *Osprey* would bring it up within the hour. He needed to somehow bring a halt to the operation.

"Bring up our diver," he said to Carlos. "I'm going to go down and take a look myself."

Surprised, Carlos replied, "You know how to dive?"

"Yes," Dussell replied. He had watched the diving operation for a few days and understood how it worked. That should be sufficient to don the equipment and descend to the seafloor. All it took was breathing and walking.

Carlos tugged on the line to the diver below, signaling him to ascend. Once the diver was hoisted onto the deck of the *Oso Negro*, he sat on a bench while the Miguel removed the helmet and helped him from the suit.

"I'm going to use your suit and go down myself," Dussell told him.

Surprised, the man shrugged. "If you know what you're doing, that's your business. I'm not responsible for keeping you alive." He moved aside so that Dussell could sit and pull on the stiff canvas marked with stitched and glued rubber patches. While they were trading places, one of the divers from the *Osprey* pulled to the surface.

"See which one that is," Dussell told Carlos.

Carlos picked up an ancient telescope. "It's the professional. The American is still down there."

Good, thought Dussell. *It will be easier to make something happen with an inexperienced man.* He sat upright as the copper helmet was lowered onto his head and tightened. Then he watched Miguel start spinning the pump flywheel. The hiss of compressed air drowned out the clamor of the deck, and he saw Carlos motion for him to stand and move to the ladder. Turning and stepping carefully through the opening in the rail, Dussell sank into the water, his weight supported by a line riven through a pulley on the mainsail boom. No one had instructed him on how to control the airflow and his buoyancy by turning the valve in his helmet, assuming that he knew what to do.

Seeing him floating helplessly, Miguel slowed the air pump to the point where the diving suit became negatively buoyant, and Dussell started to sink. A few minutes later, he stood on the seafloor, looking at the broken bow section of the *Estrella Blanca* and watched the American diver searching the ocean bottom, stopping to pick up what he assumed to be one of the uranium cubes.

*　*　*

Jerry watched as Nicholas rose toward the surface, disappearing as he ascended into the murky water above the thermocline. The diving assistant's voice came from the *Osprey* deck over the helmet speaker.

"Ready to come up too?"

"No. I have ten more minutes and can get a few more cubes." Jerry bent over to pick up another block of uranium and place it in the basket."

"Okay. But your wife thinks that you shouldn't be down there alone."

"Tell her I'll be up in eight minutes."

Maria's voice came over the headset, sounding frightened. "What do you think you're doing? You don't know enough to be down there by yourself."

With his attention diverted from his search for uranium cubes by his wife's voice, Jerry replied, "Only a few more minutes. Might as well stay down until I use up all my time. Another diver just came down, anyway, from the *Oso Negro.*"

Slightly mollified by the news that at least there was another human being on the seafloor with him, even though it was someone she had no way of communicating with, she replied, "Okay. But this is it alone. You're going to have to plan your diving so that there's always someone down there with you."

"All right," Jerry said distractedly, watching the other diver. Rather than searching the seafloor for the scattered uranium as Jerry was doing, the man was clumping toward him, ignoring two cubes on his path. The diver approached close enough for Jerry to see his face through the glass, discerning the visage of the man who had introduced himself as Ernst. One more step, and his faceplate was inches from Jerry's. He reached up and pulled on the umbilical bundle that attached to Jerry's helmet, dislodging the plug from the telephone wire.

* * *

Maria heard a crackling noise, then silence. "We've lost contact," she said in a panic. "Send Giorgios down right away."

* * *

Jerry heard Maria's voice vanish as the telephone went silent. Dussell was pulling on the air hose connected to his helmet, trying to break the seal that would flood Jerry's helmet with seawater and drown him. But his gloved hands were too clumsy to seize the hose without slipping, and the rubber to metal seal, built to withstand the pressure at several hundred feet below the surface, held tight.

Jerry pushed hard and Dussell stumbled backwards, both unaccustomed to the effort of walking. Desperate to escape, Jerry backed away a few feet, but the air hose that tethered him to the surface reached its limit and brought him up short. Dussell pulled a diver's knife from a sheath on his leg, a sharp eight-inch blade long intended to cut through rope and seaweed but easily capable of slicing Jerry's air hose and canvas suit. Clad in the worn and patched suit that he had taken from the diver on the *Oso Negro*, Dussell brandished the knife and hopped toward Jerry.

Jerry grabbed the telephone line that was swinging near his face from the bundle of umbilical tubes. Grasping the end in his thick gloves, he managed to place it above the socket on the helmet. Pushing downward, he heard a click followed by static. He twisted the socket in desperation, hearing the static stop as the connection was reestablished. Dussell approached him again, and he tried to circle around the other diver, bouncing on the sea bottom like a kangaroo.

* * *

Static filled the headset, then Maria heard Jerry's voice. The transmission was broken and garbled. "... guy's trying ... kill me. Broke ... phone line, now ... trying to ... air hose."

"The other diver's trying to kill him," Maria shouted to Tom Barber. "Stop him somehow."

"What can we do?" Tom asked Giorgios.

"He's dependent on that air pump." Giorgios pointed at the pump on the deck of the *Oso Negro*, powered by a seaman spinning a wheel at a constant speed. "Stop it, and he won't get any air. They'll have to haul him up."

Tom ran below, pulled a duffel bag from underneath the bunk, and dumped it onto the deck. A selection of Thompson submachine guns and handguns scattered over the floorboards. He selected a Colt Walker 45, an enormous revolver that he had brought to the FBI from his Texas Ranger days. Bracing his forearm on the rail of the *Osprey*, he fired at the pump on the other boat, hitting the operator by mistake. The short, stocky figure fell to the deck of the *Oso Negro* and the pump stopped rotating.

"Didn't mean to hit him," Tom said. "I don't think he has anything to do with this. If I'd had a rifle, it wouldn't have happened. But it had the right effect. No air going down."

❋   ❋   ❋

The ancient pump held pressure for a few seconds, but then began to leak, equilibrating with the atmospheric pressure when the pistons stopped compressing air. The air pressure in the hose connected to Dussell's helmet dropped to one atmosphere. A valve located where the hose attached to the helmet snapped shut, preventing the air pressure inside the helmet from dropping. The valve, a thirty-year-old rubber diaphragm, had never been needed, and the diver had neglected to inspect or replace it. The pressure on the inside of the helmet caused a bubble to appear in the center of the diaphragm, expanding as the rubber stretched, until it popped like a child's balloon.

❋   ❋   ❋

Jerry turned to see Dussell closing the distance between them, wielding the knife.

Suddenly, the unworldly figure pursuing him stopped, the legs distorting strangely and disappearing up into the torso of the diving suit. The diver's body shrank rapidly, disappearing into the opening that connected the rubberized canvas suit to the metal helmet. Dussell's body was being squeezed into the helmet like toothpaste. A stream of blood and offal began to flow downward from the tears in the canvas, attracting a school of small sharks that attacked the openings ripped out when the diving suit, sized to fit a man's body, had been pushed up into the metal ring. Pieces of flesh appeared where the sharp teeth of the sharks pulled and tore at the heavy cloth, enlarging the openings. The helmet fell to the seafloor, now a bowl of compressed meat and bone. One of the larger sharks pushed its teeth downward and pulled out a piece of flesh before being pushed aside by another.

Worried that the sharks would look for additional food after emptying the disconnected helmet, Jerry turned and continued his kangaroo hop away from the *Estrella Blanca*. He remembered the discussion with Nicholas when he was learning to dive in the Orinoco River. The water pressure at one hundred feet, when multiplied by the area of the rubberized canvas diving suit added up to a total pressure of thousands of pounds. When the air hose became open to the surface, it was more than enough to force Dussell's body up into the steel helmet.

He tried the telephone again. It worked.

"Dussell sort of disappeared into his helmet. Then a school of sharks ate what was left. Bring me up."

Turning the relief valve on his helmet, Jerry reduced the flow of air from the helmet to the water, retaining more air in the suit and causing him to slightly float. He rose slowly, pulled upward by the lifeline attached to the back of his suit.

The thirty-minute decompression stop seemed like an eternity, then finally his helmet broke the water surface. He looked upward through the glass lens on the top of the copper sphere to Maria leaning over the edge of the deck to watch him struggle up the boarding ladder. Minutes later, fresh air flooded the helmet as the assistant finished unbolting it and lifted it from his head.

"What's happening?" he asked Maria, seeing her standing in front of him, feet apart as she easily balanced on the rolling deck. She had inherited outstanding sea legs from some Italian sailor in her ancestry.

"Tom tried to shoot their pump," she said in a rush. "He hit the man pumping by mistake, but it did stop the pump."

"The one-way valve we told you about must not have worked," added Giorgios. "When the pressure dropped to atmospheric in the air supply hose, the pressure in the helmet must have popped it. That pushed him and his suit inside the helmet."

"Where's Tom?" Jerry asked.

"He went over to the *Oso Negro* with Matt once you started up. Going to search for more uranium and question Carlos."

Jerry saw a small boat with Tom Barber steering leave the *Oso Negro*, the bow pointed toward the *Osprey* as a man pulled on the oars.

As he boarded the *Osprey*, Tom said, "I left Matt talking to Carlos and came back to see how you were doing,"

"The man who was trying to kill me was Ernst. Who is he? Or who was he?" asked Jerry.

"He chartered the *Oso Negro* to bring up the uranium. He was giving the orders, and he told Carlos to bring up the other diver so he could go down. Carlos hasn't told me everything he knows yet. But he will. But first I want to find all the uranium they brought up. Then I might sink the *Oso Negro* if I don't like what Carlos tells me."

"I can help," Debbie offered. "Let me go over with the Geiger counter."

Jerry took off the rest of the diving suit, dropping it to the deck. "That's a damn good idea. Get it and let's go."

Carefully holding the Geiger counter as she stepped into the small boat, Debbie almost dropped it as the dinghy slid away under her foot. She sat down hard on the single seat, letting go of the instrument with one hand to grasp the gunnel. Jerry and then Tom boarded, and the two oarsmen moved it steadily toward the *Oso Negro*.

"You get out first, then I'll hand you the Geiger counter," Jerry told Debbie when they reached the *Oso Negro*.

Debbie grabbed the boarding ladder with both hands, steadying herself enough to stand in the rowboat. Stepping onto the lowermost rung, she climbed to the main deck of the sailing vessel, then turned to grab the Geiger counter from Jerry. When she turned the on switch, it buzzed loudly.

"How do you want me to do this?" she asked Jerry.

"Let's go below to the hold. We'll start at the bow and work toward the stern. Will it get louder the closer you get to the uranium?"

"Yes," she said. "That's how I found out that the uranium was in the *Estrella Blanca* in the first place."

Jerry and Tom followed Debbie below deck. Bending over where the sides of the vessels met at the stem, Debbie watched the dial on the Geiger counter. The vessel rolled in the swell, causing her to lose her balance and fall sideways against the wooden planks that formed the sailboat hull. Grasping the instrument handle, she held it up and away from her body and the deck.

The hold was an open space between the bow and a bulkhead twenty feet from the stern that separated the living area from the cargo space, the floor planked with thick timbers strong enough to support the weight of full fish tubs or supply crates. Sweeping the detector back and forth, she stumbled toward the stern, covering the deck from port to starboard. The intensity of the buzzing increased as she passed over a section of the deck that appeared like any other, then decreased as she moved further astern.

"It's down there," she said. "At least some of it."

"Get Carlos," Jerry said to Tom. When the captain appeared, he said, "Open that up."

"It's where we hide things that we won't want custom agents to find," Carlos said. It was obvious that he wasn't happy someone else now knew about the hiding place, diminishing its utility for the future.

He walked to one of the ribs that ran up the side of the vessel, reached for a hidden metal lever, and pulled on it. Something creaked and moved below the deck, and a section of planking tilted upward. Tom and Matt pulled the planking away to reveal a pile of the small metal cubes thrown haphazardly into the bilge water below.

"Get down there and pass them up!" Jerry ordered Carlos. The captain stepped cautiously through the open hatch, placing his feet on the planks that formed the bottom of the *Oso Negro*, and bent over to pick up two of the uranium blocks. He handed them up to Tom, repeating the process until the hiding place was empty. Then he stood upright, holding his back.

He turned to Carlos. "We're going to transfer the cubes to the *Osprey*. Stay here until we finish, and we'll let you go."

The dinghy shuttled back and forth, transferring the uranium and the four Americans back to the *Osprey*. With the cubes safely stored, Jerry added up the total. "That's about three hundred fifty cubes altogether. We'll send Giorgios down for another look to get the rest."

Matt came into the pilot house. "I radioed the airbase and they talked to Gretel again. Told her that she was on a slow boat to Marseille if she didn't tell them everything. She admitted that Ernst was the one responsible for shipping the uranium to Buenos Aires. His last name is Dussell. Becker was working on the project—and much more famous—but had nothing to do with this."

"That's why he wanted to kill me," Jerry said. "I guess he thought if I drowned, we would leave, and he could salvage the rest of what's down there. But even if we don't bring up anymore, we have some material for the project in New Mexico and there won't be any uranium going to Argentina."

"What are you going to do now?" Tom asked.

"It seems I still have a job with Pride," Jerry replied. "I'm going back to Maracaibo. The office in New York should finish processing the seismic survey in a few weeks, and if the results look good, we'll start planning a wildcat well in the delta. So Maria and I will be in Venezuela for at least another year."

CHAPTER THIRTY-TWO

The Orinoco Delta, August 1945

THE TRACTOR PULLED the drilling rig across the narrow gap between a barge wedged against the riverbank and the first plank of a board road which extended two miles north of the Orinoco River across the marshy savannah. The *Osprey,* once again moored to the bank to serve as living quarters and offices for the rig crew, had brought Jerry and Debbie back to the delta two days ago. It had been a year since they had last visited this part of the world. Jan had not been able to conceal his satisfaction when Jerry returned the *Osprey* to him in Trinidad and promised no more involvement with clandestine operations.

Another six lines of seismic data had been shot, sufficient to map the Oficina formation where it dipped a mile below the surface. The map identified a layer of porous sand ending at a fault, a place where the earth had broken and moved in the distant past—a possible oilfield. It was enticing enough to move a rig to the Orinoco delta and drill a wildcat well.

"Doesn't look much different, does it?" Jerry remarked.

"No, but the screeches at night will sound better in a steel cabin than a canvas tent," Debbie replied. She had a private cabin on the boat with room for a worktable and file cabinet, luxurious compared to the tent she had shared with two men on the geological survey.

A man in red coveralls and a weather-beaten face stepped off the barge and waved. "Hi, Jerry. Good to see you again. Hope that things are quieter this time than they were in the Everglades." Turning to Debbie, he introduced himself, "Hi, I'm Joe. Jerry says you're okay. Glad to have you here."

"Thanks. I'm ready to start catching samples. When do we start drilling?" she asked.

They watched the rig move ashore, its weight bending the wooden planks.

"It'll take us about five days to rig up, so we should spud a week from today," Joe said.

"Hurry up and wait," Debbie laughed. "I've learned that's life in the oilfield. Sometimes things go incredibly fast, and sometimes it takes forever to do something simple, like change a bit. But I've got plenty to do while you rig up. I've got a microscope, sample bags, notebooks, and chemicals to get organized."

Relaxing as the rear wheels of the drilling rig moved onto solid ground, Joe turned to Debbie. "Jerry tells me you were on the geologic survey last year. What have you been doing since you left Venezuela?"

Jerry assumed the role of a proud mentor, listening but not interrupting, as she spoke.

Accompanied by a trunk filled with samples and notes, Debbie had returned to Penn State to finish her dissertation on the shales of the Orinoco Basin, which had been published in the *American Journal of Science*. She declined a position as an assistant professor at the university when she received a letter from Mike Woods offering her a job with Pride Oil.

"Academia will always be there," Debbie said, "and I want to see more of the world before returning to Pennsylvania. I expected an assignment in New York City making detailed maps based on the seismic data but was pleasantly surprised to learn that Jerry had requested me as the wellsite geologist on the Orinoco wildcat. I wanted to come back and see this prospect through. I think it will be a discovery," she concluded.

Joe was silent for a moment, looking Debbie in the eye. He nodded his approval and returned his gaze to the dock as the tractor pulled a metal tank ashore.

"The floatplane brought us a newspaper this morning, Joe. Haven't looked at it yet," Jerry announced. He opened his pack and unfolded the paper to the front page. *The New York Times*. The headline was about a new bomb that had been dropped on Japan, obliterating a city called Hiroshima.

GLOSSARY

Curacao: island off of the coast of Venezuela, originally a Dutch colony

Geiger counter: instrument to detect radioactivity

heavy oil: crude oil that is too viscous to flow easily

Lake Maracaibo: a large saltwater lake in Venezuela with the city of Maracaibo situated on its western shore and the site of the largest oilfields in the country

milliroentgens: a unit of radioactivity, one thousandth of a roentgen

nuclear fission: the process of splitting an atom's nucleus into two or more fragments, releasing energy

Oficina Formation: a geological formation in Venezuela that contains large deposits of heavy oil

Orinoco Delta: the area where the Orinoco River, the second largest in South America, flows into the Atlantic Ocean

roentgens: a unit of radioactivity

seismic: a geologic mapping tool that uses the reflection of sound waves off of layers in the earth

shale: a rock composed of clay that is often mildly radioactive

thermocline: the boundary between two layers of water with different temperatures and densities

transect: a straight line that is determined by surveying techniques

uranium: a weakly radioactive element that can be enriched so that it be used for nuclear reactors or bombs.

wildcat well: an exploratory well in a new area

ABOUT THE AUTHOR

Stephen O. Sears grew up in South Florida, boating and fishing off the Florida Keys and in the Everglades. He studied geology at the University of Florida and earned a PhD in geochemistry from Penn State. Following a career as a petroleum geologist with Shell Oil which afforded him the opportunity to make several visits to Venezuela, Sears joined the faculty of the LSU College of Engineering in 2005. The author of over forty technical, scientific, and general interest publications on geology, engineering, and higher education, Stephen O. Sears lives with his wife, Barbara, in Mandeville, Louisiana. *The Orinoco Uranium* is his second book featuring Jerry MacDonald.